Bloodlust Voyage

Cosmic Lovers 1

Leda Palmer

Contents

1

Twisted Desires

Arda

"Get back here, you little bitch." Ren swiped at the air, a wide grin peeking out beneath the visor of her VR goggles.

"Cheeky little buggers, ain't they?" Zenda said beside her, her own arms moving just as wildly.

I chuckled lightly, blowing on my tea. It was a chai blend tonight. The heady aroma of cinnamon and licorice wafted toward me. Tea was my one indulgence. I brought real Earth-grown leaves on every voyage. Others might be happy with the micro-spliced variety, but if you ask me, it tasted like watery garbage.

"Ugh, get off me!" Zenda shook her leg to dislodge whatever virtual fiend had accosted her, the teal fabric of her skinsuit flashing in the deck lights.

These long voyages hunting for jesillium in the deepest reaches of space tended to be pretty boring, so the VR sets were a welcome distraction. Most of the time, at least. When you're hoping to relax with a delicious mug of chai—not so much.

I took a tentative sip of my hot brew, eyeing the hatch to the sleeping quarters. Perhaps I ought to leave the cheeky bitch fighting to Zenda and Ren and head—

Smack.

Ren yelped. "What the hell was that for?"

I whipped around and spotted Ren cradling her jaw on the ground. She tugged the VR set off and shoved her short blonde curls off her sweaty forehead.

Zenda kneeled beside her, rubbing her knuckles against her chest and grimacing as she pulled off her own helmet. Her brown eyes widened, her mouth agape, looking for all the world like she'd killed our tech wiz instead of just clocking her. "Gods, Ren. I'm so sorry! We must've gotten too close. I'm so sorry."

"You all right, Ren?" I kneeled beside her. When she swung her head in my direction, my nostrils flared and electricity hummed through my veins. The mug shook so badly I nearly spilled my precious chai.

"Yeah, Capt. I'll be fine." She forced a smile around her cracked, bloody lip.

She might be fine, but I wasn't. The pounding of my heart picked up speed as more blood pooled on Ren's lip, rolling down her jaw and spilling onto the neck of her skinsuit. "You're bleeding." I forced out the two words, beyond surprised my voice hadn't hinted at the roiling inferno beneath my skin.

Zenda grabbed Ren's arm and tugged her to her feet. "Capt's right. You're bleeding like a hemophiliac. Let's fix you up in the med-bay."

"Med-bay? It's just a split lip, Zenda. Stop getting your panties in a twist." Despite her grumbling, Ren allowed Zenda to lead her through the porthole toward the med-bay.

With her out of sight, my speeding heart slowed. The damn thrumming faded everywhere on my body, except for one spot. Right between my thighs.

Fuck! I snatched one of the abandoned VR sets off the deck and strode to my quarters. The lock shut with a gentle *snick*. I slammed the mug down on my desk, tugging at the neck of my gray skinsuit.

That was so close. It had taken every ounce of self-control I possessed to stay calm back there. My stomach pitched, and I drew a hand down my face. They could never know. If the rest of the crew found out my dirty secret...

No—they wouldn't. I'd been careful. I just needed to keep being careful, that's all.

I flopped down on my double bed, taking the VR goggles with me. Shaking fingers grasped the zipper at the neck of my skinsuit. But before I surrendered to the fire in my blood, the metal box on the otherwise bare wall in my cabin caught my eye.

"Verne," I barked out between heavy breaths.

"Yes, Captain Arda. How can I help you?" The ship's computer's masculine voice rang out, and a green light flickered on the box.

"Set a 'do not disturb' on my quarters. Emergencies only."

"Of course, Captain." The light blinked off.

I tore down the zipper, wrenching my skinsuit open. My overheated flesh only seemed to burn more with the action, the tan sports bra pressing against my heaving chest much tighter than usual. But I ignored it, for the moment. Instead, I plunked the VR set on my head.

A barrage of color and sound bombarded me instantly. I was transported from my plain quarters to a scene from a zombie apocalypse, rife with all the moaning and screaming one would expect. Only strangely, these zombies were not of the human variety but—spotted, short-eared bunnies?

"What the hell were they playing?" I mumbled.

Huge block letters scrolled before my eyes at the same time a menacing voice proclaimed, "Beware of Cuniculus' Curse. Do you wish to continue?"

I rolled my eyes beneath the VR set. "No. End game."

The scene shifted to an endless expanse of pure white light. It wasn't blinding, merely empty. A disembodied voice called out, pleasant and androgenous, "Do you have a program in mind, or would you like to browse the menu?"

"Play Arda3."

"This program is password protected. Enter the code to continue."

"Oolong56."

A chime sounded, and the scene shifted again, returning to the plain rectangular quarters I knew so well. The bare walls stared down at me as I reclined on my bed with my clothes half undone.

Not many people would create a VR program to model the very room they sat in. But there was one significant change.

"Hey, beautiful." A tall, exceptionally well-made man greeted me, wearing nothing but a smile. His dark-brown eyes zeroed in on mine as that smile spread across his chiseled cheeks. He stalked toward the bed, his gaze slinking across my open suit and shooting back up, full of heat.

VR was a sad excuse for a real warm body. Even a sexbot would be better, but when you're stuck out in the middle of space, you can't afford to be too picky. A bolt of lust settled in my belly as I watched the virtual stud prowl closer. Yeah. This oughta scratch that itch. I was just missing one thing.

"Pause program." The hunk stopped mid-stride, the tip of his tongue just darting out to lick his full lower lip. "Open inventory."

The entire arsenal of tools and items I'd programmed into the VR rolled past me. "Stop." I grasped the handle of a wicked looking serrated knife. The sharp metal glinted in the overhead cabin light as I tucked it behind me.

"Close inventory. Resume program."

The bed shifted beneath me as the hunk set one beefy palm down beside me. "Mind if I join you?" The rumble of his deep voice reverberated in my ears.

"You better." I grinned up at him, ignoring the blank stare that greeted me. VR might be close to perfect, but they could never get the eyes quite right.

Luckily, there was plenty to keep my gaze occupied. I watched the ripple of muscle flex as my nameless lover sank further on the bed, straddling my thighs. Fuck, he was hot. My lips curled up into a smirk as his first teasing caress traced down my belly.

He grasped the sides of my skinsuit and wrenched me up to meet his lips. With my eyes shut, I could almost forget this was all in my head. The heady, masculine scent of him filled my nose. The rough graze of his teeth caught my lower lip, then his tongue sank into my mouth. My thighs quivered as a big hand landed on my breast and tugged my nipple roughly. But it was still missing something.

I opened my eyes and slid the blade out from behind me. Loverboy released my lip with a pop and smiled, one hand still working my breast, the other sliding down my thigh, ever closer to that spot that throbbed with need.

"Do it," he demanded gruffly.

I lifted the blade.

Buzz.

I sighed. "End program." I tore off the VR goggles and wrenched up the zipper to my skinsuit. "What's the emergency?" My feet hit the floor, and I sucked in a deep breath, shoving off the last vestiges of lust.

"You're needed on the bridge," Verne's flat voice replied.

Fuck. I took a second to compose myself, then shoved the door open. A few quick strides and I was back at the bridge.

"What is it?" I asked, tamping down the annoyance spiraling through me with that damn itch still very much unscratched.

Ren and Zenda were both there, gazing at the display. Ren turned to me, excitement in her eyes. Thankfully, all signs of blood and her battered lip were gone, and my shoulders loosened a fraction. Good thing the med-bots worked quickly.

"Capt, you're gonna want to see this." Ren pointed to the display. "We've detected a rogue asteroid in our path. Scans confirm it's loaded with jesillium."

I cocked a brow, leaning closer to the navigation port. "Out here? Hm. Well, what are you waiting for? Send some mining drones over there."

"That's the thing." Ren leaned back in her chair. "The ship already did, hours ago. It's one of the auto-programs I told you about."

My brow furrowed. "So, what's the emergency?"

"They've come back empty, but scans are still showing jesillium. I want to take the hopper over there and check it out."

"And I don't think that's wise." Zenda leaned forward and adjusted her retro black cat's eye glasses. "The radiation out there is increasing the closer we come to the red giant star at the heart of this system. We're safe inside the Verne, but the hopper isn't as well insulated."

I frowned and turned back to the terminal. My fingers flew across the panel as I scanned all the data. Within a few moments, it was clear the facts lined up with the crew's story. My heart raced. There was enough jesillium on that rock to pay off my debt, and then some. Maybe even enough to splurge on a night at that sleezy brothel in the outer rim.

"Looks like we have about an hour before the asteroid moves into the deadly radiation zone," I said.

"So, I can fly over there?" Ren grinned. "It won't take that long to figure out what made the drones return empty-handed."

"You're right. Only, I'm going." I took a step toward the shuttle port.

Zenda sputtered and jumped in my path. "Capt, you can't. What if something happens?"

"You're second in command. I trust you to run things in my stead." I sidestepped around her and briskly strode down the hall. Ren and Zenda fell in on my heels.

"I don't mind going. I—"

I cut Ren off before she could finish her plea. "Ren, I need you here to reprogram the drones. If we can mine that jesillium, we'll be ahead of schedule. Way ahead. But I don't want either of you risking your health to get it."

I might risk my own skin for a night with a sex-bot, but what kind of captain would I be if I forced my crew to endanger themselves? A pretty shitty one. This was my debt. My twisted desire. I couldn't exactly explain it to them in so many words, but it was worth the risk for my continued sanity.

Zenda grabbed my arm. "Arda. You don't need to risk it either. We can head for sector G like we'd planned."

"C'mon Zen. You don't let a gift like this go to waste. It's exactly what we've been hunting for." The door to the shuttle bay slid open, and I stepped through the hatch, flashing a reassuring smile. "Nothing will go wrong. I'll be back in less than an hour."

2

Worlds Collide

"What in Dral's name is going on?" I shouted, clutching my aching skull. The alarm blared. The emergency lights flashed, and I groaned, tossing my legs over the side of the stasis pod. "Destiny, shut off the alarm!"

The ringing halted, and the lights returned to their normal muted yellow. I spun around, shoving my feet into my boots and standing on wobbly legs. "Status report."

"Ship's functions are operating at 63% nominal capacity," the soothing computerized female voice replied.

"63%! What happened?" I staggered up, leaving the med-bay and pacing through the cramped hall toward the bridge of my ship. I didn't make it more than two steps before I halted, eyes widening. A sickening scent wafted through the air.

Is that smoke?

"There's been a collision in the docking bay."

"A what?" That couldn't be right. We were in the middle of nowhere. I'd set the route myself, ensuring we weren't traveling through any populated regions before I'd settled down in the stasis pod.

"A foreign shuttle attempted to land on the hull. The auto-defenses contained it within a tractor beam before the collision occurred at approximately 12.345—"

"Enough." I turned on my heel and headed for the docking bay.

A foreign shuttle? I had to see this for myself.

Smoke curled through the air in the hall. I sucked in a deep breath, preparing myself for the worst. "Is life support stable in the docking bay?"

"Life support is at 85% and rising."

Well, that was encouraging. Thankfully the auto repairs seemed to be intact. But there was only so much the computer could handle alone. I shoved open the door and all hope that this collision would be dealt with swiftly faded.

Bent and twisted metal littered the dock, sticking out from the thick layer of foam that encased everything. I coughed, the astringent stench of the fire-retardant stinging my throat.

But I guess it was better than burning to death in a fiery ball in my sleep.

I gritted my teeth when I spotted my only shuttle, torn to pieces. The foreign craft—a big lumbering clunker that barely looked like it could fly—had ripped my sleek little shuttle in two.

"What is this thing?" I growled.

"There is a life sign onboard," Destiny announced.

"That hunk of junk was manned?" I hustled forward, determined to fish the poor fool out of its innards. I would save the idiot, then I just might kill him for wrecking my damn shuttle bay.

Kicking foam out of the way, I nearly slid racing across the dock. The clunky shuttle seemed even more strange up close. The back section sported a variety of tool attachments, half of them dangling off at odd angles, likely ripped off in the crash. I spotted drills, gripping arms, and what might have been a crude laser cutter in the mix before turning my attention to the cockpit.

The front of the shuttle appeared to have taken the brunt of the damage. I coughed again, catching a whiff of smoke still lingering around the charred, mangled vessel.

I might not need to do any killing after all. The crash might have done the job for me.

"You sure there's a life sign in there?"

"Affirmative."

Only one way to find out. I located what looked like a hatch on the craft's side and pounded on the frame. "Hey. You alive in there?"

No answer. How did this thing open? I slid my hands along the edges, searching for a way in. Might need to find some leverage and muscle it open. As I turned to hunt for a tool, a mechanical whirring bled into the air, then a *hiss*. I spun back just as the hatch cracked open.

The first thing that struck me was a sound. A voice called out, repeatedly, in a language I didn't recognize. From my vantage, I still couldn't see anyone, just a closed hatch that likely led to the cockpit. The garble of static made me quickly realize the noise was not coming from the occupant, but through speakers in the vessel.

"What language is that?" Tucking my elbows tightly to my sides, I managed to squeeze into the narrow hatch. Whatever species this ship belonged to, they were much smaller than Pherians if they built such puny hatches.

"The language is a variant of Terran, from the planet Earth—English."

"Earth. That's where we're headed. Why didn't I learn this English?"

"English is one of hundreds of Terran languages. Your lessons focused on Mandarin, spoken by one third of the planet's population."

"Great. Update my translator with English." I paused outside the second hatch, waiting for the confirmation.

"Download complete," Destiny chimed.

"Arda," I could understand the words leaking out of the comm system, finally. "Arda, come in. Are you all right?"

Arda didn't respond. Surely that didn't bode well for what I was about to find when I opened that hatch.

I slid my hands along the edges again, searching vainly for a handle, switch, or something to force the damn thing open. "What's the secret to these doors?" I grumbled.

Finally, I located a square panel on the wall. When I waved my hand in front of it, the door slid open with a quiet *whirr*.

A puff of smoky air greeted me, making my eyes water. "Hello?" I called in.

Panels with blinking lights dominated the room, and a single chair sat in the midst of it all, surrounded by enormous bubbles of pillowy fabric. Must be some kind of crude crash padding?

The occupant was shrouded from me, buried somewhere in the sea of bubbles. I brushed my fingers against the closest and stifled a gasp when it deflated at my touch. I shoved my way in, pushing aside the foam-like fabric. With each bubble I brushed aside, more of the room cleared. When I finally made it to the chair, the black leather swiveled with a gentle tug, revealing the creature seated upon it.

I was right. The Terran was puny. And female. She looked to be a good deal shorter than females on my planet, and more delicate. A rather attractive specimen if I were being perfectly honest. Long brown waves cascaded down her shoulders, framing a heart-shaped face with full lips. Her form was lush, draped in skintight gray coveralls that molded to her curves like a second skin.

A strange tingling sensation flooded my veins. But I tamped it down, refusing to linger on it while she was unconscious.

I placed a hand on her cheek and gently patted her face. Her flesh was so warm. The heat blossomed against my cool skin. "Hey. You alive?"

She was so small. Her entire face could almost fit inside my palm. I was on my way to her homeworld, but I hadn't realized her species was so fragile. No wonder they lived such short lives.

I slid my hand down her neck when she didn't respond. The gentle thud of her pulse beat beneath my fingers. I wonder what her blood—

I pulled away, not allowing myself to complete the thought. *Too long in the stasis pod. That's all this is.*

"Arda. Arda, come in!" The speakers kept blasting out the same plea.

"Destiny, is there another vessel nearby? Larger than this one."

"Affirmative. There is an H class freighter, Pioneer model at O.9 27—"

"Enough." I sighed. What in Dral's name were they doing out here?

I'll drop her off at the med-bay and come back to chat with her friends once I figure out how to work the controls on this wreck.

Nothing for it but to carry her to the med-bay. She looked to be breathing steadily, and appeared to be free from outward injury, but I couldn't be certain there wasn't something wrong with her internally. I bent down and slid my fingers beneath her shoulders. She stirred. I froze, my gaze zeroing in on her face.

Electric blue eyes fluttered open, and she stretched out like a sleepy fuciera, rubbing against my arms. She groaned, and the sound was so primal it unleashed a cascade of feral need within me. My hands curled around her instinctively, and my blood pounded.

Dral help me… I shouldn't be touching her while she's making that sound. I shouldn't—

Her gaze finally collided with mine, just as I began to withdraw and pull away.

"Ahh!" she screamed, and her tiny fist flew at my face, clipping me in the nose. I staggered back and bent beside the chair, my eyes clenched tight to stem the tears pooling in my eyes.

Damn, that hurt.

"Relax," I hissed, clutching my nose. "I'm not here to hurt you."

"Who are you? Where am I?" She scrambled out of the swivel chair and collided with more of the pillowy bubbles, which deflated beneath her. "Oh, God. I-I crashed." She rubbed her head, her wild eyes flitting around the ruined interior of her shuttle. "You—" She aimed an accusing stare at me. "You caught me in a tractor beam!"

"You can thank my auto-defenses for that. I wasn't even awake."

My words didn't seem to matter to the tiny female. She gulped loudly, and slowly backed away, popping more of those bubbles with every step.

The speakers blared out again, "Arda. Arda, please come in."

Arda spared me one last withering glare and spun to the closest panel. She tapped on a few of the blinking lights. "Ren. I'm here."

"Arda, thank God. What happened? Are you hurt?"

"I'm fine." She pounded on another button and a panel slid open, revealing a plexiglass viewport that looked down on the mess of metal and off-white foam littering my docking bay. She grimaced as she stared out, then turned back to her panels, her fingers flying as figures scrawled across the screen. "That asteroid was not an asteroid. It's a ship. I think it's gonna be a while before I can make repairs and return."

"As long as you're okay. What the hell kind of ship looks like an asteroid?"

I rolled my eyes. "Don't you Terrans know anything? It's protocol when traveling through a pre-space civilizat—"

"Arda, what is that growling?" the voice on the other end demanded. "Is someone there with you?"

Don't tell me their translators weren't up to snuff, either? No wonder the little human kept sneaking peeks at me, her expression an odd mixture of annoyance and wariness, like she was afraid I was about to pounce on her, and was not in the least bit amused by the idea.

She did it again, her blue eyes widening and her breath catching when she caught me staring back at her. But then she squared her shoulders and sent me a tentative smile. "It's fine. I'm handling it. But do me a favor, Ren. Tell Zenda I'm not gonna make it back in an hour."

Handling it... A spark of irritation flickered to life in my gut. She wrecked my shuttle. Then she punched me, when all I'd been trying to do was help her. And now she was *handling* it... The idea was laughable.

I cracked my neck and stood to my full height, letting my hand fall off my face. We'll see how much the little human could handle.

3

Torture in the Med-bay

Arda

The alien towered over me, standing to his full height. With his head practically brushing the hopper's ceiling, he had to be at least seven feet tall.

Holy hell, he was massive. Not just tall, but stacked with muscle, too. I'd hardly noticed his size, with him crouched on the ground after I clocked him. I winced internally, flashing back to the moment I awakened with his huge mitts wrapped around me and those piercing silver eyes staring into my soul.

Yeah, I hit him. Who could blame me? It's not every day you wake up while being manhandled by an enormous alien...

He spoke again, and his deep voice rumbled around the tiny cockpit, making the space feel even smaller. My heart raced as I realized I didn't have a weapon or any way to defend myself.

I doubt my fists would do much to stop this guy if he decides to stop being friendly. His nose certainly didn't look too bad, despite the blow I landed.

I tapped my neck, wondering why the stupid translator implanted just beneath my skin wasn't working.

"Your presence is required in the med-bay," a female voice announced, making me flinch and my gaze dart behind him. But after only a second, I recognized that monotone for what it was.

"Computer, you understand English?"

"Affirmative," the computer declared.

The alien's deep rumble boomed again, the tones of his foreign tongue somehow velvety smooth and guttural all at once. He still hadn't moved an inch, towering over me with his arms crossed and a flat expression plastered on his face.

Fuck, he was hot. Pale as a ghost, and gigantic, but there was no denying he was insanely gorgeous. Shoulder-length golden hair framed a face that looked like it belonged in holovids. And his body... it was hard not to notice how perfectly sculpted every muscle appeared beneath his tight black skinsuit.

The computer interrupted my lustful thoughts. "Commander Luxuth will provide you with a translator upgrade after you've been seen to by the med-bot."

My blood surged as I glanced up at the glowering giant with another cautious smile. Guess *Commander* decided my being on his ship gave him the right to boss me around.

Not like I planned on crashing here. If it wasn't for his damn tractor beam, I wouldn't be in this mess. Still, I had to tread carefully. I had no idea who this guy was, or what kind of trouble I'd just landed in.

He didn't return my smile, just kept staring, his expression giving away nothing.

But it wouldn't get us anywhere to just stand here glaring at each other... And I had just crashed. With all the adrenaline pumping through me, I wasn't feeling any pain, but that didn't mean there wasn't anything wrong with me.

Besides, the fact that he was leading me to the med-bay and not a cell had to be a good sign. I tamped down the irritation thudding through my veins and took a step closer, preparing to follow the alien hunk out of my ruined shuttle.

Get a grip, Arda.

I sucked in a huge breath as he spun around, leading the way. I blamed that damn itch. That damn, unscratched itch from earlier. No way this guy was that hot.

It was easy to tell myself that while his back was turned. Until I caught a glimpse of his ass.

Fuck. It was criminal. Perfectly sculpted and just begging to be slapped. I shook the thought away.

I must've bumped my head in the crash... No way was this stranger having such a powerful effect on me. Nope. A couple minutes with a med-bot and I'd be good as new.

The docking bay looked even worse from outside the shuttle. And my poor hopper... I couldn't bite back my frown when I got a peek at the damage. The internal readouts hadn't been good, but this would take days to fix, at least.

Luxuth grunted and bobbed his head toward a hatch on the back wall.

"Yeah, yeah, I'm coming. You don't have to go all caveman on me." I stepped carefully through the foam, burying the urge to cough.

Men. Can't say I had much experience dealing with them, but I was glad this one couldn't understand me. I'd need to cool it with the snark once our translators were fixed.

We made it out into the corridor, then he led me down a short hall lined with closed hatches. I peered around, searching for signs of any other souls onboard, but I didn't spot anyone. Silence, punctuated by the occasional mechanical whirring, were the only noises that greeted me.

Don't tell me I'm all alone on this ship with this guy...

I heaved out a deep breath, stemming the panic that fought to swell. There were bound to be more people onboard. Someone must be lingering behind some of those hatches. But then again, why would the Commander come out to investigate the crash all alone? Surely if there were more crew, they'd have made themselves known by now.

Luxuth activated a panel beside a hatch on the far side of the hall, then turned, staring at me expectantly as he loomed beside the doorway. The door opened soundlessly, and he jerked his thumb at the entrance.

The action drew my attention to his hands. I hadn't noticed before, but he only had four fingers. Except for that, the unnaturally pale skin, and his enormous size, he looked remarkably humanoid. I quirked a brow as I passed and studied him out of the corner of my eye.

What species was he? Humans had met a few dozen alien species in the last hundred or so years since we achieved faster than light travel, but I couldn't recall any mention of ones that looked like this. Hell, if word got out that there were men like him out here, there'd be a mass exodus of horny women flooding space to find them.

His voice boomed again, catching me off guard.

"Disrobe and enter the med-bot," the computer demanded in that maddening monotone.

I bristled, glancing around the neat, state-of-the-art med-bay. A sterile white box in the far corner slid open. I strode over to it and peered in. It was twice the size of the one back on the Verne, but appeared remarkably similar.

Still... I turned around and glared at the captain. "A little privacy would be nice." If he thought I was about to give him a free show, he had another thing coming.

But the giant just stood there, his eyes glued to me, their silver depths burning as they blazed a trail across my body.

And, of course my traitorous skin sizzled, and my blood ignited, practically molten. "Computer," I hissed. "Where's the translator upgrade?"

Luxuth barked out a word before the computer replied and he stalked forward. I backed away, and my ass hit the door of the med-bot.

Images of him forcibly taking off my clothes flooded my mind. Those big hands stripping me down and shoving me in the med-bot. I shivered at the mental image, and I couldn't pinpoint whether it was fear or desire that had caused it.

But instead of reaching out to grab me, he breezed past and dug inside a set of drawers, turning his back on me. I stuttered out a sigh and let my gaze wander down to that glorious ass. Yeah... mass exodus indeed.

When he turned around a second later, my cheeks burned as he caught me staring. With his face still stoic as ever, he marched right up to me.

Shit—was he pissed? With that steely expression, it was hard to say.

"I-I didn't mean anything by it." I bit my lip and rubbed my neck. "I mean, surely you must know, it's hard *not* to look at that ass of steel. Do you work out? I bet you work out, huh? I-I'll shut up now."

Damn it. I gulped, thanking my lucky stars this dude had no clue what my nervous rambling meant.

He lifted one beefy hand, palm splayed open, displaying a tiny cylinder the size of a pill. I plucked it out of his hand, unable to avoid grazing his palm.

A chill spread up my fingertips. He was cold. My hands and feet got a little chilly from time to time, but this guy was one step away from an ice cube.

I frowned at the little bead of hard plastic in my fingers. What now?

The big guy mimed sticking it in his ear.

Here goes nothing.

I crammed the device in my right ear, grimacing at the clogged sensation that accompanied it. But after only a second, it slid further in. The clog evaporated and a gentle buzz vibrated inside my skull.

"Can you understand me now?"

My eyes shot to the hunk in front of me. "Yes." My brow furrowed. "What about you? Don't you need one of those things?"

"No. And to answer your earlier questions, I get it. And yeah, I like to work out." The ghost of a smile finally tugged up the corners of his lips, and goddamn it, the sight set off a riotous flutter in my belly.

The arrogant prick! He'd heard everything I'd just said, didn't he?

Shit. My cheeks burned even hotter.

What's done was done. Yeah, he caught me staring at his ass. But then he also heard me ask for privacy too...

"Good to know." My hand shot out, pointing at the hatch. "Get out."

"This is my ship. I give the orders here." He leaned closer. "Get in the med-bot."

I crossed my arms. "If you think I'm going to strip with some alien pervert watching, you're out of your mind, buddy."

His eyes, which had flicked down to stare at my chest, popped back up to meet my gaze. "Do you expect me to leave a strange female alone in my ship? You might have a weapon hidden under there, for all I know."

I glared back, determined to stand there until he changed his mind. But then my traitorous body wobbled as a wave of dizziness washed over me.

What if I was bleeding internally? What if that flutter in my belly wasn't attraction, but blood slowly pooling around my insides?

I had to climb in that med-bot. But stripping—no fucking way. Hell, it probably wouldn't be that big of a deal, all things considered. I just didn't want to give the arrogant ass the satisfaction of me obeying his orders.

I inched away from the med-bot door and spread my arms and legs. "Pat me down."

"What?"

"If you're so worried I'm armed, then pat me down. Once you see I'm not hiding any weapons, you can leave me alone so the med-bot can fix me."

He speared me with a heated glance. "All right."

He stepped even closer and bent down.

My breath hitched.

Then he started sliding those big mitts slowly up the front of my legs, his icy fingers spreading goosebumps in their wake. His touch was methodical, patting firmly, then inching up.

Holy hell. I should've just stripped. This was torture. Absolute torture.

By the time he made it to my thighs, my legs shook, and I was having trouble keeping my arms steady.

"Are you well, Arda?" One big hand cupped my core at the same moment my name rolled off his tongue.

Fuck.

His touch didn't linger like I wanted it, just moved up, trailing across my belly.

"Fine," I bit out. "I'll be better once you're finished."

"You can't fault a commander for being thorough when the safety of his ship is at risk."

His fingers splayed across my breasts. I couldn't stop the tiny gasp as my nipples hardened from his cool exploration.

Luxuth heard it. His silver eyes shot up to mine, and I saw they'd darkened to a deep charcoal, before he returned to watching his hands trace across my body.

Get a goddamn grip, Arda.

I should not be enjoying this. This prick thought I was an assassin, or worse. One more minute and it would be over and I could make sure I wasn't bleeding internally.

His fingers burned a cold trail across my neck, then over my shoulders and across my arms, to my wrists.

"Satisfied?" I glared at him as he finished, trying to hide my uneven breathing.

"Not even close," he barked. "Turn around."

4

All Around Invasive

Lux

Torture. That's what this was.

I should've never agreed to the female's hasty demand. The feel of her perfect curves would be branded on my skin for weeks.

She shot me a venomous glare, then twisted slowly, widening her stance.

I sank down on one knee, and fought to keep my touch on the backs of her shapely legs methodical. A task made maddeningly difficult when I glanced up and spotted her curvy little ass at eye level.

My mouth watered and I swallowed thickly.

This was necessary. She hadn't bothered to explain why she'd attempted landing on my ship. I had a duty to protect my cargo. You'd think she would be happy for the opportunity to assess her health before facing an inquisition, but apparently not.

Who knew she'd be so reluctant to disrobe? Any Pherian would have shrugged, stripped, and hopped in the med-bot without a second thought.

My hands slid up to her pert little bottom. I didn't miss the involuntary shiver that whispered across her skin at the contact.

Was she enjoying this? Or was that just wishful thinking?

I certainly wouldn't mind touching her like this again. Maybe I could even convince her to lose the skinsuit next time…

"Hurry it up. Your hands are like ice," she grumbled.

Guess there won't be a next time.

A wave of something that felt an awful lot like disappointment thrummed through me, but I shrugged it off. She could be a thief or worse. I really ought to stop lusting over the little vixen before my dick got me in trouble.

All the same, I couldn't stop my brain from cataloging and committing to memory each and every curve as I finished patting her down.

Arda whipped around once my hands had their fill. "Happy?"

"Hardly," I shot back.

She cocked a brow, her pink lips twisting in a confused pout. But after only a second, her arm shot out again, her expression hard as iron. "Out."

My blood boiled. Where did she get off making demands?

But I'd agreed. And I was a man of my word.

I stalked across the med-bay and through the hatch without a backward glance.

My hands fisted at my side as the hatch closed behind me. Visions of her unzipping and peeling off that suit flooded my mind. I leaned back against the wall and sucked in a shaky breath.

A weird *clunk* sounded somewhere to my right, breaking the spell.

I stomped off to the bridge, determined to assess the damages that little female wrought on my ship.

"Destiny, I want a full damage report on the forward display." I opened the hatch to the bridge and ducked inside. The sleek room was awash with blinking monitors, each displaying various warnings that certainly hadn't been active before I laid down in the stasis pod.

I sighed. A cursory study confirmed what I'd first feared when I'd woken to the news that the ship was only performing at 63% capacity.

The shuttle bay wasn't the only thing damaged in the crash. It would take days to make repairs.

I drew a hand down my face. "Open the viewport."

There it was. The human ship hovered within view, a larger version of the rickety lump in my bay. It barely looked like it was space worthy.

The communication panel blinked, drawing my attention.

Who could that be?

I opened a channel, wondering if it was the Terrans attempting to contact Arda again, but as soon as the voice spilled through the speakers, I stifled a groan.

"Hello, Elys. What do I owe the pleasure?"

An airy chuckle set my nerves on edge. "Good, you're not dead."

"And why would you assume that?" I asked my nosy little sister.

"Your ship is hooked up to the family mainframe. I got pinged that there was a crash."

I rolled my eyes. "No need to worry. Just a little misunderstanding. I'm fine."

"Well, that's good to know. What happened?"

I rushed through a basic account of the events since I'd awoken. "And that's pretty much it. I'm assessing the damage now while the Terran is in the med-bot."

"Are the rumors true?" Elys didn't bother to hide her curiosity.

"Too soon to say," I replied.

We'd known the Terrans were there for centuries, out on their little blue green world. We watched them spread out across their system, fostering settlements on several moons and planets. But until they achieved faster than light travel, we'd left them alone to their own devices.

The Galactic Charter was clear in that regard. No interfering with developing species.

It was hard not to interfere when their species was compatible with us. With every passing year, Pherians grew closer and closer to extinction. The hope was that within a few decades of interbreeding, our species might stabilize. Now that the Terran's world was open to travel, and their decades long civil war at an end, we could finally open up trade with their system.

"Hm. I suppose not." The disappointment in Elys' voice was clear. But then she perked up. "I'm going to access your med-bot's data. Maybe I can learn something new about your stowaway."

"Don't you think that's a little invasive?"

I cringed. Who was I to talk? If anyone was invasive, it was me. I couldn't go ten minutes without rubbing my greedy hands all over her body.

I shoved the memory of Arda's warm flesh aside as my sister's laughter bounced around the bridge.

"Invasive was landing on a ship without invitation. Don't worry. What she doesn't know won't hurt her," Elys insisted.

There wasn't much I could do to stop her. Not while she was still jacked into my ship's mainframe.

I sighed. "I better sign off. Get started on the repairs."

"Talk to you later, Lux."

"Bye."

A noise in the hall outside drew my attention. Was that Arda wandering around the ship already?

I jerked out of my seat and strode down the hall back to the med-bay. I paused outside the door. She might still be in there, inside the med-bot—naked.

The thought sent a rush of blood to my groin.

Still, I promised privacy. "Destiny, is Arda still in the med-bay?"

"Negative. Arda is in the shuttle bay."

"The shuttle bay?" I muttered, turning on my heel. The minx had some nerve wandering around my ship like she owned the place. Now I had a stranger sneaking around my ship, doing who knows what. I should've stood watching while the med-bot worked, then tied her up until she answered all my questions.

The thought of Arda's wrists bound and her at my mercy was particularly satisfying. If I caught her up to no good, I might just need to make that idea a reality.

Let's go see what the little female is up to.

5

Dousing Flames

Arda

I zipped my skinsuit back up, mildly surprised Commander Luxuth didn't barge in on me in the middle of the med-bots exam.

Would that have been so bad?

My nose wrinkled at my own thoughts.

Yes. Yes, it would be bad.

He thinks I'm here to—do what exactly? Stab him while his back
was turned? Sabotage his weird asteroid in ship's clothing?

What was the deal with that in the first place? And why did our
scans show so much jesillium?

I sighed and paced to the hatch. I might as well go talk to the big guy
and put some of these questions to bed. From the looks of the damage
on the hopper, I was going to be stuck here for a while.

Maybe he had another shuttle stashed away somewhere? I could be
on it and out of here within minutes, laughing about the whole ordeal
with my crew...

Somehow, the idea didn't put a spring in my step like it ought to. I creeped down the corridor instead, past all those closed hatches.

At the far end of the hall, one hatch hung open. It didn't take a genius to figure out that's where Luxuth was. But a sound echoed down the hall as I drew nearer, stopping me in my tracks.

A woman laughing. She said something; then a second later the deep rumble of Luxuth's voice replied, too quietly for me to make out what they'd said.

I gritted my teeth and spun on my toes so fast I almost gave myself whiplash. Before I knew it, I was back in the launch bay, slamming the door to the hatch loud enough I cringed.

I drew in a deep, calming breath before I thought better of it, and coughed. That flame retardant foam was murder on the lungs.

I surveyed the damage again, taking the time to look beyond my ship at the rest of the massive chamber. The place was a wreck. A blanket of whitish goo lay atop everything, with jagged shards of metal sprinkled throughout. My hopper really did a number on the place.

If I had to hazard a guess, there were just as many repairs needed here. And from the looks of the crumpled ship my hopper smashed, it would seem my hopes to hop a shuttle out of here were equally ruined.

Well, the big guy had his crew to help him. I steeled my spine, preparing myself for days of listening to that woman laugh at all his dumb jokes.

Ugh, gag me now.

I made my way across the bay to the hopper and climbed in. Smoke still lingered in the cockpit. I waved the hazy air away from my face and sank into the pilot's seat.

Before I could even pull up the ship's damage report, my communication panel flashed.

Guess I better update the crew.

"Verne, come in."

"Arda! Where have you been?" Zenda asked, barely half a second later.

"Just got checked out in the med-bay, is all. I'm going to start on repairs to the shuttle."

"I assessed the damage report from over here. It doesn't look good."

I sighed. "Not a problem a little elbow grease won't fix."

"What about the crew over there? Will they help with the repairs? Who are they?"

"I've only met the captain so far. He's an alien, pale, humanoid." I injected as much confidence as I could into my tone. "He set me up with a translator after the crash. I'm sure we'll be able to work something out."

Zenda's voice warbled, her concern evident even through the speakers. "Are you all right, Capt?"

"Nothing I can't handle." Luxuth's scowling face flashed in my mind, but I shoved the image aside. I had bigger problems to worry about. "Listen, Zen. I need you to fly ahead to sector G."

"Without you?" Zenda squeaked.

"It'll take me days to fix the hopper. If you sit there waiting for me, we'll miss our deadline."

I didn't need to tell Zenda what that meant. We were already behind. If I missed another shipment, that meant I missed another payment. My stomach churned, worry coiling inside like the tangled mess of wires waiting for me inside the hopper.

"I-I—All right. We'll swing back for you in a few days," Zenda said, but her voice lacked confidence. "Are you sure, Arda?"

No. Not really. But we'd wasted enough time already. "Yes, I'm sure. Go."

"I'll have Verne set an alert on communications. If you need anything—anything at all—you call us and we'll come right back."

"Got it. Thank you, Zenda."

I cut the call, determined to drag my focus back to the repairs. Might as well get started.

I coughed and rubbed my stinging eyes. The smoke in the cabin hadn't lessened at all. Was it getting worse?

Heart thrumming, I leaned over the panel, my fingers flying as I studied the damage scans. There was nothing to indicate a fire... but my intuition wouldn't stop screaming.

I rose from the chair, sniffing the air. Then I slid my hands against the closest panel, testing it for hot spots where a stubborn flame might be hiding.

That was when Luxuth found me. My head was tilted back, my nose up in the air as I sniffed repeatedly. My hands caressed the shuttle wall with slow, sweeping motions.

"I hope I'm not interrupting." He halted just inside the hatchway, arms crossed, lips set in a grim line. You could almost imagine he'd made a joke, if not for his apathetic stare.

"Too bad. You are. Why don't you come back later? Or never." I snapped back.

Fuck. Foot meet mouth.

He was just so infuriating, standing there all big and sexy, while I probably looked like a complete maniac, feeling up the walls.

Thank God he wasn't bleeding from that punch I landed. There was only so much a girl could handle. If I was this attracted to him already, I don't even want to imagine what would happen if I spotted blood on that chiseled face.

I'm not sure what it was about blood that turned me on. It had been that way most of my life. A sick obsession I'd always hidden.

Maybe some people could get away with that kind of kink. But with my family's history… if anyone back home knew, they'd lock me up in a heartbeat—just like *her*.

I shoved the painful memories aside. Now was not the time.

I shifted, turning my back to Luxuth. My hands slid across the cool panel. Nothing yet. I sniffed. But the smell was only getting stronger.

"What are you doing?"

"Fixing my ship."

A low chuckle reverberated behind me, sending a wave of tingles spreading between my thighs. Fuck, even his laugh was sexy.

"You planning to rub it all better?"

My shoulders stiffened, a snarky remark on the tip of my tongue, but the sudden warmth blossoming beneath my touch made the words die unsaid.

I knew it! There *was* something burning in there.

I veered around Luxuth, ignoring his idiotic question. I opened the supply hatch, gathering the few tools from my emergency supply kit.

"Need a hand with that?" He quirked a pale brow, gazing down at the equipment in my hands.

"Nope." I breezed past him, then crouched next to the warm panel. I nodded to the hatch. "Plenty out there to keep you busy."

"Don't be stubborn," he countered, stepping closer.

"Don't you have someone else to *command*?" That girl's stupid laugh echoed in my mind. "Or do you just keep your crew around to look pretty?"

He hovered over me, watching as I unscrewed the first bolt. "No crew. Just me."

What about the girl?

I cringed inwardly. He had been on his bridge. He must've had the communication system on speaker.

The realization made my pulse race. Especially when I stopped worrying about the unknown woman on the other end of the communication and another thought struck me.

We were completely alone. Stuck on a ship in the middle of nowhere. And I just sent my crew away.

Panic rose, fast and frantic. What did I even know about this guy? I couldn't stop myself from snapping at him long enough to find out.

Tamping down the rush of jitters, I focused on the task at hand.

I'll just put out the fire, then we can have a nice, calm chat.

Three more bolts joined the tidy pile on the cockpit floor. I grimaced, tugging the panel off the wall.

Sure enough, a thick puff of smoke rushed out. I coughed, waving the cloud away from my stinging eyes. A maze of multicolored wire, electrical boxes, and exposed beams lay behind all the haze. I ducked inside, an extinguisher gripped in my fist.

"You should let me handle that," Luxuth barked behind me.

He couldn't see me roll my eyes, but he surely heard the incredulous tone of my voice. "Don't be ridiculous. I can handle it."

I could hear him grumbling behind me under his breath, but couldn't make out his words. What did the big guy want? For me to just lay back and let him save me? Get real.

Besides, he couldn't fit back here. I sucked in my breath, crawling further in, brushing a mess of wires out of my way. Hell, *I* could barely fit in. I only managed to squeeze the top half of my torso inside the wall before I couldn't go any further.

Finally I spotted a smoldering wire, in the corner of the crawl space. I pointed the extinguisher at it, and doused the flame with a sigh.

One disaster averted. I shifted, preparing to back out of the hatch.

The ship shifted beneath me, jolting sideways. My center of gravity twisted, and my body started to slide further in the crawl space.

Fuck! I felt like a fly, seconds away from colliding with a massive spider web. I'd end up strangled, or jolted full of current when I snapped the wrong wire.

Before I could fall in, Luxuth plucked me out of the hell of exposed wire bent on choking me. His big hands curled around my waist, and he lifted me like I was as light as a pillow.

Quick as it had started, the hopper settled. Luxuth set me down on my feet, his big body brushing across my back, making me shiver.

I spun around and peered up at the Commander. "Thanks." The word came out breathy, and stilted.

Had that really just happened? I fought to control my breathing while my heart continued to hammer in my ears.

Luxuth stared back at me, his pale face hard as stone. "We need to talk."

6

Bedroom Humor

Lux

Arda bristled, crossing her arms. "So, talk." Her nose was up in the air, chin tilted defiantly. It was strange to meet a female so openly hostile. I'd just saved her—again—but she kept glaring at me like I was her own personal villain.

The hunk of junk shifted again, nearly knocking Arda off her feet. I shot out a hand to steady her, and warmth rushed up my arm from her fragile shoulder.

She regained her balance and shrugged off my hand.

"We'll talk where it's stable." I nodded to the hatch.

Arda brushed past me in a huff. Once we'd both exited, she whirled around, sending a puff of foam flying. "I'm listening."

"When are your people coming to get you?"

"They're not."

I lifted a brow. "What?"

"The hopper is our only manned shuttle. I'll be out of your hair after I repair it."

Her ship was twice the size of Destiny. And they only had one shuttle? I sighed and shot a dubious glance at the pile of junk she was placing her life in. "You can't be serious..."

"You think I can't fix it?"

I pinched the bridge of my nose. "Don't you have a docking station?"

She aimed a pointed stare over my shoulder. "Do you have another one? Because it doesn't look like anything is docking there anytime soon."

I followed her gaze to my docking port. I hated to agree, but she was right. Her ship sheared off a portion of the lower hull, and the emergency seal was firmly in place, blocking space from sucking out the artificial atmosphere.

Guess I was stuck with the prickly female until we made some repairs.

"Are we done?" She stepped back toward her wreck of a shuttle.

"No." I grabbed her elbow. "Why were you trying to land here in the first place?"

She glared down at my hand until I dropped her arm. "Scans from our ships showed a large jesillium deposit. When our mining drones came back empty, I decided to investigate."

They were a mining company? That made the strange attachments on the shuttle make sense, but still... "Why didn't you turn back once you heard our radio beacon?"

Arda rolled her eyes. "I would've if there was one. There wasn't. Your ship was running silent."

I scoffed. "No, it wasn't. I programmed the beacon myself."

"Well then, it failed." She crossed her arms. "Why didn't you reach out with comms before seizing me in a tractor beam?"

"That wasn't me. It was the auto-defenses. I was in a stasis pod."

Arda frowned, then shook her head. "Figures."

I fought the urge to frown back. Was that true? Had the ship's beacon failed? The preprogrammed message should have served as a warning to any ships nearby. It sounded like Arda's mining drones had gotten the message, but her shuttle, and their larger ship didn't.

Then again, she could be lying about the beacon. If they were truly that hard up for jesillium then maybe they just chose to ignore it.

"What are you doing out here hunting for jesillium?"

"Does it matter? Look, my crew left to do some mining while I'm stuck here. I need to complete the repairs before they get back. Do you mind?"

So evasive. Why couldn't she just answer a simple question?

The hopper shifted again. From our vantage outside, I could pinpoint the cause. My poor shuttle wasn't completely done being squashed like I'd first thought. Metal screeched as the weight of the hopper settled more fully atop it.

"Yeah. I do mind." I waved my hand at both the wrecks. "It's not safe in there. Help me clean off this foam and I'll tow your hopper to a more stable location."

Her eyes flashed, and I sensed she wanted to argue, but when the wreck shifted and crunched again, she nodded.

I strode to the side of the room and opened a supply closet. "Here." I turned around holding two tools. "Your choice."

"What are those?"

I lifted the first, a long metal pole with a magnetic bucket attachment at the end. "This will collect all the metal shards." I hefted up the second, a simple wooden mop. "The foam dissolves with a little water."

She eyed the tools warily, then grabbed the magnet. I wasn't surprised the female left the dirtier task to me. But I was no stranger to a hard days' work.

We spent the next few hours in tense silence. My shoulders and lower back ached by the time we were through. Still, my lungs thanked me, once the astringent foam had all been dissolved. I spared a glance at Arda. She hadn't complained. Not once. But I spotted the weariness in her stance.

My nostrils flared as I realized the depths of my stupidity. She'd been in a wreck for Dral's sake, and I just made her clean the whole bay. She was probably ready to collapse.

"That's enough for now. You need to rest. It's been a long day."

"I'm fine," she insisted. "Move the hopper."

"Later. After you rest."

She made a strangled noise, low in her throat. "Have it your way. I'll sleep in the hopper." She shoved the tool back in the cabinet and glided across the clean shuttle bay floor.

I stepped directly in her path. "I didn't see a sleeping quarters in that wreck. Besides, it's still not stable. Come with me. There is a bed for you in the Destiny."

"Destiny. That's the name of your ship?"

I nodded and pointed to the hatch. Thankfully, Arda didn't put up a fight. She sighed then followed me out of the shuttle bay and down the hall.

I opened a hatch and stood by the doorway, waiting for her to enter.

Instead of walking past, she stopped in front of me. She rubbed her neck and sent me another one of those rare smiles she hadn't graced me with since I first found her. "I-I'm sorry for crashing into your ship. I know you weren't expecting any visitors, and you've been pretty decent about it, all things considered. So, thanks for that."

Her apology threw me off kilter. Was she really sorry, or was she just trying to put me at ease? It was hard to get a read on her. But as I gazed down into her blue eyes, I decided to take her at her word. "You're welcome."

She nodded, and her smile brightened a touch. Then she slid past, and her smile morphed into a yawn. She took a few steps inside the room before her eyes reopened. They popped wide after only a second. I watched her gaze flit over all my possessions and her relaxed, sleepy stance faded instantly.

"Is this your bedroom?" Arda flashed a glare at me. "Don't tell me. There's only one bed on this ship?"

I opened my mouth to explain, but movement caught the corner of my eye.

Arda spotted it too. She screeched, an ungodly piercing yelp that grated on my ears. "What the hell is that?"

Arda

My heart pounded as the creature hissed. It was like I'd been transported back into that stupid VR game. One of those zombie bunnies was here in the flesh, bent on eating my brains.

"Relax." The big oaf brushed past me, headed for the snarling critter. "You're scaring her."

"I'm scaring *her*?" I crossed my arms as Luxuth bent down and scooped up the hissing bundle of skin and bone. As soon as he cradled the creature within the shelter of his massive arms, it quieted, then began to purr. "What is that thing?"

"Smudge is a fuciera. You do have pets on Earth, don't you?"

"Sure. Only ours are cute and cuddly, not half-zombie."

"Zombie," Luxuth repeated, brows scrunched. "I do not have a translation for that."

I waved a hand. "It was a joke."

Something about the big guy loving on the ugly little thing had warmth spreading through my insides. I creeped closer, examining the creature. On second thought, she was much more cat-like than I'd first suspected, except for the big floppy skin flaps for ears that were much more reminiscent of a rabbit. But that purr and the way her paws flicked out to knead at Luxuth's arm were totally feline.

"Would you like to pet her? She is very affectionate when she's not being yelled at."

I scowled, but moved closer, curious to learn more about the little critter. She was a sickly shade of gray, almost like smudged pencil lead... *Wonder if that's where he got the name?* "You might've thought to warn me. Then maybe I wouldn't have been so shocked."

"Hm, yes. I see that now. You humans are an excitable species."

I almost asked him what species he was, but at that moment my hand landed on Smudge's back and I had to bite back a gasp. "She's so warm."

She was the exact opposite of Luxuth, with his icy flesh. The little fuciera's purring increased as I stroked her silky skin. A pleasant heat emanated from her, spreading across my palm and up my forearm. I stole a peek at Luxuth's face. A fond smile painted his lips, his eyes half-lidded as Smudge purred against his chest.

Any man who loves his pet so much can't be completely bad.

I brushed the thought aside as my gaze strayed to the lone bed and the memory of my earlier complaint returned.

"This is clearly your room." If the enormous alien-sized bed, or the shelves loaded with books and knickknacks hadn't clued me in, the open closet in the back corner full of huge black clothes would have. "I'm not sleeping with you."

Luxuth's contented smile slipped, his full lips curving into the first smirk I'd seen on his normally stone-like face. "If we shared a bed, there would not be much sleeping happening."

My belly tightened at the same time my mind brimmed with outrage. The nerve of this guy... I withdrew my hand from Smudge and gagged dramatically.

"What's wrong? Are you ill?" His brow furrowed, and he searched my face.

Oh man, he's serious. I massaged my temples. "I was joking, again."

"Your Terran humor is not very funny."

Fuck. It was gonna be a long few days.

"What exactly are our sleeping arrangements?"

Luxuth strode to the corner of the room and plucked a plush pet bed off the floor. "Smudge and I will stay in the med-bay. Get some rest."

"Wait." I jumped in his path before he hit the hatch. "I'll stay in the med-bay. You don't have—"

"No. Stay here." He shuffled his purring pet into the crook of his elbow and stuffed the fluffy pet bed under his arm. Then he used his free hand to gently push me aside.

My boots slid across the tile floor, and before I could do more than gape at his muscles flexing as he manhandled me, he slammed the hatch open and disappeared into the hall.

I almost sped after him, ready to shout at him for ordering me around—hell, for *moving* me just like he had that pet of his—but a yawn stopped me in my tracks.

Maybe it wouldn't be so bad to borrow the big guy's bed... I walked over to the enormous mattress and shucked off my boots. Weariness washed over me so swiftly it almost edged out the annoyance spiraling within my mind.

As I pulled the blankets over me, and sank into one of the softest beds I'd ever laid on, I closed my eyes and sighed. First thing when I woke up, I would find out what species I was stuck with. No matter how infuriating the man was, we had to learn to coexist somehow.

7

Spilling Tea

Lux

I strode down the hall to the bridge and set down Smudge's pet bed in the corner. "Here you go, girl. We need to spend a bit more time in here the next couple days."

My gaze strayed to the viewport as I sank down in the pilot's chair. Only empty space greeted me, with the bright flicker of the systems far away sun growing larger in the distance.

Arda hadn't been lying about sending her crew away. I clicked on the long-range scanners. They weren't even visible on there. Where could they have headed?

It really was mind-boggling that she'd strand herself here with me, all so her crew could dig jesillium on some wayward asteroid. Who did that? Why wouldn't they just wait for the repairs to be completed?

If only I could get out of my head long enough to hold a normal conversation with the woman. She was just so *unnerving*, the way she glared at me with those stunning blue eyes. I couldn't deny the attraction I felt for her. It was completely unprofessional.

I was headed to her planet to open up trade, and possibly find a wife. *I hope all the Terran females are not so argumentative.* Though if they all made my blood boil like Arda did, it would be easy enough to find a mate.

I scrubbed a hand across my face, and turned back to the panel. A blinking button on the communication array caught my attention. I sighed, certain it was Elys calling back to bug me again.

What luck. Just a message. I queued it up and my sister's bubbly voice blared out of the speakers.

"Hissss!" Smudge nearly jumped out of her skin.

"Easy, girl," I cooed at her with a smile, before returning my attention to the message just as Elys wrapped up her rambling greeting.

"I'm sure you're busy with repairs, so I won't keep you. I'm calling because I found something rather strange in your stowaway's genetic code. I'm sending it to a friend of mine who specializes in genetic research to examine it more. I know enough to notice something off, but I don't have the skillset to say *what* exactly it is. I just thought you should know. That Terran on your ship is more than she seems. Be careful brother."

More than she seems? What was that supposed to mean?

I nearly revved up the comms to return her call, until I spotted the clock. It displayed both Galactic Standard and the local time on my home world, Pheria. Elys would undoubtedly be asleep at this hour.

I might as well turn in too. There was a lot of work needed to fix the damage from Arda's crash. Pherians didn't need as much sleep as Terrans, but if I wanted to ensure I awakened well before Arda did, then I better get started. Until I figured out what Elys meant with her cryptic message, and Arda explained more about her purpose here, then I didn't want her wandering around my ship alone more than necessary.

I left Smudge where she was, curled up in her bed on the bridge floor, and headed for the med-bay. Probably better not to have her wandering around all the medical supplies while I slept.

I toed off my boots and climbed onto the lightly cushioned stasis pod. The pod was built for someone my size, but it wasn't nearly as large as my bed. And since I wasn't closing it to go into stasis, if I wanted to roll over, I had to be careful not to fall off the narrow edge.

Thoughts of my bed made my mind wander back to Arda. Those long brown curls would be splayed out on my pillow. Her lush curves nestled beneath my sheets. Would she sleep with her skinsuit on... or was she in my bed right now, naked and relaxed?

I couldn't stop myself from picturing her. Was all her skin that same glowing tan color? Or would it be rosy like when she blushed at something I said? My hands tingled, remembering the softness of her curves when I'd patted her down. That little gasp that escaped her when I cupped her breasts.

My dick twitched, hardening within my skinsuit. I shoved the memory from my mind. At this rate, I was going to need an ice bath to get to sleep.

"Dral help me," I muttered, right before I turned and fell off the pod, smacking into the med-bay floor.

I groaned, standing up slowly. But at least the pain killed my erection. I laid back down, determined to erase all thought of my maddening stowaway from my mind.

Arda

I was back in the med-bay, standing with my legs splayed while Luxuth knelt before me and glided those cold hands up my thighs. I shivered, my breath escaping in a gasp when I peered down my body and noticed my skinsuit was missing.

What the hell? Wasn't I avoiding getting naked? The indignation slid away. All I could focus on was those icy digits creeping ever higher.

His touch started out methodical. A pat and a squeeze, inch up, repeat. But the closer he came to my aching core the more he lingered. He rubbed his fingertips on my inner thigh with each frustrating caress, until my whole body thrummed with pent up desire.

I wobbled on my feet, and instead of standing stubbornly, I sank my fingers into his long golden hair, using him as my anchor. Luxuth hummed as I massaged his scalp, his touch drifting closer and closer to where I ached.

Bang, bang, bang.

"What's that?" I gasped as Luxuth leaned in and trailed the tip of his cold nose over my mound.

"Ignore it," he demanded.

For once his bossy tone didn't bother me. I was too mad with lust. I wanted his mouth on me next. Would it be cold, like the rest of him? Or would that one spot sizzle against my heated flesh?

Bang, bang, bang. "Time to rise. We have work to do."

I jerked awake. Damn. I was only dreaming. "I'm up," I yelled, before the object of my lust decided to burst in and caught me all hot and bothered. "I'll be out in a minute."

"Meet me in the mess. Two hatches down on the left."

I rolled my eyes as the pounding of Luxuth's footsteps disappeared down the hall. I hadn't even dragged myself out of bed and he was already ordering me around. My rising annoyance was enough to tamp down the desire throbbing between my legs.

Tugging my boots back on, I quickly used the attached washroom. I stared at my reflection in the mirror. "You can do this Arda. I know he's annoying, and too damn sexy for his own good, but you only have to deal with him for a few days."

"Do you require assistance?" The computer's droning female voice made me flinch.

"No, I'm—" I started, then shook my head, an idea forming. Why hadn't I thought of this before? "Wait. Computer, what species is Commander Luxuth?"

"Commander Luxuth is a Vamphere, from the planet Pheria."

"Vamphere," I repeated, rolling the word around on my tongue. I couldn't remember hearing anything about his species before, but the name sounded vaguely familiar. "Can you tell me about his species?"

"Vamphere are the apex predator species of Pheria. The planet is located at the coordinates 98.376—"

"Enough." I might be here all day listening to the computer spout off facts and figures. Might as well go get the story from the man himself.

I opened the hatch and slid out into the hall. Within moments I stood in the open hatch to the mess, two doors down. The room was bright and clean, the walls a shiny cream that glittered slightly beneath the fluorescent overhead lighting. A single white table that might have been made of plastic dominated the small room, with a trio of chairs wrapped around it, all of which appeared to be bolted to the floor.

The only other thing of note was the massive food processor on the far wall. The Verne had one as well—a machine capable of preparing nearly any food you could imagine using advanced alien science I did not understand. I sighed. It wouldn't come close to the Earth-grown stuff, but I was dying for a cup of Earl Grey.

There was only one problem. Luxuth was posted in front of it, his massive back blocking me from reaching the controls. He raised a cup to his lips as I closed in, seeming lost in thought.

"Excuse me. Can I put in an order?"

"Hm?" Luxuth turned, his throat working as he swallowed. My gaze was drawn to the long column of his throat. Was it my imagination, or was his pale skin pinker today?

He lowered the mug and licked his lips. My eyes traced the movement, and my stomach dropped to my feet. I blinked furiously, trying to make sense out of what I was seeing.

But even as my mind tried to deny it, my heart pounded and my skin came alive with tingles. My breath sawed in and out of my lungs. I stumbled back, knocking into a chair as I raced to leave.

"Arda? Where are you going?"

"I-I need to pee." I raced down the hall and didn't stop until I was crammed into the little bathroom again, with the door closed and locked firmly behind me.

"Oh no. This is bad. This is really bad," I muttered, pacing as best as I could in the tiny washroom.

Maybe there's an explanation. Maybe what I spotted in the cup... and on his lips... wasn't what I thought it was. I mean, its not like I waited around for an explanation.

I stopped in front of the mirror, staring into my wild eyes. My face was flush, my chest heaving, my heart still tumbling like a ship caught in a meteor shower.

"Computer?" I sucked in a calming breath.

"How may I be of assistance?"

"What does the species Vamphere eat?"

"Vamphere are carnivorous and hematophagous."

Christ, this computer is gonna be the death of me. "Define hematophagous."

"Hematophagous creatures feed primarily on blood."

Fuck. Suddenly it struck me why that name sounded so familiar. I sank down on the toilet seat, cradling my head in my hands.

First the zombie bunny-cat. Now this. *I'm sharing a ship with a goddamn space vampire!*

8

Rubbing Both Ways

Lux

I sighed, staring into my mug. The crimson fluid sloshed against the sides, its coppery scent making my stomach rumble.

The sound of a door slamming down the hall reverberated in my ears.

I'd heard humans would find our consumption of blood disturbing. Arda couldn't disappear fast enough when she glimpsed my breakfast.

Well, Elys, guess this proves it.

My little sister bet me the humans would be less superstitious than the rumors claimed, but if Arda's reaction was anything to judge by, we'd have trouble getting the Terrans to accept our dietary requirements.

I swallowed the rest, enjoying the warmth radiating through me before I headed into the hall. I paused outside my quarters, frowning at the apprehension coiling in my gut.

The little female has me nervous about entering my own room. I shook off the thought with a shrug and ducked through the open hatch. She wouldn't have left it open if she didn't mind being bothered, right?

There was no sign of Arda inside, but the muffled sound of her voice rang out behind the washroom door. Was she talking to herself in there? Had seeing me drinking blood made her that distraught?

But the answering tones of Destiny sounded next. Why was she chatting up the computer?

Bang, bang, bang. "Come out, Arda. We need to talk."

The shuffle of her footsteps preceded the door flying open and nearly slamming me in the nose. I backed away just in time, scowling.

Arda froze in the doorway, and I immediately spotted the panic flooding her blue eyes. Her chest rose and fell erratically, her skin flush.

"Vamphere." She stared at my mouth, her hands curled into fists at her sides.

I caught a glimpse of myself in the mirror behind her and winced. A drop of blood lingered on my bottom lip. *No wonder she's staring at my mouth.* My tongue darted out, swiping up the offending droplet.

Arda gasped, tracking the movement.

Now I was the one frozen. Arda's eyes burned bright, and her own tongue flicked out, licking her lips. If I didn't know better, I could almost imagine she liked what she saw. That watching me—no. Surely, that was only wishful thinking.

Arda shook off her temporary reaction. She shoved her shoulders back, standing ramrod straight, and pinned me with a withering glare. "You're right. We do need to talk. Why didn't you tell me you were a bloodsucker?"

"That's exactly why. The prejudices of your species are well known throughout the galaxy."

Arda frowned. "Prejudice? Is it prejudice if it's true? You were sucking down a cupful of blood in there, weren't you?"

"I was."

"So, it's true. Your species *are* space vampires."

I rolled my eyes. "Your Terran myths are far from the truth."

"Well then, enlighten me." Arda crossed her arms, leaning back against the washroom door.

I sighed. "No one is sure how the Terran stories about my kind evolved, but my people believe one or more of our species may have crashed on your planet long ago. There are enough similarities to suggest it."

"Like drinking blood." Arda cocked a brow. "What else?"

"The sun in your system is much stronger than our own. We can't go out in daylight on your world. Our lifespans are nearly double yours, and we maintain a youthful appearance for nearly all of it, which might give the appearance of immortality." I shrugged. "The rest of it is complete fiction, likely invented to sell more books."

"So, stakes through the heart? Garlic? No reflection?"

"I'm quite fond of garlic. And as you can see." I pointed into the bathroom and waved once Arda turned to glance at the bathroom mirror. "Stabbing a Vamphere in the chest would likely kill us, just like it would a human—but we won't burst into dust, or flame, or whatever other unlikely thing your Terran myths claim."

Arda whipped around, her delicate fingers slipping up to wrap around the slim column of her throat. "And the blood drinking? You don't—"

"No. I won't be sneaking in at night to bite you." I leaned closer, my eyes drawn to the rapid rise and fall of Arda's chest beneath her gray skinsuit. "Not unless you want me to."

Arda's breath caught. There was that burning ember in her gaze again. "Why on Earth would I want that?" Though her words spoke of disbelief, her shaky tone belied the lingering curiosity she couldn't hide. Her eyes widened as she finished speaking, and she sucked in a nervous breath.

I drew closer and planted my hands on the cold metal, boxing her in. Arda's back pressed against the door. Her chin tilted up, those burning blue orbs imprisoning my own within her gaze.

"Blood is sacred to my kind. We use the blood of animals to sustain us. But there are other uses that might interest you."

"What uses?" I was so close to her now. The warmth of her breath trailed across my skin, making me want to press against her and feel that delicious heat flush against me. I held back somehow, stopping with only a few inches of space between us.

I broke eye contact and leaned close to her ear. "When Vamphere take a lover, they often share blood."

Arda shuddered. Was it fear behind her reaction, or something else? "In our myths, that turns the human into a vampire."

"More fiction. We're born, same as you."

"Then why the," Arda gulped, "sharing?"

"Our blood has aphrodisiacal qualities." I leaned back, needing to see if that fire was still there in her eyes. *Dral help me.* The look she seared me with had my whole body burning like she'd doused me in flames. "Perhaps that is the truth behind the myth. I imagine a Terran experiencing such utter bliss would be turned off by human lovers afterwards."

Arda tensed, her gaze locked onto my mouth. For half a second, I wondered if she would rise on her toes and take my lips with hers. But then she stuck her palms on my chest and shoved.

"Puh-lease! Are all Vamphere so cocky, or is it just you?" She pushed past me, leaving me to watch the mesmerizing sway of her hips as she strode to the hatch, chuckling. "A planet full of sex gods. I'll believe it when I see it."

Did she intend to make that sound like a challenge? *Challenge accepted.*

Arda

Luxuth trailed me back to the mess, but didn't follow me inside. He grunted something about needing to visit the bridge, then left me to my own devices.

Luckily, the food processor was simple enough a child could operate it. Within minutes, I settled down with a bowl of cinnamon oatmeal and an acceptable—albeit nowhere near as delicious as I was used to—cup of tea.

My gaze lingered on Luxuth's empty mug. It sat in a bin beside several others next to a metal cabinet that I suspected hid a dish sanitizer. Did he drink blood every day? At every meal?

If that was the case...

I'm in trouble.

Why did it have to be blood? The thought should've sickened me. It likely would've disgusted a normal human woman, but not me. The sight of that blood drop on his lips had sent a bolt of lust straight to my clit. It's a miracle I didn't moan. I'd been about one second away from shoving him onto that huge bed and grinding all over his lap.

Fuck. I scooped another bite of oatmeal into my mouth.

The only grinding I should be doing is with tools, fixing my ship. I had to get out of here. I should be back on the Verne with my crew, ensuring we mined enough jesillium to secure my debt. Not trapped here with an alien sucking down blood and messing with my head.

Luxuth appeared in the hatch as I finished my breakfast. "I will move your ship now. Come." He didn't wait for a reply, just stalked off down the hall immediately.

I drew a calming breath and choked down an irritated retort. The way he just barked out orders really pissed me off.

When I arrived at the docking bay, Luxuth was already hitching a winch to the hopper. A machine hummed and clanked, jerking my ship upward. I grimaced as the full extent of the damage to his smaller shuttle was revealed. The hull had collapsed almost entirely, reminding me of a crushed can.

A wave of guilt washed over me. Luxuth might be grumpy and brash, but he'd been kind to me. Even after I wrecked his docking bay and smashed his shuttle.

He settled the hopper on the floor beside his wreck. "Should be more stable now."

"Thanks." I sent him a smile. His eyes zeroed in on my lips and I bolted for the hopper, ignoring the way my pulse kicked up.

Once inside, I sank into the pilot's chair ready to work, but the communication array blinked insistently, demanding my attention.

"Verne, come in."

"Arda," Ren replied a second later. "Where have you been? We've been dying for an update over here."

"I'm fine. Just been busy. How about you two? The mining going smoothly?"

"Yep, no problems over here. We hit a rich patch." Ren's news had relief flooding through me instantly. "So, how are repairs?"

"Slow. I had to help the commander clean up the bay before I could get started."

"The commander is working with you? Not the crew?"

"There is no crew. Just the two of us."

"Oh. No wonder the repairs are so slow. Well, is she good company at least?"

I winced. Guess Zenda didn't share the news with Ren. "He is pleasant enough, I suppose."

"Arda! A man... What species?"

"He's a Vamphere."

Ren squeaked, then shouted so loudly I covered my ears. "Zenda! Get in here."

A few seconds ticked by, then Zenda's voice joined in, "Arda. How are you?"

Ren spoke up before I could reply, her voice full of alarm. "She's stranded alone with a *man*, Zen. An *alien*. Why the hell did we leave her again?"

Ren wasn't a fan of men. The only thing she liked less was alien men. I'd listened to enough of her jokes and witnessed her lips curl up into a sneer enough times to realize it, though she'd never shared exactly why they disgusted her.

"It was my call, Ren. We can't miss our deadline."

"The mining is right on track," Zenda said. "We should be back for you in a few days."

"What the fuck is a Vamphere?" Ren's voice was so strained, I could almost picture her pacing and pulling her hair.

"Vamphere?" From the startled gasp that followed, I guessed Zenda had heard of them. "What is he doing here? Their planet is so far from Earth it takes a full year to travel there."

Seriously? I didn't realize that. The revelation sent a sinking feeling spreading through my gut. "The topic hasn't come up yet."

What was he doing here? As far as I knew, none of his kind had made a home on Earth. If men like him showed up, it would've definitely made the news. More likely, it would've set off a riot from all the women whose ovaries tingled at the sight of them.

"Do we need to come get you?" Ren asked. "Fuck the deadline. We can—"

"Ren, relax. I'm fine. Luxuth has been the perfect host." Well, he accused me of being an assassin, but we'd worked through that.

"Luxuth. Hm, sounds sexy. Is he?" I could hear the laughter in Zenda's voice. Unlike Ren, she'd never been one to turn down a visit to the outer rim brothels. I'd even snuck a peek at her chosen bot on her last trip. She hadn't gone for a human, like me, but one of the alien models.

My gaze strayed out of the viewport and found him instantly, the muscles of his back and shoulders bunching as he strained to twist a wrench. "I don't think sexy is a strong enough word for it. He's built like sin. Too bad he's an arrogant prick."

"Damn. I'm guessing that's rubbing you the wrong way." Zenda paused, then added, "Maybe he can rub you the right way, too."

Ren jumped in, "Are you insane? Don't listen to her, Arda. Nothing good can come from sleeping with an alien. Trust me on that. Stick with the bots. Much safer."

I rolled my eyes. Were we really having a debate about my sex life right now? "I'm signing off. Gotta start on those repairs."

"All right, Capt. Get off." Zenda giggled, then broke the connection, obviously tickled with herself from sneaking in one last jab.

I allowed my gaze to linger on Luxuth again. Would it really be so bad to have a little fun while we were stuck together? He certainly didn't seem opposed to the idea, judging from all his boasting. Not that I believed him about that whole sex god thing. I mean, come on. How much better than a human could he *really* be?

I sighed and pushed the thought from my mind. Ren was right. The bots were safer. I'd spent my whole life tamping down my desires. I'd seen what could happen when someone gave into them. No matter how much I craved it, I couldn't allow that to happen to me.

Lux

Arda stayed in her shuttle for hours tinkering. I left her alone, even though a part of me wanted to pull her out and make her talk. I could sense she needed time to herself. Time to come to terms with everything I'd revealed. But she couldn't avoid me forever.

"I'm going to grab some lunch." Arda hopped out of her shuttle and paused beside me, flicking her long brown waves over one shoulder. "Do Vamphere eat lunch? You know, like a mid-day meal?"

I remained seated and kept my hands busy repairing a particularly tricky piece of machinery. "Some do. I'm not hungry."

"Suit yourself." Arda disappeared into the hall.

Truthfully, I was kind of hungry. But I could eat later, alone. Watching her lip curl with disgust while I drank my lunch wasn't very appealing. Would she ever get used to dining with a *bloodsucker*?

I shuddered, recalling the venom in her voice and the sneer on her plump mouth while she accused me of lying to her. She couldn't truly be mad about that. We just met. What did she expect? Should I have introduced myself and blurted out what I'd be having for breakfast in the same breath?

I continued the repairs, lost in thought until a warm touch caressed my lower back. "Smudge. What are you doing here?" I rubbed behind her ears, and she purred loudly. "I thought I left you lounging in your bed with the hatch closed."

I lifted a brow and turned toward the hall. Smudge couldn't unlock hatches. Was my stowaway snooping?

Elys' warning rang in my ears. She'd said Arda wasn't what she seemed... What *was* she doing here? Could she be a spy, eager to stop me from completing my mission?

There were rumors of factions on Earth who weren't happy about their planet's recent inclusion in the universe at large. Isolationists who wanted to burn all the ships with faster than light travel and remain locked within their own system, and keep all the aliens out. It was one reason the Terrans weren't full members of the Galactic Union yet.

Was Arda one of them? She could be an extremist determined to send me packing before I opened trade negotiations between our species. From what I'd seen and heard, the Terrans were extremely intelligent. I wouldn't be surprised if her little "crash" wasn't a mistake at all, but a deliberate attempt to dig up dirt.

Only one way to find out.

I left Smudge curled up on the floor and tiptoed to the hall. I headed for the mess first, half-expecting her to be sitting there, quietly eating alone. She'd grin up at me as I burst in, giving me another one of those maddening smiles that sent my pulse racing. But when I halted in the doorway, I found the room deserted.

Maybe she was in her—*my*—room? A few long strides brought me there only to find it just as empty. I peeked in the washroom. Not there either.

Well, there was one place I knew she had been. I opened every hatch on my way, glaring inside each room. By the time I'd reached the bridge, I still had spotted no sign of her.

Not many more places she could hide.

The bridge hatch stood ajar. Definitely not how I left it. My heart raced, skin tingling with anticipation for her prickly welcome. I expected her to swing around in the pilot's chair when she heard my footsteps, a guilty expression on her face. But she wasn't there either.

I frowned. Where could she be? She hadn't slipped back into the docking bay without me noticing. I'd been posted right by the doorway. Unless she'd suited up for a spacewalk, that only left one place to look.

The cargo hold. A slow smile spread on my face. She wasn't an assassin, or an extremist. My pretty little stowaway was a thief.

9

Elite Treatment

Arda

"Holy shit, I've hit the motherload," I muttered under my breath. I stood in the cargo hold of Luxuth's ship, blinking furiously at the gleam of gray gold. Dozens of barrels dotted the floor, lined up in neat little rows. I'd only cracked the lid off of one, but my heart raced, suddenly certain that this was the reason for the scans that had led me here.

It took our crew days to mine the contents of a single one of these barrels. Jesillium was the rarest commodity in the universe, only found on wayward meteors and in the hearts of the occasional asteroid. It was more treasured than gold, diamond or any Earthbound gem. Without it, faster than light engines couldn't run.

Luxuth was sitting on a goddamn treasure trove! What the hell did he have all this jesillium for?

I sank my fingers into the barrel and caressed the shimmering gems. My heart sped even faster when the perfectly smooth rocks slid over my fingers. Lifting a single finger sized stone to my face, I nearly gasped.

This was not just any jesillium. The stuff we mined out in the depths of space was raw, uncut, and unrefined. The rock in my hand had been shaped and polished to the perfect shine. If every barrel here held refined jesillium, Luxuth was a very, very rich man.

The door to the hold whirred, and I spun at the sound. Luxuth darkened the door, arms crossed, his frowning face landing immediately on the rock in my hand.

"Strange lunch you have there. Are you here to steal from me, Arda?"

I shuddered, dropping the stone and smoothing the lid back in place hurriedly. "I-I was just curious. I didn't take anything."

I lifted my gaze from the lid to find Luxuth standing right beside me. He stepped closer still, forcing me to take a step back. My ass bumped into the barrel, and his hands landed on the lid, bracketing me in place.

"Do you know what they do to thieves on Pheria?"

I scoffed, meeting the hard glare of his silver eyes. "I told you, I'm not a thief."

Luxuth inched closer. Then he gripped my hips and spun me around, pressing my stomach against the barrel and tugging my arms behind my back.

I gasped, my blood boiling. "What are you doing?"

He dipped his head beside my ear. "Showing you what happens." He clasped my wrists in a single fist and clamped them against the small of my back. I struggled against his hold but his thighs pinned me in place, a shock of cold erupting across my skin as he pressed me against the barrel.

"Let me go!" I hissed, even as the feel of his weight pressing on my back sent tingles shooting across my body. My skin was too tight, my chest rising and falling erratically.

"First they'd search you." Luxuth's free hand glided over my skin-suit, going for my pockets.

I bucked against him as his hand sank into the deep pocket on my leg and worked its way across my thigh. Finding nothing, he switched his grip on my wrists and repeated the action on the opposite leg.

"I told you. I don't have anything." I squirmed beneath his touch, but that only made him press closer.

"They wouldn't stop at your pockets." His beefy palm worked its way out of my pocket. He tugged me away from the barrel just far enough to trace his hand across my stomach, leaving a trail of goosebumps in its wake. I shivered, reveling in the sensation at the same time I wanted to shove him far away. "So many places for a thief to hide such small treasures." His finger and thumb paused on the zipper at my throat.

"Don't you dare," I hissed.

He didn't listen. Slowly, he slid the zipper down to my navel. He tugged my skinsuit to the side and traced the outline of my sports bra. "Anything hiding in here?"

I bucked again, gasping as the hard outline of his cock brushed against the palm of my imprisoned hand before his hips inched out of my reach. "You can't be serious! Commander Luxuth, I'm not a thief."

His hand hovered over my bra. He dipped his head close to my ear and a wash of hot breath on my skin made me gasp. "Call me Lux."

"Lux," I whispered, feeling dizzy as the warmth of his breath brought back the question I'd wondered about since I'd awoken to that wickedly erotic dream. His cold fingers gripped my wrists, but his mouth was so *warm*. My mind swam with all the delicious possibilities.

C'mon Arda. The guy thinks you're here to steal from him. You can't be getting turned on now!

But my body wasn't listening to my inner pep-talk. My chest heaved, skin tingling with anticipation. Yet something made him hold back. I stood there teetering on the verge of craving his touch and wanting to run.

The craving won. "Do they freeze too?" I taunted.

"What?" Lux growled in my ear.

"The Pherians with their thieves?"

The hint of playfulness in my tone seemed to unlock something in Luxuth. He leaned further forward, and I tilted my head to meet his stare. He smirked at me for a half second, then his heated gaze glided down my chest.

His grip on my wrists loosened, enough that I could surely escape if I had wanted to. But I didn't. I tilted my chest toward his questing fingers as they slid under my bra.

I gasped as his icy fingertips made contact with my breast. My nipple pebbled up immediately. Lux plucked at it, and my pussy throbbed.

"Find what you're looking for?"

"Not done yet," he breathed into the shell of my ear, making shivers break out across my neck. His hand skimmed across my chest, his open palm circling the second hardened peak slowly.

I choked off a moan, enjoying this little game immensely. But how far would Lux take it? "Satisfied, now?" I asked, breathless.

"I'll show you satisfied."

Lux

I kneaded Arda's round breast, pulling a whimper from deep in her throat. That sound was intoxicating. She was like a drug, tempting me to indulge. And now that I'd finally surrendered to the urge to touch her, I felt like I'd reached new heights.

She canted her hips and rubbed against me. My dick stood at attention, straining against its confines, but I resisted the urge to grind against her curvy ass. I tore my hand away from her plump breast and unlocked her hands from my loose grasp, placing them on the edge of the barrel.

"Are thieves on your homeworld given a lot of satisfaction?" she asked, reminding me of my boast. And our game.

I eased her zipper down further. Arda inched away from the barrel, eager to allow my questing fingers room to explore. I smiled against her neck then traced a line up the warm flesh with my tongue, delighting in the way she shivered.

Oh, the taste of her. Salty and sweet. I wanted to taste her everywhere.

What was she asking?

I slid my hand inside her skinsuit and toyed with the edge of the tiny scrap of fabric covering her mound. "On my world, our elite forces train in isolation for months at a time. A pretty little thing like you wouldn't be brought to the gaoler. You'd be given to the elite to slake their lusts."

She gasped, and I couldn't be sure if it was from my words or my fingers finally slipping into her panties. I skimmed through her slick warmth, my cock throbbing as I imagined her wrapping all that heat around me.

"They would pass you between them." I slid a finger inside her. "Keep your tight cunt filled without a break."

She moaned. I pumped my finger inside her steadily and she rocked with the motion, chasing it every time I withdrew.

I gripped her chin and tilted her head back. "That and your pretty mouth."

I lifted my thumb to trace her lips, and she sucked it in. The cloudy haze of desire in her eyes and the warmth of her hot mouth suctioning the digit sent a bolt of lust straight to my groin.

Dral help me. The woman would have me bursting in my skinsuit if she kept that up.

I sank another finger inside her. She moaned again, and I pulled my thumb out of her mouth.

I jerked her bra down, exposing her full breast so I could rub my wet thumb over her nipple. She shuddered and shook, and I could tell she was close.

"They wouldn't just expect you to take their come. They'd feed you their blood too."

She stiffened. I pulled my fingers out, sliding through her wet heat until I found a spot that made her shudder and whimper when I circled it.

I pinched her hard nipple and purred in her ear, "They'd keep you so high you'd lay back and beg for more, no matter how many men claimed you."

She squirmed, her hands clenched on the barrel. "Lux. *Please.*"

I thrust my fingers inside her and she moaned so loud the delicious sound sank into my veins.

"Would you like that, Arda? Having your sweet cunt filled," I punctuated each word with a hard thrust, "over and over?"

"Yes," she shrieked. "Yes, fuck!"

Her cunt pulsed around my fingers, and she shook in my arms. I kept pumping until she rode out her release and her hips stilled.

"Hm. Too bad you're not a thief then." I pulled my hand out of her panties and took a step back. "I think that was a long enough lunch break, don't you?" I grabbed her shoulders and spun her towards the hatch. "Stay out of the cargo hold. We don't want you getting tempted to earn your place with the elite."

Arda scowled, wrenching her skinsuit closed. I thought she might throw a smart remark back at me, but all she did was race away. I sucked in a deep breath and followed more slowly, my cock throbbing so much it was painful.

The hatch to the docking bay slammed as I emerged into the hall. I smirked and headed for the washroom. As soon as the door closed, I tore down my zipper and gripped my rigid cock in my fist. With the memory of Arda fresh in my mind, and the smell of her on my fingers, I stroked myself.

I pictured her laid out on my bed, stripped naked, legs spread. That hot, wet cunt just waiting for me to fill it. Those breathy little moans of hers serenading me as I claimed her.

It only took me a few pumps to find my release. The pleasure coiled up my spine and my whole body tingled. I groaned as I came, spilling my seed into the toilet.

In the aftermath, doubts swam in my head. I still didn't know Arda well. Yet when I'd found her in the cargo hold, with her luscious mouth parted in shock and her chest heaving, she just looked so sexy.

Before I knew it, my hands were all over her like they had a life of their own. I almost left her there before it went too far until she leaned into me and started teasing me, showing me she craved my touch.

But though I wasn't certain of her intentions, I couldn't find it in myself to regret what happened between us. We were both adults. Nothing wrong with blowing off a little steam. I smiled as I zipped up and headed for the docking bay.

10

Widespread Blowout

Arda

I hurried out of the cargo hold and into the docking bay. My cheeks burned as Lux's parting words rang in my ears. "We don't want you getting tempted to earn your place with the elite."

Asshole. It's not like I really wanted to be some aliens' sex slave. I'll admit, the thought of it was pretty damn hot when he was whispering about it in my ear while he played with my pussy. But in real life... no fucking way.

What *was* that back there? When he found me holding that jesillium, I was certain he would scream at me and lock me up somewhere until my crew came back to pick me up. Not make me come while painting a very vivid picture in my mind.

He hadn't kissed me, or even let me touch him, except for that single accidental graze. Was he just toying with me? Punishing me for stepping out of line?

If that's what passes for punishment on Pheria, I bet crime is widespread.

I chuckled at the thought, then climbed into the hopper's cockpit and started on the repairs. A few minutes later, Lux sauntered in. He met my gaze through the viewport, his face hard and unsmiling, then turned away, heading for the same broken equipment he'd been working on all morning.

Guess he's back to ignoring me. Whatever.

The repairs were enough to occupy my hands and my mind, and I sank into the job, burying thoughts of my infuriating shipmate. Unbolting a panel from the wall, I settled on the floor to tinker inside the bowels of the ship. I was so engrossed with the task that I was totally blindsided when something nudged my ass.

"Ahh!" I screamed loud enough to wake the dead, my heart thumping to life. "Oh, it's you."

Smudge cocked her head beside me, her floppy ears bouncing as she stared up at me.

"We've got to stop meeting like this," I said, while petting her ugly little head. She started purring instantly, her toasty flesh vibrating beneath my fingers.

"Arda!" Lux burst into the cockpit, his normally stoic expression replaced with widened eyes and a deep frown. He stalled out as he spotted me on the floor with Smudge. "I heard screams."

"Sorry. Smudge snuck up on me." I smiled at him, feeling sheepish. Still, I couldn't resist needling him a little. "Were you worried about me?"

He leaned against the wall, crossing his arms. "I wouldn't be a good commander if I didn't see to the welfare of my passengers."

"Is that what you were doing in the cargo hold? Seeing to my welfare?" The words popped out before I had time to think them through.

"I did not hear you complaining."

What the hell kind of non-answer was that? Ugh, the man was infuriating.

I rose to my feet and stepped closer. "You know what? I *do* want to lodge a complaint. Who do I talk to about that? Who the hell sent you out here to manhandle unsuspecting women out in the depths of space?"

Luxuth rolled his eyes. "No one sent me." He sighed heavily. "Complaint noted." Then he stalked out of the cockpit.

A blast of shame seared me where I stood. My damn temper. I shouldn't have bitten his head off like that.

It's not like I hadn't wanted it. I'd been a willing participant in the hold. My pussy tingled as the memory of his touch rose in my mind. Those thick, icy fingers sliding across my heated skin and pumping inside me.

The dirty fantasy he'd whispered in that husky voice replayed in my ears. When he'd mentioned blood... that got me hotter than I'd ever been in my life.

Then when I'd screamed, he'd run to check on me. He tried to play it off as nothing, but damn if that didn't make my heart squeeze a little.

Fuck. I better go apologize. I left the cockpit, hoping I could keep my foot out of my mouth long enough to take back my harsh words.

Lux

I marched out of the docking bay and into the mess. Arda's angry face played in my mind and her insistent complaint rattled against my skull.

She wasn't fooling anyone with that nonsense. I'd felt her fall apart in my arms. She'd wanted me to touch her. But it still stung, knowing she was willing to brush aside all that had happened between us.

I'd raced inside her pitiful excuse for a shuttle, thinking of nothing but her safety—certain that flying piece of junk had wounded her somehow—and all she wanted to do was complain about me.

I sighed, punching in an order on the food processor. I might not be able to wash away Arda's regret, but at least I could relieve the hunger burning in my gut. The machine dinged, and I grabbed the mug and took a sip. The delicious tang exploded on my tongue and slid down my throat to spread warmth through my veins.

"Lux?"

I spun around. Arda stood in the mess hatch, her gaze downcast.

Oh, no. Why does she look so sad? I couldn't stand to see the defeat in her posture and to hear the tiny tremble in her voice.

"Do you need to lodge another complaint?"

"What? No." She stiffened and shot me a hard glare.

That was better. I'd take her anger over her sadness any day.

Her gaze flicked to the mug in my hand, and her expression shifted. The anger was still there, simmering under the surface, but something stronger overpowered it in an instant. Her chest heaved and her cheeks pinked. Her eyes glazed over, just like they had when I'd thrust my fingers deep inside of her.

How intriguing. Was Arda not disgusted by my diet, but *turned on*? Maybe all my talk of the intoxicating effects of Vampherian blood had sunk in, making her eager to experiment.

"Does it bother you watching me drink blood?" I gulped down a mouthful, keeping my gaze trained on her the whole time.

She didn't look away. She stared straight at me and licked her lips. My cock twitched.

Arda shook her head. "I-I didn't come to talk about that."

I drained the mug and set it in the bin next to the sanitizer. Arda calmed the moment the cup left my hands. I sank into a seat at the table. "What did you come to talk about, then?"

She marched over to the table and sat across from me. "I wanted to apologize for what I said earlier." She stared at me directly. "And I want to formally rescind my complaint."

I wasn't expecting that. I leaned back in the chair, studying her. "All right. Consider it rescinded. Apology accepted."

She twisted her lips. I was certain she would bolt then, but she surprised me again. "Can we start over?" She stretched her hand across the table. "Hi, I'm Arda."

I quirked up a brow and glanced down at her hand. One of Destiny's lessons on human etiquette came to the rescue. She wanted me to shake her hand. Should I grab onto the chance she was giving me? A part of me was insulted that she wanted to wash away everything that happened between us to *start over*.

But the desire to not spend the next few days with her sniping at me won out in the end. I grabbed her hand. But instead of shaking it like their Terran customs demanded, I gave her a Pherian greeting. This one was normally only used for potential mates, but Arda wouldn't know that.

I dragged her hand across the table to my face. Leaning over, I took a deep sniff of her skin and placed a firm kiss on her wrist. Her pulse pounded beneath my lips, racing like a fuciera escaping a predator.

"Arda. I'm Lux." I released her hand, and she snatched it back, cradling in against her chest.

She sent me a wobbly grin and gulped. "I'm really sorry about crashing into your ship, Lux. You see, my crew and I are jesillium miners. When we spotted your ship in that camouflage, we obviously jumped at the chance to mine it. It was an honest mistake."

Arda's expression was so earnest, I believed her. "I see."

Her smile brightened a little. "So, what brings you out here? From what I hear, Pheria is a long way away."

"I'm headed to Earth. Someone needed to open trade with your planet after we discovered your civil war had ended, and I volunteered to go."

"Oh." Her eyes widened. "So, all that jesillium is for what? To buy stock from Earth to send back to your planet?"

"Exactly."

"Hm." She drummed her nails on the table as she considered my words. "I don't get it, though... What does Earth have that you'd come so far for? Aren't there other planets in the galaxy that are closer and cheaper to trade with?"

"It's simple. They want the same thing I'm hoping to find on your world." My stomach clenched as the words spilled out. I kept a close watch of Arda's face, suddenly extremely curious to see her reaction to what I had to say next.

"What's that?"

"A mate."

Arda

"A mate..." I repeated slowly, sitting perfectly still while a dozen questions bombarded my mind, but in the end all that came out of my mouth was a squeaky, "on Earth."

"Yes. I believe you Terrans call them spouses." He bent one leg and crossed it over his knee casually. "I have need of an heir. Our species are compatible." He shrugged like it was of little importance, but his gaze stayed glued to my face.

"All that jesillium is meant to purchase brides?" I cocked a brow. "How many heirs do you need?"

He chuckled dryly. "They're not all for me. Our population has been steadily declining for centuries. We expect that interbreeding will be a boon to both our species. We're hoping to convince some of your females to relocate to Pheria. That will take time and plenty of funding to arrange."

"Why is your population declining?"

"Our long lifespan means longer pregnancies. Our females rarely have more than one child. Your females are said to have no issue birthing many."

Well, that made a strange amount of sense. Back home, after decades of civil war where men were the primary casualties, females outnumbered men twenty to one. There were bound to be plenty of Terran women eager to take the Pherians up on their offer. It would mean an actual partner, instead of a life spent screwing sex-bots and raising their children alone using donated sperm.

"And you're planning to find love while you're at it."

"Love has nothing to do with it. I need an heir, that's all."

"You make it sound so romantic." I rolled my eyes.

Lux leaned back. "I'm not flying to Earth seeking a lover's mating. I have a need, and I'm satisfying it."

"I don't get it. Why go to all this trouble? Can't you make an heir back on your planet?"

"I could. But Terran females are better suited to my particular needs." He waved a hand. "Besides, someone needed to be the first Pherian to mate with a human. I'm prominent enough on my world to lead by example."

I scoffed. "Big sacrifice on your part."

"I'm glad you see it that way."

Guess sarcasm isn't a thing on Pheria.

"What are your particular needs?"

Heat sparked in his eyes. "You're awfully curious about me, aren't you?"

"Fine. Don't answer." I moved to stand, but Lux grabbed my hand and tugged me back down.

"On Pheria when you choose a mate, you're bonded for life." His gaze burned into me. "I am told it's the same for you Terrans."

I gulped and nodded. "Usually, yes."

"I need an heir, but I do not wish to be tied down for longer than necessary." He let go of my hand and leaned back. "If I select a spouse who is close to the end of her fertility cycle, then it will likely only mean a few decades spent together."

I jerked back. "Wow. I don't really know what to say to that."

He was planning to knock up a woman in her forties so he wouldn't be stuck with her for long. *I'm definitely out of the running. Twen-*

ty-four is a long way away from forty. Shock reverberated through me. How could anyone be so calculating in finding a partner?

At the same time, a tinge of something I didn't want to examine too closely pinged around my chest. Something that felt an awful lot like disappointment.

I stood, and this time he let me. "Good luck on your cougar hunt. Just do me a favor, Lux."

"What favor?" He rose and followed me as I walked toward the hatch.

"I realize she meets your age requirements, but stay away from my mother. If I have to call you Daddy, I might puke in my mouth."

I thought he might laugh at that, but he only stared blankly, his silver eyes swimming with confusion. "What about you?" he asked finally. "What brings you out here, hunting for jesillium?"

I grinned, halting in the hatch. "Simple. My ships not paid off. I gotta meet my quota or I'll lose it." My smile fell at the reminder of the deadline hanging over my head.

Luxuth nodded. "I've always wanted to explore space. I envy you that."

"Why don't you?"

"Family. Responsibilities." He shrugged. "But one day I'll pass the company on to my heir and be free to enjoy my retirement exploring."

I bit my lip. It was kind of sad that Luxuth wasn't free to live his life how he chose. I could certainly relate.

I loved exploring. But the reason I chose a life in space wasn't entirely for the thrill of discovering new worlds. It was easier to escape the whispered words and side-eyed glances of the people who knew about my family's checkered past out here.

I shook off the thought and sent Lux a tight smile. "Glad we got that cleared up. I'm gonna get to work on the repairs."

"I will meet you there shortly." Lux turned on his heel and stalked off with no further explanation.

My boots clunked loudly down the hall as I fled in the opposite direction. I'd learned a lot about Luxuth today, but I still felt like I didn't know him at all. At least we'd turned a corner and moved on from all that naked hostility.

If only I could stop thinking about getting him naked...

Now that I knew he was hunting for a wife—and I didn't come close to meeting his odd qualifications—it was time to stop fantasizing about anything more happening between us. Nothing good would come out of it.

That twinge tugged at me again, but I ignored it and shoved open the docking bay hatch.

11

Coded Secrets

Lux

I opened the bridge hatch and stormed in. The disapproving look on Arda's face as I'd explained my plans replayed in my mind. She just didn't understand what it was like for me. There were certain expectations I had to meet for my family. For our future. Once I met them, I would be free to follow my own path. Sure, my plans didn't fit in with her feminine ideals of romance and love, but they would get the job done.

The communication panel blinked, drawing me from my thoughts. Elys again, no doubt.

"What can I do for you today, sister?"

"I'm glad I caught you. How are the repairs?"

"Progressing smoothly."

"That's good. I contacted the mayor and let him know you'll be delayed. They asked for an update on your timeline."

I sighed. "I'm not certain yet how long this will set me back. I can't engage the FTL engine until I complete the repairs."

"I understand. Keep me updated."

"I will."

Silence stretched out, and I wondered if she might leave it at that. But of course, she couldn't let me off that easily. "What about your stowaway? Have you learned anything else about her?"

"I've learned enough. I don't know what you discovered from her DNA, but I doubt she's a threat."

Elys gasped. "Lux... Do you *like* her?"

I rolled my eyes. How could she be so perceptive from light years away? "She's far too young for me."

"You act like you're older than dirt." Elys scoffed. "You're barely thirty, Lux. She can't be that much younger than you."

I bristled. "It doesn't matter. She's returning to her ship once we complete repairs and I'm going to Earth."

"That's too bad. I guess you don't want to know what my scientist friend discovered about her then."

I swiveled in the pilot's chair, making sure I'd closed the hatch behind me. "Wait. Tell me."

She chuckled. "Yeah, I thought so." I could picture the smug smile she likely wore. "I was right. There is something unusual about her DNA. My friend said she has markers that other humans don't."

"So, she's not human?"

"I asked the same question. She is human, but it's like someone tweaked her genetic code. Hers, or one of her ancestors."

My stomach clenched. The galactic charter banned DNA manipulation of sentient beings. Were the Terrans experimenting with forbidden sciences?

"And get this," Elys continued. "Guess what species those markers resemble?"

The question hit me like a starship collision. "Don't tell me... Vamphere." All of Arda's strange reactions when she caught me drinking blood suddenly made sense.

"You guessed it."

I leaned back, rubbing my temples. "What does that mean?"

"I don't know. But unless I'm completely off base, you like her. You should tell her what we've discovered."

"What if she already knows?" I groaned. "She'll want to murder me for digging into her genome in the first place."

"And what if she doesn't know?" Elys replied. "My guy said this was buried deep. It's not something that would show up on normal scans."

I thought back on our interactions together, trying to make sense of them in light of this revelation. The way she'd been so blindsided when I first told her who I was—when I explained who Vamphere were—certainly seemed to suggest she had no clue about her unique heritage.

"I think you're right. I don't think she knows."

"Well then, tell her. She deserves the truth."

I sighed. "You're right. She does. I better go."

"Keep me posted. Good luck," Elys said before breaking the connection.

I watched the communication panel's light flicker off, then closed my eyes. How could I break the news to Arda that her DNA was hiding such a massive secret? And worse, I'd need to explain how I learned of it in the first place—letting my sister send off the med-bot's readings—without her consent.

Something told me she wouldn't be happy. I rose from the chair, feeling like I was headed to my execution.

She's going to kill me. Can't say I blame her.

Arda

I should've gone back to work on the hopper when I returned to the docking bay, but I found myself pacing towards the outer hull of Lux's ship. From up close, the damage to the docking port didn't look so bad.

In fact, I knew exactly how to fix it. I smiled to myself and climbed into the hopper to grab my tools. Then I returned to the task, so engrossed with the repair that time slipped by me unnoticed.

Lux found me there sometime later. "What are you doing?"

I aimed a grin at him, ignoring the way his deep voice set off shivers down my spine. "I'm almost done, actually. I repaired the seal. The outer hatch should be back in order," I shifted back to the electrical panel and dripped a few more drops of solder, connecting the last wires, "right now."

"You didn't have to—" he grunted.

"I don't mind," I cut him off, shrugging. "Besides, I'm the one who wrecked it."

"Listen, Arda." Luxuth glared at me, that unreadable expression of his firmly in place. "We need to talk." Those words and the grim frown that briefly curved his lips sent a spike of fear up my spine.

He was gone for so long. What if he got bad news? My mind raced, throwing out worst-case scenarios like grenades, each one more explosive than the last. I slammed the panel back in place and lurched forward. "My crew. Is something wrong?"

Lux grabbed my arm before I made it back to the hopper. "No. Your crew is fine. This is about something else."

I spun to face him. "Go on, then. Spit it out."

He sighed. "Everything on this ship is connected to our family mainframe back on Pheria."

My gaze immediately darted to the ceiling, searching for cameras. "You sick fucks. Was someone watching us in the cargo hold?" I shuddered, picturing a bunch of aliens gathered around a screen watching Lux get me off. Incredibly, the thought sent a wave of lust crashing through me instead of disgust.

I nearly groaned. *Guess I can add being watched to the list of things I didn't realize turned me on...*

Luxuth grimaced. "Not like that. I mean the equipment. All the computer readouts and data are sent back for remote access."

"Okay..."

"The med-bot readings too."

My brow furrowed. "The med-bot gave me the all clear." Unless... "Did someone mess with the readings? Is something wrong with me?" I dragged my hands down my torso, like that might help me figure out what was wrong. Obviously, it wasn't that simple. There's no way I would feel it through my skin if something was off inside my body, but I couldn't stop my hands from frantically groping in a panic.

Lux groaned and grabbed my wrists. "Stop that. You're fine."

"Then what is it?" I snapped, trying to wrench my hands from his grip. Of course, it was no use.

"It's your DNA."

I stilled and shot him a disbelieving look. "My DNA?"

"Yes. We've had it analyzed by a geneticist on Pheria. There are markers in your genetic code that shouldn't be there. Markers that most humans don't possess." Lux let go of my wrists and grabbed my hands gently.

"You're kidding, right? This is a joke." I chuckled, but the thready laugh held no humor.

"I'm sorry, Arda. I wish I was."

I shook off Lux's hands and backed away slowly. "What markers? What does that even mean?" I frowned. "And what gave you the right to dig around in my DNA?"

Lux scowled. "It wasn't my idea. As long as Destiny is jacked into the mainframe, our crew back on Pheria can do what they want with the data."

I crossed my arms, glaring at him.

"I'm sorry, okay?" Lux stepped closer, and I backed up, keeping the same distance between us. He sighed. "The markers. They're Pherian."

"What does that mean?"

Lux shook his head. "I do not know. It might be genetic manipulation. To you or one of your ancestors."

Eyes widening, I bit back a gasp. If that were true... *Oh, fuck!*

"Arda, it will be all right. I will connect you with the genetics expert my sister found. He can run more tests and get to the bottom of things..."

I nodded numbly as he rambled on, but my mind wouldn't stop whirling. The revelation should have been shocking. It should have rocked me to my very core. Instead, a bright sense of relief rushed through me. It made a bizarre kind of sense—more than anything ever had in my entire life. It might even explain what drove my grandmother to commit such heinous crimes.

I opened my mouth to cut off Luxuth's string of reassurances, only to be silenced by a deafening blare.

Lux winced, covering his ears. "What is that?"

My blood ran cold. "The hopper's alarm. There's only one thing that could set that off. My crew's in trouble."

12

Frantic Distress

Lux

Arda raced into her shuttle. I followed, cringing while the alarm continued to blare.

She slipped into the pilot's seat and slammed a button on the dash, shutting off the noise. I sighed, but Arda's frown only spread as she scanned the ship's readouts.

"What is it?" I asked.

She ignored me in favor of firing up her communications system.

"Verne, come in," she yelled, voice tight with panic.

When no reply came, her hands started to shake. She frantically scanned the readouts, flicking from one screen to the next so quickly I couldn't make sense of it from where I crouched behind her.

"Arda," I spun her chair and grasped her shoulders. "Tell me what's happening."

Wild blue eyes met mine. "I don't know. They sent a distress call but didn't explain." She kicked at the floor, trying to spin back. "Let me go. I need to help them!"

"Take a deep breath," I demanded, refusing to let go.

Fire burned in her gaze. I was positive she was about to slap me and return to pounding on the controls. But then she sucked in a shaky breath. "Fuck! I sent them out there. This is all my fault."

"Another, Arda."

She obeyed, the breath sawing in and out of her lungs slowing considerably.

I released her shoulders and spun her back around. "Get their coordinates."

I didn't wait for her response. My boots slapped down on the docking bay floor and I hurried over to the machinery I'd left half-finished this morning.

Arda bounded out of her shuttle a moment later with a tablet in her hand. "I have it."

"Destiny," I said, keeping my hands and eyes trained on the repairs.

"Yes, Commander," the ship's computerized voice droned.

"Give Arda access to the bridge and all controls."

"Access granted," Destiny replied instantly.

Arda's jaw hung so low it was practically dragging on the floor.

"Go to the bridge and input the coordinates into the navigation system," I said.

She hurried off, and I grabbed a set of wire cutters. I couldn't fix the FTL right now—not completely—but if this worked, it might be enough.

The panic in Arda's gaze back in her cockpit tore at me. I couldn't just sit by and do nothing while she was so worried. This plan wasn't without risk, but if something happened to her crew and I didn't do everything in my power to save them, then what kind of man would that make me?

Arda appeared in the hatch just as I'd finished. "The coordinates are set."

"Good." I bent down, hefting the bulky component in my arms with a grunt.

"What can I do?" Arda rushed over, her brow furrowed.

"Grab my laserspanner," I muttered, as I shoved the part back where it belonged.

Arda handed me the tool and watched as I secured the seal. "Did you fix the FTL already?"

"No. Rerouted through the emergency backup. It will get us one jump." I nodded at the newly repaired hatch. If the docking port had even a tiny defect that prevented the seal from closing, it would be a death sentence once we activated the FTL. "You sure the repair to the docking port will hold?"

She bristled and crossed her arms. "Yes."

"Then we're all set." I shoved the spanner back in my tool kit and headed for the hall. "Come, Arda. We must strap in for the jump."

Arda trailed behind me, hurrying to keep up with my longer strides. I whistled sharply. Smudge darted in front of me and I scooped her up.

I secured Smudge in her carrier inside the bridge, then myself in the pilot's chair. Arda perched on the co-pilot's chair, her knuckles white from clenching the arm rest.

I leaned forward to start the jump, but before I reached the panel, Arda spoke. "Lux. Thank you."

The gratitude shining in her eyes made my heart stutter. We hadn't even left yet, and she was already beaming at me like I was her hero.

I can get used to her looking at me like that. I brushed off the wayward thought with a shrug.

"Don't thank me yet." I grinned. "Let's save your crew first."

Arda

The FTL fired up, and the jump detonated like a bomb blast. Adrenaline raced through my veins, my heart and mind at war, while the ship quivered and shook. It was the same every damn time, like the entire universe slowed down to super slow mode for a split-second while simultaneously racing at super speed. The dichotomy sent a sickening wave of dizziness through me.

But just as fast as it started, it was over. That was the good thing about the jumps. It felt like shit while you were in the middle of one, but they didn't last long.

Lux scanned the display as soon as the Destiny stopped shuddering. It took a moment for the navigation drive to catch up to our new place in the universe.

I jabbed a finger at the screen. "There!"

The unmistakable shape of my ship floated on the readout.

"If that's there, then..." Lux paused, slamming a button on the controls. The viewport shimmered and turned translucent.

I gasped. "Fuck! That's not even on the scans!"

My blood boiled as I surveyed the elongated sleek vessel currently attached to my poor Verne. With its massive size and distinctive torpedo shape—just like a gigantic dick—it dwarfed my little mining ship by at least ten times.

"The hell are they doing?" I yelled. "Who the hell are they?"

"Looks like Garcuks," Lux answered. My face must've shown my confusion. Lux glanced at me and continued, "They're notorious in this sector. Thieves and slavers. They must be cloaked. Probably snuck up on your crew without them realizing it."

"Giant dick sounds about right," I mumbled to myself.

"What?" Lux's brows shot up.

"Doesn't matter. Have they spotted us?"

Lux shook his head. "We're disguised like an asteroid, remember?"

How could I forget? "What are we going to do? They could be in there trying to capture my crew right now."

"You're probably right."

I twisted my nose, barely holding back a groan. "I don't need you being agreeable right now, Lux."

Where was the cocky asshole when you needed him? I could sic him on these invaders.

Granted, the way he took charge and flew us here, when I'd been awash with panic, was kind of insane. I was practically a stranger to him, and here he was, putting his ship in danger to help. I shoved the thought aside before I swooned like a proverbial damsel in distress. Fact was, I couldn't keep relying on Lux to solve my problems.

Think, Arda. Think!

"What weapons do you have on board?" I asked.

"Plenty. But nothing we can use while they're docked together."

"Fuck!" I lurched out of the co-pilot's chair and started pacing. "It hasn't been long since we received the distress call. Zenda and Ren might still be okay. They'll go after the jesillium first." I tapped my chin. "Maybe they'll come after us instead of hunting for my crew, when my ship's readouts ping your supply…"

Lux frowned. "These guys are not the type to do any mining. They want the easy grab." He scratched his head. "We could drop the disguise and send out a distress call of our own. Might convince them to abandon your ship and come to us."

"That could work. We can blast them as soon as they undock."

Lux turned back to the controls. "One problem. I can't scan for life signs. Their cloak is interfering with the readout."

"Wouldn't matter, anyway. We knew this might happen. There's a hidden panic room in the Verne. If Zenda followed protocol, then they're in there, hidden from the Garcuk's scanners, too."

"You sure that's a chance you want to take with your crew's lives?"

I blew out a shaky breath and rubbed the back of my neck when a sudden thought struck me. "Maybe we don't need to chance it. How close can you get us?"

"How close do you need?" Lux tapped on the console, bringing up the navigation controls. "What's the plan?"

I smiled, a rush of warmth flooding me as Lux's gaze connected with mine. He might be a jerk sometimes, but this was priceless. His willingness to help, to let me make the plans, showed I could count on him in a way I sorely needed right now.

Averting my eyes, I focused on the ship violating my poor Verne through the viewport. I rubbed the little square just under the skin on my neck. "If we fly within range, my implant will connect to the Verne. It's short range. I've never tested exactly how short…"

"Let's find out." Lux started the ship in motion.

I pressed down on the implant, activating the receiver. "Zenda, Ren. Come in."

No response.

Ren gave me a massive amount of shit when I splurged for the implant last year. I can still remember her curled lip and laughing taunts. 'Why would you want to be tagged like a dog?' When this worked, I was going to make her eat her words.

My heart raced as Lux slowly maneuvered the ship closer, keeping on a straight trajectory that wouldn't out us as a ship—hopefully. If this didn't work, then we might give ourselves away to the slavers before we could put our plan into action.

"Zenda, Ren. Come—"

"Capt?" Zenda hissed, her voice bouncing around my head.

"Zen. Thank God! Are you all right? What about Ren?"

"We're fine. Holed up in the panic room."

My shoulders slumped. "Good. Hang in a little while longer. We're going to get you out of there."

"There's still a bunch of them onboard. I can hear them stomping down the corridor. The jesillium, Arda—"

"Don't worry about that now. We'll need to move out of my implant's comm range to lead them away, okay? Don't panic if you can't reach me."

"Okay. Be safe, Capt."

"Are they hidden?" Lux asked.

I nodded. "Yeah. Let's blast these fuckers."

13

Tricks and Lessons

Lux

I leaned over the controls, setting everything in motion. Within a few moments, Destiny's asteroid disguise would shift back, and the distress call would reach the pair of ships currently locked together.

The Garcuk were a disgusting race. A species that would rather steal to survive than work an honest living. I'd met a few in the past and I could honestly say each experience was worse than the last. On our first exchange, they'd swindled me out of a lucrative trade deal. And then there was that time on the third moon of Zoimia. My lower lip curled as the smug look on Saenov's face rose in my mind.

I shoved the memory aside and smiled, pleased to be the one doing the tricking for a change. If Arda's plan worked, we could teach those slimy Garcuk a lesson they wouldn't soon forget.

We didn't have to wait long. A bare minute after Destiny shifted, and the call went out, the big, oblong ship detached from the Verne and blasted in our direction. I plucked at the controls, shifting our trajectory while maintaining a careless path that would hopefully still look like a ship in duress.

"What are you doing?" Arda's brow raised.

"I need to be sure the Verne won't get caught in the blast when we hit them."

"Smart." She flashed me a quick smile before returning her attention to the readouts.

My cold flesh warmed at the compliment. That was high praise from her.

By the time the Garcuk vessel flew within firing range, I'd flipped Destiny around. I readied the weapon controls, waiting for them to zero in on the docking bay.

"It's working," Arda whispered.

Just one more—now.

I fired up the torpedoes and aimed. A *whiz* sang in my ears as the system engaged. Then the concussive blast hit the Garcuk ship in an explosion of light.

"Yes!" Arda whooped with glee.

The Garcuk ship immediately reversed course, rushing out of weapons range. But not before it sent a parting gift right at us.

"Lux," Arda squeaked.

My fingers flew, sending Destiny sideways. "I see—"

I didn't have time to finish the sentence before the Garcuk's blast exploded beneath us. The quick maneuver saved us from a direct hit, but from the way Destiny shuddered and alarms shrieked to life, it was clear we'd taken damage.

"Are you all right?" I scanned Arda as she nodded, a hand splayed on her chest.

"That was it? It's over?"

I bent over the controls. "The Garcuk are cowards at heart. I suspected they would run once we put up a fight. But look," I tapped on a nav readout, "they're heading to the nearest planetary system. We must have done some serious damage if they're being forced to land."

"Good." Arda grinned. "Maybe we can sneak up on the fuckers and snatch my jesillium back."

"Destiny, damage report," I demanded as Arda tapped on the comm panel, attempting to open up a channel with her crew.

"We are operating at 78 percent optimal capacity."

"Display the damaged systems on my screen."

It wasn't too bad. Nothing affecting life support. No hull breeches. Only...

"Slight problem." I winced when Arda shot me a glare. "Our landing gear is out of commission. We won't be chasing after the Garcuk anytime soon."

Arda's face crumpled. "Oh." She sighed. "All right. Head for my ship instead. I need to check on my crew."

I nodded and changed course. I should've been happy. I was about to return Arda to her crew. Now that she'd fixed the docking port, there wasn't anything stopping her from returning to her ship. Her shuttle was still stuck in my bay, but I could arrange to have it fixed and returned once I arrived on Earth.

But though the thought should have bolstered my spirits, knowing I'd soon be back on track, I couldn't stem the sick wave of regret that washed over me.

I don't want her to leave.

I buried the thought and stared ahead as Destiny's auto-targeting engaged with the Verne's docking port. Then I watched her ugly little ship fill my viewport and forced a smile. "I guess this is goodbye."

Arda scoffed. "Goodbye?" She bounced out of the co-pilot's chair and her hand landed on my shoulder, sending a tingle down my spine. "You're not getting rid of me that easily. Come on. Let me introduce you to my crew."

I trailed Arda down the hall into the shuttle bay, watching her curvy backside sway. Clacks and bangs reverberated from inside, then the *hiss* of atmosphere pumping into the docking port.

I sucked in a deep breath, preparing myself for the journey through the slim tube now connecting our two ships. Not much fazed me, but small, tight spaces were not my favorite place to be.

When hurried footsteps echoed, I realized I wouldn't be cramming myself into the walkway just yet. A blur topped with cropped blonde curls bounded out of the hatch, colliding with Arda and wrapping her arms around her. She was taller and slimmer than Arda, with stained fingers that matched the black splotches on her green skinsuit.

"Ren," Arda said. "Fuck, it's good to see you."

A second woman arrived a moment later. She brushed a lock of bright red hair off her forehead and straightened her unusual glasses before clasping her arms around the pair.

"Zenda. I'm so glad you're safe." Arda's voice was strained, filled with a note of distress beneath her obvious relief. "When I spotted that big dick on top of the Verne I almost pissed myself."

I raised a brow, unable to halt the chuckle that rumbled through my chest at her crude description. My laughter startled the females into action. They broke apart, and all three turned to stare at me with wide eyes.

"This *him*?" Ren asked with a frown.

"Wow, you weren't kidding," Zenda murmured out the side of her mouth to Arda. Then she thrust out a hand to me. "I'm Zenda and this is Ren. Pleased to meet you, Commander Luxuth."

I took her hand in mine and shook the way I'd seen in the holovids of Earth I'd studied. But though I noticed the warmth of her skin, the woman didn't send any tingles over my flesh like when Arda touched me.

"Zenda. Ren. It's a pleasure to meet you as well." I nodded at both of them, deciding to forgo offering my hand to the scowling Ren, then peered behind them down the tube. "Should we go meet the rest of the crew?"

Arda shifted beside me. "No, this is everyone."

"You don't have any male crew?"

"Fuck no." Ren made a strangled sound in her throat that had my hackles rising. I nearly rushed to her aid until I remembered Arda's joke in the med-bay and it clicked that Ren was only gagging for effect.

"What Ren means to say is that most Terran men don't travel out of the system much," Arda explained. "With the shortage of men after the war, our government decreed any man who provides genetic samples regularly would be granted a generous stipend."

"All they're good for, if you ask me," Ren grumbled.

Well, it's pretty clear she's not a fan of men. A weighted silence fell over us, and I was trying to think of something to break the tension when Zenda shrieked and my pulse leaped into overdrive.

"Cuniculus!" She jumped, reaching an impressive height despite her short legs, and landed in a fighting position.

"What?" I whirled around, spotting nothing unusual.

"Relax, Zen." Arda giggled and jabbed her thumb in my direction. "That's his pet, Smudge. She scared the shit out of me too, when I first got here."

My heart slowed as my gaze landed on my fuciera cowering beside Arda's wrecked shuttle. I crossed the room and scooped her up in my arms. "Smudge is harmless, I promise."

"Sorry." Zenda blushed, dropping her fists.

Ren rushed forward, her gaze locked on the wreck. "My poor hopper." She skimmed a hand reverently along the craft's dented hull, her voice taking on a sweet lilt. "Mama will fix you."

"I'm heading to Earth. I can have your shuttle repaired and returned once I arrive," I offered.

"Fuck that," Ren said, all trace of sweetness gone. "The hell if I'm letting some stranger fiddle around inside her."

I turned to Arda. "Surely you'll be wanting to return to your ship now?" I held my breath, my stomach churning as I awaited her response.

She bit her lip and opened her mouth, but Zenda spoke up before she replied.

"Capt, about the jesillium." Zenda rubbed the back of her neck, her gaze downcast. "We mined enough to meet our quota before they came, but now... I'm so sorry. They took it all. They damaged the mining drones, too. I don't know if there's time to fix them, even if we can locate another batch of jesillium rich asteroids."

Arda's face fell, but then she flashed her crewmate a wobbly smile. "It's okay. You two are safe. That's all that matters. We'll think of something."

Warmth spread through my chest as I watched Arda console her crew. It was obvious all three cared for each other a great deal, and the theft equally discomforted each of them. If only there was something I could do...

"Did you see they were headed for the nearest planet?" Ren asked.

Arda nodded. "Yeah, we were gonna chase them, but the landing gear on Lux's ship was damaged in the blast."

Zenda perked up. "The Verne's landing gear still works."

"True." Arda glanced at me. "How quickly can we pull these ships apart?"

A vise clenched around my heart. She *did* want to leave. "I'll go with you." My reply came out unbidden, shocking me almost as much as it seemed to affect Arda.

"W-what?" Her eyes bulged so much they looked like they were about to pop out of her skull.

"You've never dealt with the Garcuk before. I have. Your crew will stay here and complete the repairs while we're gone."

Arda bristled at my command. It was a miracle she didn't immediately argue.

Ren chimed in, "I can handle the hopper repairs, Capt." She nodded to me. "I'll look at your landing gear, too."

"And I'll help. You know I'm no good in a fight." Zenda grinned impishly. "I'm more likely to punch one of you instead of the enemy. Take him with you." She spun to face me. "Thank you, Commander."

I quirked a brow at Arda, set Smudge down gently, and took a step toward the docking port. "Come, Arda. Let's go get your jesillium."

14

Sneaky Deals

Arda

The plush cushion of the pilot's chair in the Verne sank beneath me, and I sighed. It was like the first time laying in my own bed after spending ages bouncing from hotel to hotel. *Perfect.*

The co-pilot's chair squeaked, and I spared a glance sideways. "You don't have to come, you know. I can handle myself."

"Hm. Noted." Luxuth busied himself scanning the readouts, his brow scrunched.

"You look worried."

"The Garcuk are not a species to take lightly."

I jerked my head to the hatch. "Feel free to go back and help with the repairs."

Lux grunted and stayed stubbornly in place. His oversized body made the co-pilot's chair appear so comically small, I bit back a grin.

I shrugged. If he wanted to stay, I wouldn't force him away. It was oddly comforting having the big guy backing me up. And honestly, he was right. I didn't have a clue how to handle these dicks. With any luck, Lux would have something up his sleeve. Either way, I was getting my jesillium back. I couldn't lose the Verne, not when exploring space was the only thing keeping me sane.

I activated the navigation system and set our destination. A tingle of anticipation spread through my belly as the Verne jerked into motion. I pulled up the scans of the small blue world ahead of us. "I've never been on an alien planet before."

"You haven't?"

I shook my head. "I've been to all the settlements in the Sol system. Europa, Mars, Luna. And dozens of asteroids, of course."

"I'll take you to Pheria one day," Lux offered casually. "It's much like your Europa. A world of snow and ice."

I swallowed my surprise at his offer. He couldn't *really* want to take me to his home world. He was probably just making small talk. "Why are you going to Earth then and not Europa?"

"I cannot meet my goals there. Earth is the center of commerce in your system. Besides, I have been assured the new underwater settlements will be a pleasant enough environment for my species."

I bit my lip, studying him out of the corner of my eye. "No sunlight down there. Makes sense. Will the light be a problem for you on this world?"

"Hm, let me see." Rather than key up the information on his own display, Lux planted one of his big paws on my thigh and leaned over to stare at my screen. His cold touch set off a flurry of sensation on my skin.

"Well? What's the verdict?" I forced my voice to remain steady as his fingers caressed my flesh.

His drawled answer tickled my ear, reminding me of the last time he'd whispered to me in the cargo hold. My pulse kicked up, drumming through my veins like a pulsar. "I will be fine. The sun in this system does not shine as strongly on this world as your Sol shines on Earth."

I gulped, his words barely reaching my brain beyond the lust lighting up my skin from his simple touch and his enormous body hovering so close.

Fuck. I needed to shove him off. It was *so* not the time to be getting horny. But before I worked up the nerve, he retreated, removing his hand and leaning back in his seat.

"Look, we've arrived." Lux nodded to the viewport.

My breath caught in my chest as we began the descent. The little world was smaller than Earth. According to the readouts, the gravity would be much more in line with the pull on Mars, and the atmosphere was breathable.

"It's so blue." I squinted, trying to see past the gauzy cloud cover. "Is the entire world covered in water?"

Lux bent over the scans. "Doesn't look like it. And most of the water is shallow, it seems."

As we sank lower in the atmosphere, my gaze picked out the first rocky outcropping dotting the endless sea of lakes, and my eyes widened. "The planet's blue, too." I grinned. "I've never seen anything like it."

Lux grunted noncommittally. He flicked on the nav screen and jabbed a finger at the readout. "The Garcuk ship landed here. Their ship is damaged badly. We'll land nearby and offer our aid in exchange for the return of your cargo."

I crossed my arms. "And that's going to work?"

"The Garcuk's homeworld is weeks away. I was very deliberate with where I aimed my blast. I'm willing to bet both their FTL and comm systems are down."

I punched his shoulder with a grin. "So sneaky. I love it!"

The corner of his lips inched up a fraction at the compliment. "Like I said before, they are cowards. They'll take the deal if it will save them weeks of being stranded."

The phallic shape of the Garcuk's ship appeared on the horizon, punctuated by the clack of the landing gear descending.

"I hope you're right, Lux. Time to make a deal."

I landed the Verne without issue and we made our way through the ship silently. All the while, anticipation buzzed through my veins. The outer hatch hissed open, granting me my first glimpse of an alien world. Heart thrumming, I paused with my foot hovering above the blue rock we'd landed on, feeling strangely giddy.

"What is it?" Lux halted beside me, eyeing my raised boot.

"I feel like I ought to have something pithy to say. One small step, one giant leap, ya know?"

Lux smirked and stepped out of the ship, the planet's low gravity making his stride ridiculously long and high. "Giant leap sounds about right."

I grinned and followed, forgetting all about finding the right words in my eagerness to explore. I bounced over the ground, feeling superhuman—if a bit wobbly. After a few strides, I got used to the sensation. When I tore my gaze off my feet, I stopped in my tracks. "Wow, this world is gorgeous."

From up above, it'd appeared an almost uniform blue, the rock and water blending so well it was hard to tell where one lake ended and another began. On the surface, glimmering flecks of violet and midnight dotted the rocky hillsides, and the still waters shimmered with aqua highlights. But for all the beauty, it was eerily silent, except for the occasional splash of water in the distance.

I tucked an errant brown curl behind my ear when it dislodged in the gentle breeze. "I figured that with the atmosphere here, this world would support life."

"It does. They have not evolved to live on land yet."

I stole a glance at Lux, admiring the way his silver eyes sparkled against the grayish-blue of the cloudless alien sky.

"Have you been here before?"

"No, but someone on Pheria must have. That information was in the scans back on my ship." Lux's gaze raked over me just as intently as I'd scanned the landscape. A pulse of need erupted in my belly when I spotted the heat in his expression. But he was quick to douse it, turning aside and waving an arm ahead. "The Garcuk ship is this way."

He waited for me to bounce forward before joining me. Dread coiled in my stomach as we rounded the hillside and the metallic hull of the Garcuk's ship came into view. "Are you sure this plan will work? What if they shoot us before we get our offer out?"

Lux lifted the sleeve of his black skinsuit, revealing a thin golden wristlet. "Personal deflector field. I widened the range. Stick close to me and you'll be covered."

I gaped at his wrist. "Put that thing away. Don't those cost a fortune? Those thieves will be after you next."

He rolled his sleeve back down and tilted his head. "Eager to keep me safe, I see."

"I'm already rescuing my cargo. I don't need to add rescuing you to my agenda."

Lux grabbed my shoulder just as I bounced ahead, using the momentum from my leaping step to plaster me against his side. "Just admit you like me, Arda. I like you too."

My first instinct was to tear myself off of him and tell him where he could stick his demand. But then my traitorous heart fluttered. He *liked* me?

"Halt," a gravelly voice boomed. "State your purpose or you will be fired upon."

I flinched, whirling toward the sound. A bald alien stood between us and the Garcuk ship, a blaster cocked at us. Once I peeled my gaze away from the weapon, my eyes widened and I nearly burst out laughing.

Why didn't I look up the Garcuk before now?

The creature ahead of me was bipedal and humanoid, though his arms and legs were gangly and oversized, giving him an almost scarecrow-like visage. But that wasn't what had me dying inside from self-contained laughter. In place of a nose, the Garcuk's off-white face had a puckered orifice that resembled a certain part of human anatomy almost exactly.

"They're not giant dicks, they're giant assholes," I muttered out the corner of my mouth, jabbing Lux's side with my elbow. "Why didn't you warn me?"

Lux choked on a laugh, but smoothly shifted into clearing his throat. "Take us to your captain. We have a deal to negotiate."

The Garcuk tapped his neck, then fired off a string of words, likely a code, for I couldn't understand any of it, even with the translator. After waiting for a reply, he nodded curtly and said, "Come. The captain will see you."

Lux

The Garcuk soldier led us through a sleek metal hall. Crew bustled through the large vessel, dressed in identical brown skinsuits. Curious bald heads watched us pass, peeking around the bends of corridors and sneaking glimpses from open hatches.

Arda marched beside me, her body quivering more with each alien we passed. She must be terrified. Terrans were new to exploring space. I'd bet anything this was the first hostile encounter she'd experienced.

I tugged her into my side, seeking to calm her just as we passed another onlooker. This Garcuk didn't keep a respectable distance like the others. He leaned forward and his circular nostril flared while he sniffed noisily.

Arda stiffened, a strangled sound echoing in her chest.

Was she about to cry? Her jaw was clenched, fists balled up tightly. But it wasn't fear I spotted in her eyes. No, she looked like she was seconds away from bursting into laughter.

Her head tilted to the Garcuk as he sniffed even louder. "Where I come from, people say excuse me," she whispered, covering her smile with her hands.

My brow scrunched up, but then I remembered her muttered insult outside the ship. *"They're not dicks, they're assholes."*

Dral help me, this woman... I'd lived and worked with aliens all my life, so the Garcuk's unusual nose wasn't anything I'd ever given a second thought to. But now that she'd planted the visual in my mind, I had to admit—she was right.

When the next Garcuk we passed followed suit, leaning forward and opening his puckered nose to sniff deeply, Arda wasn't the only one choking down giggles. As my shoulders trembled and Arda sent me a conspiratorial wink, a blissful contentment washed over me.

What is this female doing to me?

I couldn't remember the last time I'd shared a private joke with someone. This should be one of the most stressful moments of my life. I was surrounded by a shifty species who'd take any opportunity to screw us over, but instead of my balls shriveling up inside my belly, I was fighting back laughter.

She'd brought humor and passion into my life. Something I hadn't even realized I'd been missing, but now that I'd gotten a taste, I couldn't stop craving it. Craving more of her addictive smiles. More of *her*.

The soldier halted in front of a hatch, then punched a panel beside it. A robotic voice spilled into the air, spouting more of their indiscernible coded chatter. After a few moments of back and forth, the hatch slid open silently, and the soldier ushered us inside.

Hazy dimness shrouded the cool interior. A gangly figure sat tall in a straight-back chair behind a barren desk. Piercing black eyes met mine and a jolt of recognition hit me square in the chest.

"Saenov. Funny finding you here."

Arda crossed her arms, her gaze flicking between me and the smiling Saenov. "You two know each other?" Her smile curved up in the dim overhead light until she spotted the deepening scowl I couldn't stop from overtaking my face.

"We're acquainted," I said. How could I forget the sneak who stole one of the most profitable trade deals of my life out from under me?

"Luxuth, my old friend." Saenov rubbed his bald head, a smarmy grin painting his face. "So that was you playing that dirty trick out in space? Why am I not surprised?"

"Cut the crap, Saenov. We are not friends." I stalked over to the desk the coward perched behind like it was a shield. I slammed my hands on the surface, biting back my smirk when the idiot flinched. "You have one chance to give Arda the cargo you stole, or I'll leave you here to rot on your broken ship."

Saenov blubbered, and his nose hole pinched shut for a split second. Then he waved a hand. "My crew is more than capable of completing repairs in time."

I laughed. "Sure, *in time*. But how much time?" I leaned closer. "Do you have replacement parts for your FTL and comms or will they be rewiring them from scratch?"

Saenov frowned, giving me all the confirmation I needed.

"Your ship uses a T9-A6 FTL and a Barradia Comms, doesn't it?" I asked, already knowing the answer. I thanked the stars for all the mind-numbing research I did on the Garcuk back when we began dealings with them. "So does mine, and I have fresh replacements in my hold. I can have you back in space before the day is through."

Saenov eyed me suspiciously. "Why would you do that for a few measly barrels of unrefined jesillium? What game are you playing, *friend*?" He hissed out the last, seeming to enjoy the word as it spilled out of his rotten mouth.

My gaze flitted back to Arda. She watched the argument unfold beside the soldier, a perplexed tilt to her brow.

"Ah, I see," Saenov cut in. "I often forget your race is driven by your incessant biological urges." He chuckled darkly, and I was a second away from blasting my fist into his ugly face until he spoke up again. "All right. I'll take your deal." He turned to the soldier and barked out more code, then spun back to me. "He will lead you to the storeroom. Take your cargo and get me off this useless rock."

Ha. I knew the promise of an easy return to working order would sway him. "Glad you could see reason."

I straightened, then returned to Arda's side. She clapped her hands together and gifted me the most gorgeous smile. It was like a visible weight lifted off her shoulders. Seeing her relief and happiness bloom made dealing with that slimy bastard worth it.

I followed the soldier out of Saenov's office, hoping it'd be the last time I'd have to see him.

Something tells me I won't be that lucky...

Arda

As Lux and I trailed behind the Garcuk soldier, my chest practically burst with relief. I was one step away from getting my cargo back. The safety of my ship and crew were secure, and I wouldn't have to worry about another missed loan payment. It didn't get much better than that.

I can't believe that actually worked...

I stole a glance at Lux, the marvelous, big alien. He'd been so confident back there. So demanding. Watching him stick up for me made my heart flutter in a way I'd not been expecting. I'd spent so long on my own. It was truly comforting having someone in my corner for a change.

I stepped lightly down the hall, doing my best to ignore the crew's stares—and sniffs. But the further we walked, the more that lightness vanished, replaced with a niggling sense of dread.

It all felt a little too easy.

The thought had barely formed in my mind when we rounded a corner and found ourselves surrounded by a trio of armed soldiers.

Maybe they're just passing by—

One of them lifted the butt of his blaster and smashed Lux in the temple.

Fuck!

I darted sideways, avoiding a blow aimed at my skull. The soldier hit the wall instead. His blaster reverberated with a *clang* and flew out of his grasp.

Holy shit. That hit would have dropped me easily.

Though Lux's attacker put as much force behind his blow, Lux didn't fall. His fingers lifted to his brow, and I spotted a flash of red on his fingers before his hand curled into a fist. My heart immediately kicked up, blood thrumming through my veins and pooling in my loins.

Goddamn it, Arda! Get it together.

With a roar, Lux leaped into motion, kicking the Garcuk whose blaster was lifted for a second strike. The alien slammed into the wall and slid down, a groan on his lips. Lux spun to the next and popped him in the neck. The soldier clasped his throat with a pained gasp that turned into a gurgle.

I shook off my surprise and tamped down the fresh wave of lust that blasted me at the sight of Lux's blood. I lifted my fists, ready to do my part taking out the assholes, but before I joined the fray, a hard arm clamped around my neck and the terrifying point of a blaster kissed my temple. My stomach dropped as I realized the sneaky fucker who'd been leading us had slipped in behind me.

Lux whirled toward the third Garcuk who'd attempted to hit me with menace in his eyes. The soldier stood from a crouch, his shaking hands gripping his retrieved blaster.

"Stop or I'll shoot," demanded the soldier at my back. I choked down a whimper as he pressed the blaster into my throbbing temple.

Lux shifted and spotted the bastard holding me. His face morphed, his normal stoic expression turning positively feral. "Touch her and I'll rip your throat out."

I shivered at the intensity in his voice. The man's grip on my neck tightened, making me flinch.

Lux growled in the back of his throat, the sound so menacing my eyes widened involuntarily. But then he dropped his fists at his side. "What do you want?"

The soldier's grip loosened, and I sucked in a sharp breath. I felt his head jerk. It must have been a signal which caused the soldier beside Lux to jam the point of his blaster into Lux's back.

"Follow me," he demanded gruffly.

Before I knew what was happening, they shoved us into a tiny, dank room in the bowels of the ship, and slammed the door closed. No word of explanation. No demands. Just me and a pissed off, bleeding alien, all alone.

And of course, the second that gun lifted from my temple, and they left me alone with Lux, my body flew into overdrive. Blood dripped down from a cut on the side of his head, and instead of feeling remorse for his pain, or queasy at the sight of all that red, I was burning up with lust.

What the hell was I going to do?

15

Notorious

Lux

The door slammed closed, leaving us in a barren room barely big enough to be a closet. I pounded on the metal, knowing before my fist connected to the cold steel that the action would be useless. There was bound to be someone standing guard. If I forced the door open, they'd only cram us somewhere else. Pain radiated up my wrist, and the door stayed stubbornly shut.

A whimper in the corner gave me pause. I whirled around and spotted Arda crouched on the floor, her head in her hands. *Dral's bones.* If that bastard hurt her, I would hunt down the entire crew and slaughter them one by one.

I took a deep breath and gentled my voice when all I wanted to do was scream. "Arda, are you all right?" I bent beside her, trying to catch a glimpse of her face beneath the curtain of her dark curls.

Arda flinched as my hand landed on her shoulder. "Don't touch me."

I backed away, acceding to her wishes while my blood boiled. She'd seemed fine. But maybe that soldier's hold on her neck had been tighter than I'd thought.

"Where did he hurt you?" I demanded, digging through my pockets and coming up empty. There was nothing. I didn't have a damn thing to help, and she wouldn't even let me hold her.

"I'm fine," she bit out. "I-I don't want to hurt *you*."

I suppressed a chuckle. Did I miss her hitting her head? "You won't hurt me."

Arda lifted her face and met my eyes. Her pupils were blown, her breath coming in short pants. Her gaze landed on my temple, and she licked her lips. "The blood, Lux. God, I can't stand it."

All traces of my rage evaporated, but my blood didn't cool. It heated further, the molten liquid pulsing beneath my skin. "I know what this is."

"You do?"

I grabbed her elbow and tugged her to her feet, ignoring her hiss of discomfort.

"I told you, don't touch me." She jerked her arm, trying to escape into the corner again, but I held firm.

"That's not what you need." I gripped her chin, forcing her to meet my eyes. "This bloodlust won't just fade away. If you had grown up on Pheria you would know what this means."

Her gaze flitted between my eyes and the small trickle of fresh blood I could feel trailing down my cheek. "This," she gulped, "lust, it's part of being a Vamphere?"

I nodded gently. "If you don't give in, it will only get worse."

She shook her head violently. "I-I can't. I'll hurt you." She ripped her arm away and backed up. "I'll hurt you just like her."

"What are you talking about?"

Arda answered, her voice barely a whisper, "My grandmother. God, I can't believe I'm telling you this." She flicked a glance at me, and continued, "My grandmother was Cora Jenson."

I frowned. "Am I supposed to know who that is?"

She searched my face and cringed. "If you lived in the Sol system, you would. She was the most notorious serial killer in the last century. The media dubbed her The Bathing Butcher. She murdered over a dozen men during the war." Arda drew a deep breath and straightened her shoulders. "Sh-She bathed in their blood. She targeted men leaving for the front, and with all the confusion during that time, it took authorities years to catch on."

"I'm sorry, Arda." My mind spun, all of her reactions to blood suddenly making sense. "Not that it makes it right, but I have a feeling the genetic manipulation must have contributed to her crimes."

Arda nodded. "When you told me about my DNA, I thought that might be the case. But don't you see? If I give into these feelings—this lust—I might end up just like her." Her lower lip trembled. "I don't want that Lux. I don't want to hurt you."

"You won't." I grabbed her hand and placed it on my chest. "The feelings you have are natural for a Vamphere. I can teach you how to handle them so they don't grow out of control. I imagine that's what happened to your grandmother. She suppressed her instincts until she had no choice but to unleash them violently."

"You would do that, for me?" Arda tipped her head up, her blue eyes wide pools I could easily lose myself in.

I caressed her cheek and nodded. "It would be my pleasure."

Arda

"Are you ready for your first lesson?" Lux asked.

My breath flooded in and out in rapid pants. I nodded quickly, ready for anything that would ease this ache. My skin felt stretched taut, begging to be touched. Even the tender caress Lux trailed across my cheek had my body burning up.

There hadn't been much time for me to consider the revelations into my DNA. But everything Lux told me made so much sense. The vile crimes my grandmother committed had always brought me so much shame. My mother dragged us all over the world, then from planet to planet, trying to escape the stigma, the side eyed glances of people who learned of our infamous relative. But no matter how far we traveled, before long, someone always figured it out.

When I'd grown into a teen and started having feelings of lust every time I spotted blood, that just made it so much worse. I couldn't quiet the tiny voice in my mind that whispered I'd never be normal. I'd always be a freak who could only get off with the thought of blood in my mind.

But now, I finally had an explanation. I finally had someone telling me that I wasn't a freak. This craving for blood while I had sex wasn't just some sick kink. No, it was normal. A natural part of being part Vamphere.

"What do I need to do?" I asked.

Lux pulled me against his chest. He traced his thumb against his temple and picked up a drop of blood, then gripped my chin. "Open."

I stared at the bloody digit hovering in front of my lips, my mouth watering.

Was I really about to do this? If there had ever been a turning point in my life, this was it. Could I give into the demands my body had always craved?

I opened my mouth and sucked in his cold thumb. My eyes rolled back in my head from the exquisite flavor bursting on my tongue. I'd expected a coppery tang, but Lux's blood was decadent and rich, unlike anything I'd ever tasted. It sent a flurry of tingles straight to my core.

My pussy clenched, and I sucked harder. Lux growled deep in his throat, then pulled his thumb out with a *pop.*

"What now?" My eyes widened. Fuck, did that husky voice belong to me?

"Relax and just feel," he whispered. Then his lips crashed down on mine.

I moaned into his mouth and melted into his embrace. Lux's lips felt like sin, and when he slid his hot tongue against mine, I trembled with desire. God, the man could *kiss.* He took his time, stroking languidly into my mouth while his cold hands trailed down my back.

His touch floated over my ass, feather light, then he gripped the globes and jerked me up against his chest. My legs clamped around his waist and I gripped his neck tightly as he shoved my back against the wall. Then he lined his cock up to my core and grinded against me and I swear I saw stars.

"Fuck, Lux," I moaned into his mouth. "You feel so *good.*"

He trailed hot kisses over my cheek to my ear, his hips pulsing in a steady rhythm. "So do you, Arda." He nibbled on my lobe and whispered in a voice thick with lust, "I can't wait to taste you."

I stiffened involuntarily. "Do you need to taste my blood, too?" My voice trembled, and I wasn't sure if it was fear or anticipation causing it.

Lux pulled back far enough to meet my eyes and smirked. "No, Arda. That's not what I'm planning to taste." His hips stilled, and I groaned, immediately missing the friction between my legs. But then the meaning of his words hit me, just as he planted my feet on the ground and gripped the zipper of my skinsuit.

He wrenched the zipper down in a single swift motion, making me gasp. Then he dropped to his knees and lifted my leg. Before I could even suck in a breath, he'd shucked off my boots and my skinsuit dangled off my arms, gaping wide open, my legs bare.

Lux licked his lips and stared at the triangle of fabric covering my mound. "Spread your legs," he ordered gruffly.

Fuck. My mind flashed back to that wicked dream. I'd woken up swollen and throbbing that morning, but having him here in the flesh, those sinful silver eyes staring up at me, ready to devour me—God, it was so much more intense. My pulse pounded between my legs and I knew without having to look that my panties were drenched.

"Arda." His voice carried a note of warning, full of strain as he waited for me to obey.

That was one order I was happy to concede to. I kicked my legs out wide and held my breath, dying for his touch. For his hot mouth to descend.

"Good girl," Lux said, a smirk on his lips. He leaned forward, his gaze zeroed in on my panties. He planted one big hand on my stomach and pushed, pressing my upper half against the wall. Then he bent down and trailed a line of kisses up my thigh.

I moaned, desperate for him to drag his mouth to my aching core. But he only placed one leisurely lick where my panties met my leg and moved onto the other thigh.

"Lux, *please*." I squirmed, trying to thrust my pussy closer to his warm mouth, but his icy hand splayed tighter on my belly, keeping me from making contact.

"Please what?" Lux asked between kisses. "Does your greedy cunt need my tongue?" I shivered, nodding and moaning at his dirty words.

"Tell me what you want, Arda," he ordered, just as the tip of his nose trailed over my soaked panties.

My rubbery legs nearly gave out. If not for his hand on my stomach, I would have melted into a puddle on the floor. "Lux, if you don't lick me right now, I might die."

The bastard chuckled and moved away from my core, the low rumble of his voice doing crazy things to my belly. "We can't have that now, can we?"

He tugged my panties aside and spread me lewdly with his fingers. I gasped at the icy sensation of his cold fingers chilling my overheated flesh. The vision of his big body kneeling before me, the pure lust in his eyes as he stared at me spread for him, nearly made me come right then and there.

Lux groaned, his gaze glued to my pussy. "Mm, your cunt is so wet, Arda." He licked his lips and dove in, moaning with me on the first stroke.

"Fuck, Lux. Don't stop." My legs trembled, pleasure shooting through me with every flick of his talented tongue. I dug my fingers into his hair, keeping him right where I wanted him.

Lux slid his icy fingers through my heat, and my eyes rolled back in my head. "Oh God, Lux. That feels so fucking good." He quickly brought me to the edge with a hot lick, then an icy stroke, over and over. The contrast of temperatures on my clit was unlike anything I'd ever felt. "You're driving me *insane*."

Before long, I was a trembling mess, rolling my hips against his face and moaning uncontrollably. I don't know if it was his blood, amping me up like he'd claimed would happen, or if it was just *him*. Every delicious lick and stroke made me quiver and jolt. It couldn't have been more than a minute before I was ready to explode.

"That's it. Come for me." Lux curled two fingers inside me at the same time he sucked my clit into his hot mouth.

That was all it took. I screamed, coming so violently I almost blacked out. Wave after wave of pleasure collided into me until I was practically boneless.

Lux stayed with me through it all, pumping his fingers and lightly stroking his tongue, extending my orgasm far longer than I thought possible. It went on and on until my head thrashed against the wall and I screamed again. Finally, it subsided. Lux slid his fingers out of my pussy and smiled up at me.

As I stood there catching my breath, I took stock of my feelings. That annoying, unending ache I always felt was completely gone. Even when I caught another glimpse of the dried blood on Lux's face, it didn't bother me.

This beautiful, generous man. He just gave me the most intense orgasm—somehow curing me of the constant affliction I'd struggled with for my entire adult life—without even a single thought of his own pleasure.

My gaze immediately fell between his thighs, eyes widening at the size of the bulge straining against his skinsuit. I licked my lips and opened my mouth.

The door to the room flew open without warning. Lux let go of my stomach and lurched up, blocking me from view with his big body. My cheeks burned, and I scrambled to right my clothes.

"Well, well. I was worried you two wouldn't enjoy the accommodations, but I see that you're making the best of things," Saenov drawled in a slimy voice.

16

New Accommodations

I scowled at Saenov's maddening smirk and adjusted my skinsuit. *That's one way to kill an erection.*

"What in Dral's name are you doing, Saenov?" I stood to my full height, blocking Arda's delectable body from view. The Garcuk weren't compatible with either of our species, but that didn't mean the creep deserved a free show. I wanted to tear out Saenov's eyes for stealing that single glimpse.

Saenov aimed his blaster at my chest, amusement painting his ugly face. He clearly thought I should quake in my boots from the threat. Normally I would be—I'm not the kind of idiot that stares down the barrel of a deadly weapon for fun—but the personal shield hidden beneath my skinsuit gave me the confidence I wouldn't be harmed.

Still, I made a show of eyeing the blaster and grinding my teeth. Wouldn't do to let the bastard in on the tricks up my sleeve—not when that shield might be the only advantage I had left.

"It's unfortunate my crew stuffed you in here. I promise the guest room we've prepared is much better suited for the long journey to Pheria."

"Pheria," Arda squeaked behind me. I flicked a glance at her just as she shoved her feet in her boots and glared at me. "What the fuck is he talking about?"

Although I was happy to see her re-clothed, Saenov's announcement soured my mood. I should've known he had something sneaky planned.

"Don't worry, sweetling," Saenov cooed, aiming a grin at Arda. "You can have your pitiful haul of raw jesillium back when we arrive at Pheria. After all, you've brought me something much more valuable."

Arda frowned. "I'm not your sweetling. And damn right you're giving me back my cargo. But you're fucked if you think I'm going to Pheria." She nudged me with her elbow. "Why is he talking about Pheria, Lux?"

I let out a weary sigh. "Ransom, I'm guessing."

"You always were a smart one, Luxuth." Saenov chuckled, a nauseating sound that made me want to wrap my hands around his throat. "The Vamphere will pay handsomely to have one of their royals back."

Arda jolted, and she backed up a pace. "Royal? What the fuck!"

I ignored her, cutting a hard glare at Saenov. "You're insane if you think this plan will work. You can't even get off world without my help."

Saenov snorted with his grotesque nose. "Your ship isn't the only one with compatible parts." His gaze swung back to Arda. "Luckily, my crew are well suited to hacking security systems. It will take a little longer, but we'll be on the way within a few days."

Arda's fists balled against her leg. "Stay the fuck away from the Verne!"

Saenov cocked his blaster at Arda. Growling, I pushed Arda behind me. "Don't," I said, my voice laced with menace.

Saenov turned the blaster on me. "Your mate will be safe so long as you cooperate."

"Mate," Arda grumbled behind me. "I'm not his mate."

Saenov snorted again, the odd blare echoing in the tiny room. "Could have fooled me with what I walked in on."

I drew a deep breath, tamping down the conflicting emotions swarming through me. Now was not the time to worry about why the thought of Arda as my mate warmed something deep inside my chest—or the fact that she was so quick to dismiss the idea.

"You said you have a better room. Let's go then." I grabbed Arda's arm, tugging her close to my side.

Saenov shifted out of the doorway, keeping his blaster trained on us. "By all means. After you."

Arda

I paced down the hall, my lungs burning with the need to question Lux. From the tight set of his jaw and the firm grip he kept on my shoulder, it didn't take a genius to clue into his anxiety. So I kept my mouth shut, but once we were alone, he would have some explaining to do. Immediately.

Royalty... What the hell was he thinking, keeping that to himself? Didn't a girl deserve to know the alien she's stranded with is goddamn *royalty*? I could've caused an interplanetary incident, colliding into his ship. My memory kicked into overdrive, replaying all of our early encounters.

No wonder he was worried I was a spy...

"Stop here." Saenov trailed behind us, his blaster aimed at Lux-uth's back. He angled his body sideways and punched a code into a control panel on the wall. A hatch slid open, revealing a brightly lit cabin, easily three times the size of the tiny barren closet we'd just left. Saenov waved us in. "There's a food processor and a washroom. All the amenities you'll need for a comfortable voyage. Make yourselves at home."

With that, he slammed the hatch, leaving us alone. I resisted the urge to pound on the door and demand he release us, and inspected the room. One wall held a small food processor and a door which likely led to the washroom. A tiny table and single chair sat bolted to the floor in the corner. A full-size bed covered with crisp white sheets dominated the rest of the space. This was clearly a cabin built for one.

"Tell me you have a plan, Lux. I can't go to Pheria. I'll miss my deadline. I'll lose the Verne." I groaned. "Assuming those fuckers don't tear my poor ship to pieces before that."

"You must be hungry. What would you like?" Lux strolled over to the food processor and punched in an order.

"Are you seriously worried about eating right now?"

As the processor whirred, working on Lux's order, he cocked a brow, his hand hovering over the keypad.

"And what about that whole royalty thing, huh? You didn't think I would just let that slide, did you?"

"Order something," he drawled.

The command stiffened my back, and I stared him down. A second ticked by. Two. Then three. Lux stood silently, waiting.

"Fine." I brushed his hand aside and punched in an order for tea and toast. "There. Now talk."

Lux grabbed the mug the processor spit out and sank on the edge of the bed. "I have a plan." He took a long pull from his mug.

"Care to elaborate?"

Lux nodded to the processor as it finished my order. "I'm going to take that apart and reconfigure it to contact my ship. Are you sure you ordered enough to hold you over?"

"Oh." Comprehension rolled over me like a bomb blast, and I cringed. I quickly punched in a request for a few protein bars, just in case. Then I grabbed my toast and tea—peppermint this time—and settled down at the little table. "And the other thing?"

Lux chugged from his mug, then waved a hand. "Yes, that. Technically, it is true."

"Technically? What does that even mean?"

"I'm a distant relation of the Royal line of Pheria. Thirteenth in the line of succession. I'm surprised Saenov knew about it."

A fluttery sensation spread through my stomach. It sounded like he'd likely never rule, but I'd just had alien royalty kneeling for me. The realization made my heart thump like crazy.

"So he's right. They'll pay a ransom to get you back." I bit off a corner of my toast, willing my pounding pulse to slow.

Lux chuckled, and the deep vibration sent a shiver down my spine. "No. Pherians don't deal with terrorists."

I swallowed. "Seriously?"

Lux nodded. "I'm afraid so. No matter. We will not be flying to Pheria."

I had to give it to Lux; his confidence was sexy. If only he could pull it off...

I furrowed my brow, scrutinizing the room. Despite the furniture, it wasn't much better than the little closet. Bare walls loomed around us, devoid of any shelves. There were no tools, not even a decorative knickknack to aid us. "How do you plan to take that thing apart?"

Lux lifted his sleeve and slipped the wristlet off his arm. "Don't worry, Arda. I'll have your pretty little ass back in your pilot's chair before the day is over." He sent me a wink and stood.

I watched his broad back flex as he made his way toward the processor. And even though it seemed not just impossible, but utterly inconceivable, that Lux would get us out of this mess, I believed him.

Leaving my half-eaten toast behind, I sidled up beside Lux. "All right. How can I help?"

17

Mad Plans

Arda

"What do you mean, it's not working?" I stared down at the mess of wires and components littering the floor, my insides just as jumbled as the interior of the food processor.

We'd been at it for what felt like hours. Well, mostly Lux. After he popped off the back of his personal shield wristlet, destroying the shockingly expensive item without a second thought—nearly giving me a coronary—I watched him use the sharp bits inside like a makeshift screwdriver, giving him access to the guts of the processor.

Don't get me wrong, I know my way around a ship. I can handle basic repairs to just about anything—food processor included. Whatever Lux was doing was an entirely different story. He reminded me of Ren, utterly focused and working at a genius level to bend the machine to his will.

But apparently it still wasn't enough...

"It's not working *yet*," Lux corrected with a cocky gleam in his eye. "It will."

I nodded, pacing the floor. My gaze darted to the door for the hundredth time. I couldn't stop envisioning one of those ass-faces flinging open the hatch and ripping away all of Lux's hard work. That and the ugly bastards tearing apart my poor ship. Those two images played on a loop in my mind, ratcheting up my anxiety to a fever pitch.

We'd bet everything on this mad plan working. Without Lux's personal shield, we were utterly defenseless. And there was nothing for me to do except cross my fingers and pray that Lux knew what he was doing.

"There goes that idea," Lux muttered, tugging his head out of the processor's innards.

I halted in place. "No. Don't tell me this was all for nothing?"

Lux met my eyes, his expression grim. "I cannot connect with Destiny. All the hardware is aligned, but she's not answering my hails."

"Fuck! Try again."

"I've already tried a dozen times." Lux leaned back on his knees and sighed wearily.

"Oh no. This is not good." I picked up my pacing, rubbing my hand on my neck. "This is not good at all."

Lux watched me ping-pong across the room, then his gaze zeroed in on my neck. "Wait. Your personal communicator. I might be able to use that." He ducked back inside the processor. "Let me just tweak the frequency and amplify the signal..."

I tuned him out. All the technical jargon went over my head, anyway. Instead, I tapped on my neck, activating the implant.

"Ren? Zenda? Come in."

No response. I kept trying, repeating the plea on a loop, then waiting for a response that never came.

We were so far away. My communicator was only meant to work at short distances. Could Lux really work some wizardry to make a food processor amplify the signal?

When his hands stopped working inside the machine a few moments later, my heart sank. Still nothing.

"Arda? Is that you?" Ren's voice boomed in my mind.

I winced and gripped my skull. *Damn, that's loud.* Maybe the amplification worked a little too well.

"Did they answer?" Lux asked, at the same time a wide grin split my face.

"Ren. I'm here. We need your help."

"Are you still on world? I don't see the Verne on the nav screen."

"Yes, we're on world and we're in trouble." Ren called Zenda over, and I gave them both a quick rundown of the events since we'd landed. "And that's the gist of it. So, can you guys fly down here and break us out? Lux says his ship has enough firepower to make the Garcuks hand us over."

"That's gonna be a problem," Ren said. "We're dead in the water up here. I haven't completed the repairs on the engines yet." Her voice was thick with remorse. "I kind of just tore them apart. I had to power down the ship's AI too. It will take me another day to fix everything."

That explained why Lux couldn't reach Destiny. "Fuck. The Verne will be toast by then."

"I might have a solution," Zenda said, her excitement evident. "I've been reading up on the Garcuk. What if we could get all of them to exit their ship? Then you two could sneak out and grab our jesillium on the way."

"How will we manage that?"

"The Garcuk have unusual mating habits. They're only fertile during a brief window on their home world, during the high summer.

The extreme heat triggers a chemical change in the females, one that is irresistible to the males."

Zenda was always learning about new species, but the biology lesson was beginning to grate on my nerves. I forced myself to reply calmly, "Ok. That's interesting, but how does it help us?"

"Get this, they only mate in water. If we can spike the temperature on the ship—"

I gasped, cutting her off. "All those lakes. You're a genius, Zenda!" I quickly relayed the plan to Lux, bouncing on my toes.

"I like it. There's only one problem," Lux said.

"What?"

"I can't hack into the temperature controls. Not with what I have here."

Fuck. "It's a no go." I repeated what Lux said. "Any other ideas?"

"Wait," Ren said. "You *do* have what you need to hack in. Listen carefully and relay this to Lux."

I nodded and obeyed, echoing Ren's instructions, and though they were totally incomprehensible to me, Lux lit up when she'd finished explaining.

"Yes. I can do that." Lux bent beside the processor and began shuffling components around. "Your crew just saved us."

"Ren, Lux says it will work. Thank you both."

"Great," she replied. "I'll talk to you when you get back. Good luck!"

"Wait, you don't have to say goodbye. What if we need your help?"

Ren chuckled. "I should've known that would be Greek to you." The humor in her voice dissipated. "I'm sorry, Arda. It's the only way."

"Huh?"

"The part we need," Lux drifted closer and traced a finger over my neck, his silver eyes shadowed with a glimpse of something strange, "you have it."

18

One Thing Missing

Lux

I finished tinkering with the machinery, following Ren's instructions carefully. Then there was only one thing missing.

Standing up, I brushed the knees of my skinsuit, my gaze immediately seeking Arda across the cabin. She paced the floor, her boots tapping in time with the pounding beat of my heart.

I tamped down my excitement, determined to not scare her, even though every cell in my body was alive with the knowledge of what was about to happen. "Everything is in place."

Arda halted and spun to face me, her hand raising to encircle the graceful curve of her neck.

"Are you sure you want to do this?" I asked.

She inhaled deeply and pressed her shoulders back. My dick took notice, leaping against its confines when her full breasts lifted.

Dral's bones. Calm down, Lux.

"Yes. I'm ready." She tugged her long locks out of the way and met my eyes.

"Here." I pricked my finger with the sharp shred of metal I'd been using as my lone tool.

"What's that for?" Arda's face flushed and her breathing picked up as she stared at the drop of blood pooled on my fingertip.

"This will hurt—a lot. My blood will dull the pain. Give you something else to concentrate on."

She nodded and sucked my finger into her hot little mouth. My body thrummed with pleasure, my mind flashing back to the last time she'd tasted me—and then I tasted her. *Was she remembering too?* My tongue lapping up her cream. Her thighs clenching my head as she came—so damn hard.

When her eyelids drooped, the bright blue orbs heady with lust, I withdrew my hand. "Mm, Lux," she cooed, trailing her palms across my chest. "Come here."

She didn't need to tell me twice. I dipped down and captured her lips. She tasted so sweet. The lingering flavor of my blood coated her tongue, making my head swim. This female—I wanted to stay wrapped around her for hours, licking inside her delicious mouth. Stroking her silken skin and tasting every inch. I wanted to *devour* her.

But that would have to wait.

Her zipper sang as I tugged it down. Then I plucked her questing hand off my chest and slid it inside her skinsuit.

She tore her mouth off mine. "What are you doing?" With our hands entangled, I traced the smooth curves of her belly.

I dragged my tongue up her neck to her ear just as I slipped her fingers inside her panties. "Showing you where to rub your hot little cunt."

She shook her head and tried to tug her hand out from under mine. "No. I want you."

My balls throbbed at her request, but I held her fast, sinking her fingers into her slick heat. "I want that too. After, I promise. I need my hands free. Touch yourself, Arda."

I couldn't tell if her gasp was from the pleasure of her touch or the reminder of what I was about to do. But when I pulled my hand away, she kept hers in place, rubbing and flicking her tender flesh.

I leaned back and allowed myself a second to watch. Her face was flush, her chest heaving. Her little body tensed as she circled the spot between her legs. I'd never seen anything so sexy. It took everything in me to step away while I was dying to tear her clothes off and sink into her.

I hurried into the washroom. I cleaned my hands and the metal shard carefully in the sink. All the while, Arda's breathy moans filled my ears. "That's it. Don't stop."

My hands shook when I returned to the room. She'd stripped out of her skinsuit and kneeled on the edge of the bed in her bra and panties. My gaze zeroed in on her hand, tracing little circles between her thighs.

Don't get distracted...

I almost didn't listen. Especially not when Arda's gaze locked on the bulge in my skinsuit and she let out another throaty moan.

I carried a towel in from the washroom and balanced the folded rectangle of cloth on Arda's shoulder. "Close your eyes."

She obeyed, her eyelids flicking closed, her moans increasing as I traced the square implant on her neck.

I could feel the hard shape just below her skin. It was tiny, the size of the smallest nail on Arda's cute little toes. The cut wouldn't need to be big—but there would be blood.

My mouth watered. Dral's teeth... I hadn't even cut her yet, but the thought of her blood made my dick throb. *Would she let me taste it?*

No—I shook the thought away. *I have to save her.* Save us both.

I lifted the shard of metal and pricked her neck. Blood dribbled down immediately, and Arda's moan changed tone, the pleasure mixing with a gasp of pain.

I wet my lips, watching the delicious droplet roll down her neck to land on the white towel. *What a waste.* My mouth watered, desperate to lick up the trail. But I buried the urge and focused. I had to pull the implant out.

I sliced a shallow cut, just wide and deep enough to push the hard square free. Blood gushed out, coating my fingers in warmth. The tang of copper reached my nose and made my vision cloudy. I shook my head and massaged Arda's neck, maneuvering the implant closer to the cut.

Arda groaned, her eyes pinched tightly, fingers stroking steadily inside her panties.

"Good girl," I whispered. "Keep rubbing that perfect cunt. The pain is almost over."

I plucked the implant free and pressed the towel tightly to Arda's neck. "It's out. Hold this."

Arda opened her eyes and untangled her fist from the blankets, then gripped the towel. Her other hand stilled between her legs.

"Did I tell you to stop?" I growled.

She licked her lips. "I thought you were done?"

I chuckled, stroking my thumb across her round breast. "No, Arda. I haven't even started."

She gasped as I pinched her nipple, eyes glazed.

I clenched my fist, and the hard implant dug into my palm. "I'll be right back and you better be ready for me." I reluctantly backed away, sending Arda a wink before I bent beside the processor and got to work. It took barely a moment to fit the implant in place. With all the prep work I'd done before, that was all I needed to crank up the temperature. A few hours and it would feel like a sauna in here.

And I know just what to do while we're waiting.

"Did it work?" Arda asked, her voice husky.

I stood. "Yes." I turned. "We should celebrate."

Arda's breath hitched, her fingers flicking again under the drenched triangle of fabric. "We should."

"I want you naked. Now."

She met my eyes and slowly shook her head. "You first."

Arda

Lux stared me down, his giant body hovering over the edge of the bed, motionless. When my hand stilled, he shot me a glare, nostrils flaring. I tugged my hand out of my panties and cocked a brow, waiting just as calmly. If I weren't still holding the towel against the bloody gash on my neck, I would've crossed my arms too.

The big guy might be stubborn as hell, but I was stubborn too. I hadn't been fully bare yet, but he'd gotten plenty of peeks at my goods. I wasn't about to let him go another round without seeing what he had hidden under that skinsuit. If the size of that bulge was anything to judge by, it would be an impressive sight.

As if spurred on by the thought, my gaze flicked down. I licked my lips, clenching my thighs with anticipation.

Lux groaned and reached for me, but I scooted further back on the bed.

"Nuh uh, buddy." I shook a finger at him. "I said, 'you first,' and I meant it."

For once, Lux's stone-like expression was gone. His gaze flicked over me hungrily, a feral gleam in his eye. I half-expected him to tear his skinsuit to shreds. Or to grab me and rip my bra and panties to bits. But when he finally moved, his hand trailed up his hard body in slow-motion. He gripped the zipper and slid it down the center of his chest, revealing inch after inch of pale, muscled skin.

His pace was torturous. By the time he neared his hard length, my legs quivered, rocking the bed beneath me.

A tinge of fear sparked somewhere deep in my mind. Sometimes it was easy to forget that the gorgeous man in front of me was an alien. He'd claimed we were compatible—hell, my body certainly hadn't ceased singing from his touch—but I knew next to nothing about his species.

I'd heard stories about some of the alien species we'd discovered Terrans could procreate with. There was even a planet full of men with *two dicks*.

Fuck. What would I do if Lux whipped it out and there were two… How did that even work?

He might have anything hiding under there. A tentacle, or a massive, hairy shlong he wants me to lick like a lollipop. Why didn't I think this through before my horny ass insisted he get naked?

I mean, I'd still want him naked, but maybe I could've prepared myself a little better. Was it too late to ask for a dick pic? My heart sped up, and I tamped down the sudden visceral panic as his zipper reached his bulge.

My breath caught in my throat as his cock sprang free.

Only one—thank fuck!

Lux shrugged his shoulders out of his skinsuit and then began slowly peeling it off. My belly flooded with lust. He was magnificent, packed with hard muscles and pale creamy skin I itched to touch. His cock jutted out proudly, looking remarkably similar to a human's. Not that I had any experience with those—but the sex-bots *were* based on human anatomy.

The two main differences were color and size. Lux was a big guy—nearly seven feet tall, I'd guess—and his package was definitely proportionate. My pussy clenched as I pictured his veiny, blue-tinged cock sliding between my thighs. Maybe his size should've frightened me, but I'd always been up for a challenge.

I grinned, scooting closer as Lux tossed his skinsuit aside. It was his turn to stop me. "Strip," he demanded, fists clenched at his sides.

Fair was fair. First, I lifted the towel off my neck, sighing when I realized the shallow gash had stopped bleeding. I tossed it aside and trailed my fingers slowly to my bra, determined to give him the same tortuous striptease, but something in Luxuth's posture made me think twice. His stare flicked from my neck to my breasts and back again, his entire body spooled tight. He was like a coiled spring, ready to launch.

I whipped off my bra and panties in about two seconds flat. Then I lay back on the bed and let him drink me in.

His big hand fisted his cock, and he pumped leisurely, his gaze roaming across every inch of me. His silence was unnerving. I stretched like a cat, arms above my head, watching as his silver eyes flicked to my breasts.

"What do you think?" I spread my thighs, giving him a clear view of my pussy.

His nostrils flaring was the only warning I got before he launched forward, his knees slamming into the bed on either side of my legs. "Beautiful." He leaned forward, capturing my nipple with his lips.

I moaned, arching closer to his hot mouth. His hand landed on the other breast. Icy fingers plucked my hard nipple. The contrasting temperatures set off a flurry of sensation. Pleasure zinged through my skin and pulsed between my thighs. When he switched sides, hot mouth soothing the cold nipple, and icy fingers chilling the burning heat he'd left on the other peak, my eyes rolled back into my head.

"Fuck, Lux." I moaned. My hips shot off the mattress, attempting to grind into his hard body. But the bastard held himself out of reach, his hand and mouth the only parts of him touching me.

I unclenched my hands from the sheets and sank them into his silky hair. He groaned around my nipple and awarded me with a little nip when my nails gently scraped his scalp.

"Please. I need to feel you." My clit ached, desperate for contact. "If you don't touch me, I'll do it myself."

Lux growled deep in his throat. His hands shot out lightning quick, and he pinned my wrists to the bed. "No, you won't. That cunt is *mine*."

Holy fuck. Something else to add to the list of things I didn't know turned me on. Hearing Lux's possessive demand, those silver eyes staring into my soul, made my pussy clench.

He tugged my hands above my head and clamped my wrists tightly with one big hand. Then his lips descended on mine in a blistering kiss. I met him stroke for stroke, tangling my tongue with his until I felt like I might melt into a puddle of lust beneath him.

His free hand trailed down my side. I panted into Lux's mouth, dying for him to rub my clit. He refused to rush. Just like when he'd stripped, his fingers grazed my flesh maddeningly slowly. His mouth moved just as deliberately, trailing a line of hot kisses across my cheek to my neck. Then those icy fingers halted their movement, directly above where I needed them.

Lux groaned and pulled back. His gaze locked on my neck, his whole body tensing.

I met his gaze, seeing an echo of the same lust I'd glimpsed in the mirror so many times. Clarity washed over me like a meteor shower.

If I was so turned on by blood, and I was only part Vamphere, then the sight of my bloody neck had to be driving him crazy. I concentrated on the spot and sensed a tiny trickle of heat dripping down my skin. Had all the thrashing I'd been doing against the pillows started me bleeding again?

Either way, I instinctively knew what to do.

"Taste me."

Lux's eyes shot to mine. He gulped, then flicked a glance down at my pussy. I looked down too, and the sight of his big hand resting right next to my spread thighs nearly had me going along with his assumption.

"No. My blood. You want to taste it, don't you?" I angled my head sideways, giving him better access. "Taste my blood like I've tasted yours."

"Are you certain?" Lux licked his lips.

I stared directly into his silver eyes and nodded. "If it will make you feel half as good as your blood feels to me, then I want you to taste me."

Lux groaned, dipping his head down to my neck. He released my wrists and tangled his fingers in my hair, holding my head steady. His hand that still hovered beside my pussy shifted to my hip, gripping me tightly. I closed my eyes, burying the disappointment at his fingers leaving when they were *so damn close* to where I wanted them.

But the next second, he washed away every lingering trace of dismay when his tongue flicked out. Lux's moan vibrated across my neck, and his hips shot forward. His cold cock slid between my thighs, making me jolt and moan even louder than he had.

"Lux." I rocked my hips, panting as his cold length slid against my slippery clit. "Fuck, you feel *so good.*"

He suckled my skin with bruising intensity, pulling fresh blood from the wound. But the tiny sting barely registered. Not when his hips rocked, rubbing my tender flesh with his hard cock.

I gasped, feeling something deliciously hot cutting through the chill. I tugged my head away from Lux's fingers and peeked between our body's, but I couldn't see anything with him pressed against me so tightly.

There it was again. My legs trembled, toes curling from the pleasure coiling between my legs. "What are you doing to me?" I asked with a gasp.

Lux lifted his head from my neck, his eyes hazy and half-lidded. He aimed a lazy smile at me and lifted his upper body on his forearms.

This time, I had a clear view of his big, blue cock-head slipping across my folds. I moaned at the erotic sight. As I watched, a little bead of precome gathered on the top. Lux angled his hips, sliding back down, and the bead rolled off and landed directly on my clit.

I gasped, my thighs shaking at the bolt of pleasure that struck me. Holy shit! *Yep, that's it. The man has heated sperm.* Just like the inside of his mouth, his come spread warmth over everything it touched.

Lux noticed my reaction. He leaned back, gripped his cock, and smirked down at me. "Do you like that, Arda?" He tugged hard, gathering a bigger drop of precome. "Should I rub my come on your greedy cunt?"

"Yes." I moaned, clutching his hips and trying unsuccessfully to drag his big body back to mine. "Give it to me."

My eyes were glued between our bodies, watching as he pumped. He aimed his cock at my clit and spread the hot bead of liquid with his hard length, making us both groan. Then he rocked against me with his icy flesh. I whimpered and arched into his touch.

If he feels this amazing just rubbing against my clit, what will he feel like inside me? The minute the question left my mind, my pussy clenched. I wanted to find out—immediately.

"Stop screwing around and fuck me," I demanded.

The bastard chuckled. My eyes shot to his, and he must have seen something in my expression that had the ghost of a smile falling off his lips. He drew in a deep breath, lined his cock up with my entrance and pushed in on a hard thrust. I stiffened, feeling fuller than I'd ever been with his icy cock impaling me.

Lux stilled. "Arda. Are you all right?"

I gripped his hips, keeping him in place before he could pull out. "Just give me a second. You're a lot bigger than the sex-bots I'm used to."

His eyes widened slightly. "Is this your first time?"

"Of course not. I just told you about the bots." I grimaced. "It's basically the same."

Lux grunted noncommittally, but stayed silent. After a moment, I relaxed enough that I felt a burning urge to move.

"I'm good now."

Lux grumbled under his breath, "Dral *something, something.*" Then his hips started moving.

I gasped, the pleasure quickly building. After only a few thrusts, I had to admit, Lux was right. This was nothing like fucking a sex-bot. It was so much *better*. Lux's scent surrounded me. His delicious muscles bulged and flexed. His hands were everywhere, and his drugging kisses had me on the edge within minutes.

"I'm so close," I moaned in his ear.

Lux slid his palms under my thighs and gripped my ass, changing the angle of his thrusts. When he bottomed out, grinding his pelvis against my clit, the first quaking flutters of my orgasm washed over me.

"That's it, Arda. Come with me."

My eyes rolled back in my head as Luxuth exploded inside me. Heat pulsed out of his cock, drenching my inner walls. He groaned, his thighs shuddering and chest heaving as he pounded me with ice again, setting off another rush of bliss.

"Oh, God! Oh, fuck!" I screamed. Wave after wave of pulsing desire detonated in my core, so intense I nearly blacked out.

After I came down from the high, I giggled. Lux lay heavily atop me, totally spent. He lifted his head and wheezed out a breath.

That was amazing, but it was certainly over fast. Not that I was about to complain after the man gave me an o that left me feeling boneless.

I wiggled out from under him, intending to grab a washcloth.

"Where do you think you're going?" Lux gripped my hips and flipped me on my belly.

"I-I was just going to clean up." I moaned as he tugged my ass up in the air, his big hands squeezing the globes roughly.

"I'm not done getting you filthy yet." An icy finger traced my pussy, then something much thicker.

I peeked behind me, biting back a gasp when I spotted his cock standing at attention. "I thought you came?" *Hell, I know he came. I felt his hot seed spilling inside me less than a minute ago.*

"Do your males only come once?" he asked with a smirk.

"Umm, yeah."

Lux rammed his cock back inside me and leaned close to my ear. "Not me. Your perfect cunt will be drenched before we're through."

Holy. Fuck.

Lux's boast about his species' special attributes suddenly replayed through my ears. *"I imagine a Terran experiencing such utter bliss would be turned off by human lovers afterwards."*

Maybe there was a bit of truth to his whole Vamphere sex god brag, after all.

I knew one thing. I was going to have a lot of fun finding out the truth behind the rumors.

19

Who's Counting

Lux

Arda sprawled out beside me on the bed, her luscious curves slicked with sweat. Images of the last few hours flicked through my mind. I'd had her in nearly every position imaginable, her breathy moans turning to screams of pleasure so many times I lost count.

I reached for her, and she swatted away my hand. "Jesus, Lux. Give a girl a break. You fucked me half to death."

I chuckled and dodged a second half-hearted swipe, then tugged her into my arms. "Hush and let me hold you."

Arda only stiffened for a split second before she stretched out against me. "Oh, your cold skin feels so good right now. It's so hot in here."

I skimmed my palm down the heated flesh of her back. "That means our plan is working. Won't be long now before the Garcuk abandon ship."

Arda giggled. "Guess we won't be the only ones having sex today."

I brushed a sweat soaked lock off her forehead. "I wouldn't exactly call what the Garcuk do sex..."

"What do you mean?"

"I'm sure you'll see soon enough. Let's just say there's a good reason why our species aren't compatible." I rolled off the bed and stood. Then I leaned down and scooped Arda in my arms.

"Lux! What are you doing?" she squeaked.

A few quick steps brought us inside the washroom. "Cleaning us up. We better get ready to leave." I set Arda down inside the ionic shower. She clutched my arms, steadying herself on wobbly legs. "You first."

"I can wash myself," she insisted, making a grab for the shower wand.

I snagged it first, my grip like iron. "Let me take care of you." I stroked a finger over the cute little wrinkle on her brow. "I want to."

She pursed her lips but then she sighed and said, "Ok."

I started the shower, wishing it was a normal spray of water like we had back on Pheria. The thought of Arda's curves, drenched in water and sudsy with soap, made my dick twitch.

Relax. She needs a break.

The ionic shower worked swiftly, blasting away the sweat and dirt from her smooth skin with its spray of invisible particles. Arda bounced on her feet as I directed the spray over her face. "It tingles," she whispered.

"Almost done." I aimed the wand at her breasts, not bothering to hold back my tiny grin when she sucked in a gasp. Then I bent to one knee and trailed the wand lower. "Spread your legs."

Arda bit her lip and slowly widened her stance.

Dral help me.

My come dripped down her thighs and glistened inside her lower lips. The sight was so erotic, I had to fight the urge to leap up and press her against the shower stall. Instead, I swept the spray over her legs, my stomach twinging as I watched the evidence of our lovemaking disappear.

A sudden thought had me reeling. I rushed through the rest of Arda's shower, not even bothering to linger over her perfect cunt like I'd originally planned.

I climbed back to my feet and set down the shower wand. "Arda." My serious tone made all traces of lust vanish from her eyes. "The Garcuk aren't compatible... but we are. We never discussed what might happen after we coupled. I want you to know—"

"Let me stop you right there, big guy, before you go getting all valiant on me. I can't get pregnant."

"You cannot?" I frowned, my heart lurching. "I'm sorry."

Arda waved her hand. "It's nothing like that. I'm not barren or anything." She picked up the shower wand and aimed the spray at my chest. "I'm on birth control." She tapped her arm between her elbow and shoulder. "An implant. Makes things easier in space without having to worry about getting a period once a month."

I nodded, the human anatomy lesson Destiny taught me filling in the gaps. "I see. Well, that's—thank you for telling me."

Arda grinned up at me, the shower wand trailing over my stomach. "No worries. Your plan to knock up an old lady isn't in danger from me."

Looking down at her cheeky grin, suddenly my meticulously thought-out objective seemed like the stupidest thing I'd ever committed to.

I sank my fingers into her hair as she bent down on her knees, sweeping the wand across my thighs. "What if I told you I am not so sure about that plan any longer?"

Silence stretched between us. Arda gazed up at me with those gorgeous blue eyes.

A commotion in the hall broke the trance we'd fallen under. "What the hell is that?" Arda hopped up, then cringed, rubbing her ear with one hand.

"If I'm not mistaken, that's a Garcuk mating call."

Arda

I thrust the shower wand into Lux's hands and backed out of the shower stall. "I need to get dressed."

That awful caterwauling was even louder in the cabin. If a howler monkey and an elephant ever mated, they'd probably sound just like it, only with the Garcuk's disgusting, flatulent snorts acting as a strange bass note among the shrill shrieks. I barely suppressed the urge to cover my ears while I slipped my skinsuit and boots back on.

Lux joined me moments later, proudly strutting across the small space in all his naked, muscled glory, without an ounce of shame. Not that he had anything to be ashamed of. The man was built like a dream. Even now, after countless rounds of screwing, his cock was stiff, ready for round ten—twenty? Who's counting? Certainly not me. I lost count after the third mind-blowing orgasm. Especially when they just kept coming, one after the other.

Fuck. It's really too bad he's headed to Earth, determined to find a mate. I shook off the thought. Now was not the time to worry about Lux's future wife. Don't even get me started on that look in the shower...

I winced as a particularly loud cry rang out in the hall just outside our door. "Zenda said they would do that outside."

Lux zipped up his skinsuit and strolled across to the far wall. He pressed his ear against the metal hull. "I think they are. Sounds like some of them are out there already."

"Really?" I raced over, leaning my ear against the wall. I smiled as a hint of yowling reached me through the hull. "Jesus, they're loud."

Lux perched on the bed and stuffed his big feet into his boots. "Won't be long now before they are all out there."

I nodded, my heart racing and my feet beginning to pace without me telling them to. "What do we do next? We're still locked in here." I tugged at the neck of my skinsuit, a bead of sweat dripping down my back. "Shit, we need a plan. Why don't we have a plan?"

"I can get us out of here. And I know exactly where the cargo bay is located.

"Seriously?"

Lux calmy tightened the fasteners on his boots. "We will grab your jesillium and get you back to your ship. I promise."

My heart stuttered from his quiet vow and the molten look he sent me. "All right. Let's do this." I sucked in a shaky breath, adrenaline bleeding through my veins. "What do you need from me?" I turned to the mess of parts littering the floor from the torn apart food processor. "Should I help you gather some of this so you can hack the lock?"

Lux stood from the bed and strolled to the hatch. "No."

"What do you mean, no? How are you going to open—"

The word died on my lips as Lux lifted his huge tree-trunk of a leg and pounded on the hatch. He kicked once, twice, three times. Nothing happened.

"That was an impressive show of brutality, but I don't think—"

Lux ignored my babbling and shifted, aiming a fourth kick at the hinges.

My mouth dropped open at the same time the hatch blasted outward. "Holy crap!" I stacked my hands on my hips, glaring at him. "Are you telling me this whole time we could've broken out of here, easy as that?"

Lux smirked. "Pretty much."

I sputtered, my eyes flicking back to the bed where he'd spent hours fucking my brains out. "I thought we were stuck here." Would I have let him keep me all but tied to the bed if I'd known it was that easy to break out of our prison? Maybe not...

What a waste that would've been.

"We were." He shrugged. "Now we're not. Come on."

I followed Lux into the hall, my heart pounding. Surely it was too much to hope that all the Garcuk had left. Clearly, not everyone would be affected by the females' pheromones. But the further I tip-toed down the silent hall, the more my speeding blood pressure eased. "Did they really all leave? What about old folks, or kids?" I whispered.

Luxuth shrugged. "This is a working ship. I doubt they have any elderly or children on board."

"Lucky for us, I guess."

"Indeed." Lux led the way down the corridor, not pausing even when presented with forking tunnels that looked identical to me.

I quirked a brow. "How do you know this ship so well?"

"This model is well known. The Vorill manufacture them."

"The Vorill... Don't they make skinsuits too?"

"Yes, and many other things that we rely on to run the universe." Lux rubbed the back of his neck. "I'm close friends with one of the men who runs their main manufacturing company. He shared the specs of this vessel with me when the Pherian military were considering purchasing new ships for the fleet."

Lux is friends with what has to be one of the richest men in the universe and he makes decisions for his planet's military? Not like that's a big deal, or anything...

The reminder of Lux's lofty lineage nearly made my head spin, but I guess that explained his knowledge of the ship. I wasn't about to complain while he was leading me exactly where I needed to go—I hoped.

And thanks to the Garcuk ladies' irresistible snatches, we were left alone to wander down the halls. Our boots clattered loudly, but I'd take that any day over our last trip through the ship, with dozens of eyes watching and all that nasty sniffing.

"Here we are," Lux announced. He found a panel beside a wide hatch and activated it. Then my breath flooded out in a rush as the door opened and I spotted an enormous problem.

"Holy mother of Jenga." Except for a small space at the very front, the entire cargo hold was packed, nearly floor to ceiling, with crates, boxes, and barrels. I almost expected it all to come tumbling into the hall and crush us; that's how densely packed it was.

"Mother who?" Lux asked, a perplexed expression on his handsome face.

"Never mind, not important." I pinched the bridge of my nose before balancing on my toes, gazing this way and that into the pile of insanity. "You're telling me my jesillium is in *there*?" No matter which way I bent, I couldn't spot a way in. "How are we supposed to find it?

We'll be here for decades. The Garcuk babies they're out there making will be walking and talking—hell, they might be making kids of their own before we're through searching this mess."

When Luxuth only answered with an unamused stare, I contemplated strangling him. I mean, the guy could fuck like no one's business, but that didn't mean he needed to breathe, right? *Right?*

Finally, he let out a deep sigh—the kind of sigh you save for when someone was being a complete fucking idiot, mind you—as I stood there seething. He strode just inside the massive stuffed chamber and turned to a second panel on the wall. Five seconds later, the entire surface of jam-packed cargo began to move, and I bit back a gasp.

What the hell kind of wizardry is he pulling?

But when a pair of familiar dented barrels somehow ejected from the mass of junk and landed at our feet, all my annoyance vanished. "Oh, you beautiful man! Thank you!" I raced forward and tore open the closest barrel's lid. Irregular, black rocks glimmered dimly in the fluorescent light, and a weight lifted off my chest.

The relief I was feeling only lasted a split second. "All right, big guy. Now, how do we get this out of here and back to my ship?"

20

Nice Moves

Lux

Arda stared up at me, her disbelief clear from her closed off stance and hard glare.

Females... You hand them a lilza on a platter and they demand to know how you'll cook it. *Lucky for this female, I always have a plan.*

I pushed a few more buttons on the control panel. Out of nowhere—or more accurately, out of the hidden storage units in the floorboards—a hovercart ascended, appearing just beneath Arda's jesillium barrels.

Arda squealed. Then I hit the code to activate the outer hatch. Arda's smile widened and her eyes lit up, even as she cringed when the Garcuk's mating calls assaulted our ears. "You really do know this ship, huh?"

"I do." A few more tweaks to the controls and a walkway appeared through the cargo. I led the way, tugging the hovercart behind me with a grunt. Even with the cart doing most of the work, it was a heavy load.

Jesillium wasn't exactly light. But after only a few steps, I noticed Arda wasn't following. She lingered beside the control panel, blue eyes wide like the rings of Hunyria. "Arda, come."

"Are you crazy?" she hissed. "That junk could crush us at any minute."

I flicked a glance up at the piled supplies. The ship's cargo system shifted enough to make us a round tunnel to the wide-open doors on the far wall. But there was so much cargo shoved into the hold. Barrels and boxes hovered just above my head, using nearly all the vertical space in the massive chamber.

I had to admit, the longer I stood there, the more claustrophobic I felt. But it was the only way we were getting out with the jesillium...

"It's perfectly safe. The cargo system is state of the art."

Arda just stood there, breathing erratically and shaking her head. I left the hovercart and retraced my steps, stopping beside her. "Come, Arda." I held out my hand. "We will go together."

Arda's delicate fingers slipped into my hand. She met my eyes and exhaled. "I don't trust that junk, but I trust you."

Dral's bones. Why did that simple statement make my heart hammer madly?

I held Arda's hand and led her back to the hovercart. Together, we tugged the heavy load across the cargo bay and out into the bright blue landscape.

The planet looked much the same as it had on our last hike. Endless stretches of blue rocky hills littered with lakes by the dozen. But whereas last time, it was devoid of any life—except for the few fish and microscopic beings hidden in the water—now it buzzed with Garcuk.

"What the hell are they doing?" Arda giggled. "They look ridiculous."

Female Garcuk crouched thigh deep in the lakes, completely nude. The male Garcuk still wore their skinsuits, but all of them gamboled about on the lake beds, screeching, snorting, and dancing like madmen.

"This is their mating ritual. From what I understand, the females choose a partner based on who can sing and dance most pleasingly." I pointed to a cluster of Garcuk gathered in front of a lone female. "The most desirable females have the most suitors. Once they choose, the rejected males will move onto another. The process can take days with a group this large."

"Huh, that's kind of like how some birds do it on Earth. Do they lay eggs too?"

I cleared my throat. "It is not an egg exactly, but that's probably the closest comparison I can think of. They—"

"You know what? Forget it. I don't need to know." She pursed her lips. "What's important is, will they stop us?"

I shook my head. "No. This is a mating frenzy. They'll ignore everything until they have satisfied it."

The volume of shrieking rose nearby and Arda wrinkled her nose. "Ugh, they call that *singing*?"

I shrugged. "Not a fan, I gather?"

"Are you kidding? Though I have to admit, they've got some nice moves…" Arda grinned as she watched a group of Garcuk fight to out shimmy each other, their gangly arms and legs swaying hypnotically. "How about you, Lux? Gonna put on a little dance for me?"

I leaned close to her ear, delighting in her reflexive shiver that my closeness provoked. "Mm, I might have some moves for you." I grabbed her elbow. "Later. Let's return to your ship first."

I held my breath as we passed the first group of Garcuk. But even though we passed close enough that we could've reached out and grabbed the closest dancer, we were completely ignored. We hiked quickly, the hovercart blessedly doing most of the heavy lifting. Still, by the time we made it to the Verne, sweat beaded on my forehead.

Arda crested the last hillside just before me. "Oh no, my poor ship! They broke in!"

Arda

The outer hatch to the Verne hung off its hinges, clearly the victim of Garcuk sabotage. "My poor ship." I started forward, intending to burst in and rip each one of the horny fuckers out, but Lux's tight grip on my shoulder stopped me.

"Wait. If they entered before the female's pheromones changed, then they won't be affected like the others."

I ripped my arm out of his hold. "I won't just stand here while they tear my ship apart." I took a leaping step away, the planet's low gravity aiding me in my quest to arrive quickly.

Lux followed on my heels. "Arda. We need a plan."

"I have a plan. We go in there and throw them out."

Lux rolled his eyes, then sighed. "It might be enough just to leave the inner hatch wide open. Garcuk have an excellent sense of smell. If they catch a whiff of the mating—"

"Yeah, I get the picture. C'mon." I cringed as I ducked beneath the broken outer hatch. Luckily, the inner hatch was intact, so we'd still be safe to leave the atmosphere. I paused just outside of the inner hatch. "Verne, it's Arda. Respond."

"How may I help you, Captain?" the computer's voice replied.

I sighed, a hand on my heart. *Good, we won't be running in blind.* "How many lifeforms are onboard, excluding me and Lux?"

"Six."

"Shit," I muttered. "Locations?"

"They are all located in the engine room currently."

I tapped my chin, then slapped the control panel, activating the door. "This way." I punched a code on the panel in the hall, ensuring the inner hatch remained open when we left.

Lux followed me silently. Having him there calmed a bit of the rage boiling inside of me. Those greedy, nasty fuckers didn't get to tear my ship apart. Not happening. Not today, not ever.

I opened the door to my bedroom and motioned Lux in. He eyed the bed with a smirk. "Don't start," I whispered, before he could sneak in a cocky remark. I slid the hatch closed as quietly as possible. Then I strode to the far wall and activated the hidden panel.

The mechanical trap door opened with a *hiss*. I pulled out two Niroblian blasters and handed one to Lux.

Lux flipped the small gun in his beefy fist. "Correct me if I'm wrong, but aren't these stun blasters?"

"Yeah." I shrugged. "We're a mining ship. Excuse me for not having a well-stocked armory."

Lux grimaced, then exhaled. "Hm. Not much on a diplomatic vessel, either. We'll make it work. Where is the engine room?"

"Not far. But listen, I have a plan that might get them out of here without fighting. As much as I want to teach those assholes a lesson, six against two aren't the best odds." I lifted the blaster. "Even with these."

"Smart thinking. What do you need me to do?"

My heart clenched. No arguing. No demanding to know every little detail of my plan. Lux's instant support was doing funny things to my insides.

I cleared my throat. "Can you hide outside of the engine room? I'm going to the bridge. I'll have Verne flood the engine room with air from the surface. Once they smell the females, they'll all hightail it out of there."

Lux nodded. "Yes, that could work. And I'll be there to pick off any stragglers that don't get the message. I doubt there will be, but it's better to be safe."

I quickly supplied Lux with directions, then paused by the door. "Verne, are the other lifeforms still in the engine room?"

"Yes, Captain."

I squared my shoulders and sent a quick nod to Lux. He met my eyes and nodded back. Then I eased out of the hatch and tip-toed into the hall.

"Arda," Lux whispered, his voice impossibly soft and his gaze like molten iron, "stay safe."

"I will," I whispered back, "you too." Then we split up, Lux stalking off toward the engine room as silent as a cat. Who knew the big guy could move so stealthily?

With a determined stride, I lifted my blaster and creeped forward. It was time to get those asses off my ship. I made my way down the hall of the Verne until I reached the bridge. I breathed a sigh as I opened the hatch and found it empty.

At least the Garcuk hadn't been in here. I'd half expected to find the room in tatters, all the intricate displays ripped apart and reduced to scrap, but my fears were unfounded. A few lights on the control panel blinked lazily, signs of a ship at rest.

I settled down in the pilot's chair and cracked my neck. But before I could set my hands on the panel, intuition made the hair on my neck stand on end. I whipped around in the swivel chair only to come face to face with an ugly bastard creeping up on me from the corner.

"Saenov!" I hissed, grabbing for the Niroblian blaster on my waist.

"Uh, uh, uh," he drawled, aiming his own gun—one I could tell from a distance wasn't a stun-gun, but a lethal laser variant—directly at my head. "Drop it or you're dead."

I fumed, but obeyed, slowly bending and setting the blaster on the floor.

"Kick it over here," Saenov demanded.

My boot connected with a dull *thud*, and the stun-gun skidded across the deck.

Fuck. How the hell had he snuck up on me? It didn't make any sense.

But as Saenov bent to pick up my blaster, I bit back a gasp as I spotted the tiny device strapped to the pocket of his skinsuit. It was a small oblong cylinder, the same size and shape of the cloaking apparatus I'd spied in Luxuth's engine room when I'd been poking around.

Saenov had a miniature cloaking device! No wonder he hadn't shown up on the Verne's scans. And I'd just traipsed in here, right into his slimy clutches.

There was no way he would let me touch the controls. Our plan was foiled and unless I wanted to chance a laser blast, those assholes would keep tearing my poor ship into bits.

Think, Arda, think! There had to be something I could do to distract him. Maybe if I got him talking, I could buy enough time to use the controls. I knew my ship like the back of my hand. It wouldn't take me more than a few seconds to fire up the correct panel and input the command.

"You'll never get away with this," I said cooly. "Luxuth will be here any minute to beat your ass to a pulp."

Saenov chuckled, the hearty sound interrupted by a nasty snort halfway through, making me cringe. "Ha. It's funny you think that idiot Vamphere has any loyalty to you. I looked you up, *Arda Jenson*. A Terran commoner—a scandalous one at that—and a Pherian lord?" He snorted again and shook his head.

My stomach churned. Was any of that true? But I shook off the doubt and eyed him brazenly. "You don't know Lux."

"And you clearly know little about Pherians. Their royals only make political matches. He might be happy to make use of you while he's stuck with no one else to serve his baser instincts, but that's where it will end. You're nothing more than a—what do they call it on your world?" He tapped his chin. "That's right—a whore."

I clenched my fists so hard my nails were likely drawing blood. "Listen here, you gigantic ass. You better shoot me now, because no one insults me on my own goddamn bridge and lives."

Saenov rolled his eyes and strolled closer. He jammed the barrel of his gun against my forehead and if not for the anger roiling through every cell of my body, I probably would have wet myself. Instead, I just stared up at him defiantly, my gaze so hot I'm surprised it didn't sear him where he stood.

"You need to learn your place. You humans are worse than gilats. Disgusting vermin spreading through the stars. You should stay where you belong and rot on your ugly little world."

"Fuck you," I said. Then I spit right on his slimy face.

Crack. Saenov smashed the gun across my cheek. Pain exploded, washing away the satisfaction I felt at the utter shock on his ugly mug when my spit landed on his smirking lips.

I groaned, my head lolling sideways and my hands rising to cradle my stinging cheek. Saenov backed away, wiping his mouth with his sleeve.

"You're going to pay for that," he hissed.

What the hell? A pistol whip wasn't payment enough?

I knew I should make nice. I should've played it safe. Calmed him down with sweet words and found a way to distract him, like I'd planned.

But me being me—goddamn awful temper and all—I smirked back. "Bring it on, asshole."

21

Out Of Tricks

Lux

I hid behind the open hatch to Arda's med-bay, down the hall from the engine room. I'd chosen the hiding spot both to listen for the departing Garcuk, and to monitor the air quality scanner I'd scrounged up among the medical equipment.

I shook the little device, frowning at it as the dial remained stubbornly fixed in place. The sounds from the engine room continued on uninterrupted. Clangs and grunts of exertion mixed in with the occasional muffled string of chatter and the answering laughter of thieves none the wiser.

They certainly didn't sound like the men had back on the Garcuk vessel, shrieking their mating calls at the top of their lungs.

I shook the scanner again. Either the gauge was broken or... *Something must be wrong.*

Heart in my throat, I set the device down carefully and snuck back into the hall. What was taking Arda so long? The Verne claimed no one else was onboard, but who knows what could've gone wrong on her way to the bridge? Visions of her nearly being choked to death on the wiring in her busted shuttle rose to plague me.

Dral's bones. She probably took it upon herself to complete another repair and got tangled up in trouble. I bit back a grin, picturing the scowl on her cute little face when I arrived to help her.

But as I approached the bridge, the unmistakable sound of Arda groaning in pain made my blood run cold. And when a man's voice spoke up a second later, I halted in my tracks. I couldn't make out what he'd said, but I'd know that sleezy voice anywhere.

"Saenov," I muttered under my breath.

He was *dead.* Whatever he did to make her cry out like that—I didn't even want to know—all I knew was he was about to be bleeding at my feet. I covered the hall's remaining length in a blur of motion.

Just as I lifted my hand to the hatch, I heard Arda call out defiantly, "Bring it on, asshole."

I shoved the hatch open and burst in with a roar. Arda and Saenov spun toward me, wide eyed. Arda rested on her pilot's chair, a hand clutched on her reddened cheek and Saenov towered over her, wiping his face, a gun pointed at her.

The bastard! I zeroed in on Saenov, crossing the small room in a few leaping strides.

Light flashed and a shooting pain erupted in my shoulder, but I brushed it aside like a mere insect's sting. I screamed, landing on the squealing Garcuk in a tangled heap. His gun went flying and my fist slammed into his face.

Time slowed around me. All that existed was my fists and his flesh. Again and again, skin met skin until all that remained was the wet squelch of blood splattering the floor.

"Lux." Arda tugged my elbow, her sweet voice cooling my rage. I left Saenov in a gurgling puddle and leaned back on my knees. Then I shifted sideways, grabbing Arda's arms.

"Are you all right?" I gently traced the bright red mark marring the tan skin on her cheek. A dark purple bruise was already beginning to swell beneath her eye. My blood boiled, and I nearly spun back around to land a few more hits on Saenov.

"Me?" Arda bit her lip and swallowed. "He *shot* you. Lux, I think you're in shock."

I shook my head and glanced down at my shoulder. Blood dripped from a hole in my skinsuit, mingling with the flecks of Saenov's blood splattered all over me. "Huh, looks like he did."

Arda shot me a strange look, then she ducked under my arm. "C'mon, I'm taking you to the med-bay."

"Wait, the Garcuk—"

"I flooded the ship with surface air while you were fighting." She grunted, struggling to help me stand. Now that the adrenaline was wearing off, my legs wobbled, and I was glad for Arda's help.

"What about *him?*" The last word escaped like a curse, full of venom.

Arda chuckled. "Are you kidding? We'll need to peel him off the floor to drag him out of here. He's not going anywhere." She tugged my elbow firmly, but still I wouldn't budge. "And I locked the controls. If he wakes up while we're gone—which I seriously doubt is happening—he won't do any damage."

I sneered, giving the bloody wretch a final once over. He was unconscious, breathing uneasily but steadily. "I should—"

"After we patch you up," Arda insisted, her tone brooking no argument. She tapped her pocket, outlining a bulky shape hidden inside. "I have the blasters and his cloak. He's all out of tricks."

I nodded curtly, allowing her to turn me away from Saenov and toward the hall. From somewhere deep in the ship, a familiar sound rang out. The first shrill echoes of Garcuk mating calls.

Arda grinned at me. "It's working." She slammed the hatch closed and input a code into the keypad. "A little extra assurance won't hurt. Saenov's locked in."

I breathed deeply through my nose. Fresh adrenaline coursed through me—the ship was still crawling with Garcuk—but the pain in my shoulder had begun making itself known. Luckily, a shot from a laserblaster cauterized the wound, leaving minimal bleeding.

Shrill cries echoed down the hall. "Hand me Saenov's blaster."

Arda pulled it out of her pocket and passed it to me. She lifted one of the stun guns, then we inched forward cautiously.

Six wild-eyed Garcuk burst into the hall. I stiffened, aiming the gun at the closest alien. He didn't spare me or the weapon a second glance. Each of the Garcuk behaved the same, lifting their ugly noses into the air and sniffing deeply. Then, like a vorhound with a scent, they tore off, screeching and stumbling toward the outer hatch.

"Well, that worked better than I'd expected." Arda led me to the med-bay, where she propped open the door to a tiny stall in the corner.

I eyed the interior dubiously. It clearly hadn't been manufactured with a being of my stature in mind.

"Go on. Strip." Arda grinned mischievously, making no move to avert her eyes.

"You don't want to pat me down first?"

Arda giggled and licked her lips. I couldn't help flashing back to our first meeting. My fingers itched, recalling the soft imprint of Arda's curves sliding along my palms. When her cheeks pinked, I stepped closer, certain she was remembering too.

"Oh no, big guy." Arda backed up, and gestured at the med-bot. "Fix that hole in your shoulder, then we can talk."

I held Arda's gaze as I shucked off my boots. When I winced, she rushed forward.

"Here, let me help you." I kept still as she peeled off my skinsuit. The fire in her eyes when she spotted my hard length didn't make leaving her alone any easier. I wanted to bury myself inside of her. After hearing her cry out in pain, knowing that bastard was hurting her, I needed to have her again. The urge to take her burned so much I nearly slammed her against the wall and tore off her clothes. But the sharp pain radiating up my arm made me think twice.

"There." Arda glanced up as she finished tugging the skinsuit off my legs. The sight of her kneeling in front of me while I was fully naked made my dick twitch. "Get in."

I scowled, then bit back a curse as I crammed myself into the puny box. It was a tight squeeze, but after crouching, I made it work. My elbows and knees pressed painfully against the walls, and I could barely see through the glass viewport with my head jammed against the ceiling, but at least I was in. Arda secured the door. The machine whirred and after only a second something sharp poked me in the rear.

"What in Dral's name was that?"

Arda peeked at me from the med-bot's control panel, her voice muffled but loud enough to reach me. "That would be the sedative I ordered."

"Sedative!" I bucked inside the med-bot. With the door shut firmly and a wave of wooziness quickly washing over me, it only rattled the device. "Wh-why would…"

"It's for your own good," Arda insisted. "This will take a few hours and it won't be pleasant. You might as well get some rest while the machine does its thing."

I opened my mouth to complain. To demand she unleash me from this coffin and slap a bandage on me until we were safely back in space. But the fleeting urge floated away before I could form the words. My eyes fluttered closed and darkness consumed me.

22

Sweet Dreams

Arda

I smiled as I watched Lux nod off inside the med-bot. A twinge of guilt pinged my chest, but I brushed it aside. Sure, he'd probably insist on staying conscious through the surgery if I'd given him the choice, even if it meant withstanding excruciating pain. Yeah—not on my watch.

Sweet dreams, Lux.

I slid into the empty hall. "Verne, life signs and locations. Report."

The ship's computerized voice replied, "There are three life signs currently onboard. One on the bridge, one in the med-bay, and one in the main hall."

Exactly what I'd been hoping to hear. "Close and lock the outer hatch."

In the distance, banging reverberated dully. "Task complete."

Now that I didn't have to worry about any more unwanted visitors, I strode to the engine room. Time to see what kind of damage those Garcuk had left.

The hatch slid open, and I peered inside. I groaned as I took in the damage. They'd certainly been busy. Dozens of parts were stacked on a hovercart by the door. But on the bright side, everything was still there, just not where it needed to be for the ship to fly.

"Fuck, it's gonna take me hours to fix this," I grumbled to myself as I picked up the closest part and began the tedious task of setting everything back in its proper place.

At least it would give me something to do besides worry about Lux. What was he thinking, rushing in and attacking Saenov like that? Don't get me wrong, watching him burst in and put that asshole in his place had been one of the hottest things I'd ever witnessed. Lux had been positively feral. I shivered, recalling the savage way he'd beaten him off with his bare hands.

Then after, when I pulled him off, the tender way he'd touched my cheek, and the sweet way he'd asked if I was all right—I almost swooned right there. Definitely would've if not for the lack of concern the big guy had for his own health.

Sometimes when he looks at me, I almost wonder...

I shook off the thought. Lux had been perfectly clear about his intentions. It would be foolish of me to imagine anything serious would come out of this—whatever it was—happening between us. He'd never made me any promises other than helping me come to terms with my Vampherian heritage.

He'd certainly helped me with that. A few days ago, the sight of all that blood while he'd pounded Saenov to a pulp would've rooted me to the spot, dizzy with lust. But after slaking our desires together, the crimson flecks were easy to ignore.

How am I going to give that up? How am I supposed to give him up?

The big alien had gotten under my skin. He might be cocky and demanding, but he was kind and giving, too. Whenever he touched me, all my senses came alive.

I shook my head as Saenov's words rang in my ears. A Pherian lord and a scandalous jesillium miner from Earth—no matter how much I might want it to, it would never work. He was on his way to Earth to offer himself up as the first husband of another species.

What would it say about him if he chose someone like me, a nobody—no, worse than that—the granddaughter of the infamous Bathing Butcher?

It wouldn't look good. With their species' need for blood, and their obvious reluctance about focusing on that little detail, it would look pretty damn awful.

No, I had to come to terms with the fact that no matter how wonderful this time spent with Lux was, it was temporary. Maybe if I reminded myself enough, it would be easier to swallow.

Soon, all thought of Lux fled my mind as the complexity of the repairs increased. One part put in backwards, or a single connection made incorrectly, could be the difference between a successful takeoff and a crash landing. I focused completely on the machinery in my hands, querying Verne frequently to test my work.

By the time I fitted the last piece in place, my back ached and my fingers throbbed. But it was done.

After a quick confirmation from the Verne, I snuck back to the med-bay. Lux's eyes were closed inside the med-bot. I held back a giggle at the sight of his bulky body scrunched up inside. He would likely wake up with a few kinks in his back, but it was better than getting an infection from some foreign bacteria on this uncharted little world.

I scanned the med-bot's readings. They predicted Lux would need another hour before his treatment was complete. With a sigh, I closed the door to the med-bay and strode to the outer hatch.

"Verne, I'd like an update on the condition of the lifeform on the bridge."

"That lifeform has not moved in many hours. It appears to be unconscious."

I grimaced. I had half a mind to drag Saenov out myself and toss him off the ship. Then again, as much as I wanted that slimy fucker gone, I wasn't in the mood to toss my back out. Moving Saenov could wait for when Lux woke up.

That only left one thing for me to do. I had to grab the jesillium from where we stashed it on the hillside, and cart it back into my hold where it belonged. Hopefully, I could avoid another run in with more Garcuk while I was at it.

Lux

I woke with a dull ache in my lower back, the painkillers pumping through my veins doing nothing to soothe it. *This med-bot will be the death of me.*

Scanning in vain, I searched for a way to open the tin can when the door popped free on its own. I groaned as I hopped out, blood rushing to my tingling feet and fingers. My whole body was like one big cramp after spending who knows how long crammed in that puny box.

After a few stretches, and a cursory peek at my shoulder to make sure the med-bot "did its thing" as Arda so casually put it, I tugged my clothes back in place and set off to find her.

Anger seeped out of my pores, and I bit back a snarl as I threw the hatch open. How could she knock me out without my consent? 'For my own good,' she said. What about *her*? Anything might have happened to her while I was out of it. If she had one hair out of place on that pretty little head when I found her, I swear I *would* murder someone this time.

The fact that Saenov was still drawing breath ate at me. I'd let Arda talk me into leaving him alive, when all I'd wanted to do was choke the life out of him with my bare hands. The thought of him touching her... I paused outside the door to the bridge. Was he still inside? Maybe I ought to finish what I started.

Footsteps echoed behind me. "There you are. Looks like the med-bot fixed you up." Arda sashayed beside me, an easy smile on her gorgeous face. Seeing her whole and unharmed eased some of the tension rocketing through my body. "I'm glad you're here, actually. I just finished securing the jesillium in the hold—"

"You what?" I bit out.

Eyes widening, she cocked her hip. "My jesillium. I went outside and got it."

My jaw ticked, and I sucked in a deep breath through my nose. "You went out alone?"

"Yeah." She rolled her eyes. "I can handle a thing or two on my own, you know."

Before I knew what was happening, I had her pinned against the wall. I crowded her in, a hand on her throat. Her breath hitched, her pulse pounding beneath my fingers.

I placed my lips so close to hers I could feel the heat radiating off her skin. I didn't close the gap, but hovered just out of reach. "Anything could have happened. It's just you and me down here, against all of them. Don't be so stupid."

I inched closer, desperate to feel her soft curves flush against me, but something hard rammed into my gut instead. I tore my gaze off her lush mouth and peered down between us.

The little temptress. "Why are you aiming a blaster at me, Arda?" I flicked my gaze back up at her face.

Her chest heaved, her eyes burning holes into me. "I'm going to give you three seconds to take your goddamn hands off of me before I show you how fucking *stupid* I can be."

That mouth. *Dral's bones*, what I wanted to do to that mouth of hers.

I lifted my hand off her throat and backed up, giving her space. She grinned triumphantly, and waved the blaster as if to say 'see, told you I can take care of myself.' I let her have her moment—exactly that—a moment.

She opened her mouth to say something, but I swooped in. I knocked the blaster out of her hand and pinned her against the wall—by her wrists this time. The dull clang of the weapon echoed down the hall as my lips descended on hers.

Arda gasped, and I slipped my tongue in her mouth. The gasp turned into a moan as her little tongue flicked across mine, sending need coiling down my spine.

It would be so easy to sink into her. To claim her again, right here against the wall in her ship. But I needed her to hear what I had to say. Though it pained me, I broke the kiss and squeezed her wrists—hard. Her breath escaped in a hiss.

I pulled back just enough to meet her eye and let her see a glimpse of the feral anger I kept painfully leashed. "Terrans are not the only species at the top of the food chain anymore. I will have you safe while you're with me, Arda. Understand?"

For a second, I was certain she would argue. I could see it in her eyes. Her temper was a match for my own, and her stubbornness as well. But then her shoulders slumped, she sucked in a deep breath, and nodded. "I probably should have waited. I'm sorry if I scared you."

I dropped her wrists and drew back, startled more than I wanted to admit by her apology. Was I scared? I went searching for her, only concentrating on my anger, but if I really dug deep down to my bones, that was exactly what caused it all. Fear—for her.

When I started pursuing Arda, I assumed we'd just have a good time together, but what did it mean if I couldn't stand the thought of her being in danger?

Oblivious to the way her apology had just sent me reeling, Arda patted me lightly on the chest and slipped away. She stopped in front of the bridge hatch. "Glad we cleared that up, big guy. Now, do you mind helping me haul that asshole off my ship so we can get the fuck out of here?"

23

Devious

Arda

I ducked inside the hatch, half expecting that idiot to lunge at me like something in an old Earth horror vid. But the universe gave me a break, for once.

Saenov sprawled on the floor in the same position we'd left him in. I winced as I took in his swollen, blood-crusted face. I really shouldn't be feeling any sympathy for the guy, but damn—Lux had really done a number on him.

I flicked a glance beside me as Luxuth walked in. A muscle in his neck twitched, and if looks could kill, Saenov wouldn't be wheezing for breath right now.

I squeezed Lux's forearm. "Hey. You can help me drag him out of here without murdering him, right?"

Lux sneered down at Saenov, then gently traced my bruised cheek with a finger. "Why shouldn't I kill him? He deserves it."

My heart thudded wildly, and my thighs clenched. *Holy fuck. Why is that alpha bullshit such an incredible turn on?*

I frowned and brushed his hand away. "I won't be responsible for an interplanetary incident, that's why. Correct me if I'm wrong, but isn't homicide a crime according to the galactic charter?"

Lux stared at me intensely. "He needs to be taught a lesson about touching what doesn't belong to him."

My body thrummed strangely from that statement, and the heat in Lux's gaze. *Cool it, Arda. He isn't saying you belong to him... he's just pissed.*

"I'm pretty sure you taught him that with your fists already." I sent him a wicked smile. "Besides, I have something much more torturous planned for our friend than a quick death."

Lux cocked a brow. "You do?"

"Yep." I walked over to Saenov and grabbed one of his boots. "Help me drag him to the outer hatch and I'll show you."

Lux strolled over and barked, "Put him down."

I dropped Saenov's foot and shifted toward his face. "I can grab his head if you'd rather—" I bit my tongue as Lux hefted the unconscious Garcuk off the floor with a grunt and tossed him over his shoulder.

Guess he doesn't need my help... won't catch me complaining.

I followed the pair out of the bridge and down the hall into the docking bay. "Set him down here." I gestured to a wall of cabinets where we stowed our mining gear.

Luxuth dumped Saenov on the floor. I located a bag of heavy-duty twist ties and passed a couple to Lux. "I'll get his hands. Can you secure his feet?"

Lux got to work immediately, but not without asking, "Why are we tying him up?"

"I figured the least we could do for our buddy Saenov would be making sure he has the galaxy's worst case of blue balls."

Lux's brow pinched. "Blue balls?"

I chuckled. "It's an old Earth saying men use when they're turned on and denied satisfaction."

"Oh." Lux smirked. "Devious."

I tugged the twist tie shut tightly and dug into my pocket. I pulled out the syringe I'd pilfered from the med-bay and lifted it for Lux to see. "Let's toss out the trash. Then I'll make sure sleeping ugly is alert enough to hear all those lovely mating calls."

Lux hefted the hogtied alien in his arms. "With the way the males compete for females in his species, they won't untie him until the frenzy is over."

"Poor guy. Can't say I'm upset there won't be any little Saenov's running around in the next generation of Garcuks." I worked the controls to the hatch, then we stepped out onto the alien planet once more. Night wasn't far off, washing the blue world in shades of midnight and violet.

From the sound of it, the mating frenzy was still in full swing. Shrill cries echoed on the wind, but from our sheltered valley, we couldn't see any Garcuk. *Thank God for that. The last thing I need is an alien orgy burned onto the backs of my eyelids.* I shuddered at the thought.

"You all right?" Lux asked.

"Yeah. Let's get this over with."

Lux bounced a safe distance from the ship, then plopped Saenov on a rocky hillside. I hop-stepped over and kneeled beside him. I wasn't trained in medicine like Zenda, but for what I had to do, the instructions were simple enough.

Here goes nothing.

I stabbed the needle into Saenov's chest and injected the meds.

A second passed. Two. Three.

Saenov gasped and jolted awake. The eye that wasn't swollen shut flicked wildly, and he groaned in pain. Then that ugly nose gaped wide and sniffed deeply. A crazed look overtook his pained expression. He opened his mouth and shrieked, his mating cry sounding more desperate than the rest as he tugged uselessly at his bindings.

"Not much fun being held against your will, is it?" I patted the shrieking Garcuk on his bloodied cheek, making him wince. Then I stood and grabbed Luxuth's elbow. "C'mon. Our work here is done. Let's get off this rock."

Arda

The clang of the docking module clicking into place reverberated through the Verne's shuttle bay. Except for the pulse pounding moment of fear when starting the engine, my mind alive with worry that the repairs wouldn't hold, the return to space had been uneventful. Now all that was left was to reunite with my crew onboard the Destiny.

As soon as the hiss of air pouring inside the tube faded, I shoved my way into the walkway and out the hatch.

"Capt." Zenda slammed into me as I popped into Destiny's shuttle bay. "I'm so glad you're all right."

I hugged her back fiercely. Despite being together for less than a full year, spending day in and out with the same people forged an unbreakable bond. I knew Zenda needed the comfort of a hug from me, and I wasn't about to be stingy.

At the same time, I knew Ren would normally do anything to avoid a physical greeting. I'd nearly died of surprise when she'd hugged me after the Garcuks invaded the Verne, but I guess nearly being captured by slavers would make anyone eager for a little affection. I settled for sending her a smile and a nod.

Surprising me, she approached and tentatively squeezed my shoulder. "You had Zen worried Capt." After a few halfhearted pats, she backed away with a grin. "Not me though. I knew you could handle those pricks." Her gaze darted to the hatch as Luxuth unfolded himself from the cramped space. "Commander. Good to see you're back."

Lux nodded at Ren. "Good to be back. Oof."

Zenda detached herself from around my waist only to collide with Lux. "Thank you for keeping Arda safe."

Lux returned Zenda's hug, resting his arms lightly across her shoulders, but his heated gaze speared into me. "It was my pleasure."

A riot of meteors collided within my belly. Even with his arms wrapped around my crewmate, the man could make me squirm. It was entirely uncalled for.

Ren cleared her throat loudly. "Zen, let the commander breathe."

Zenda chuckled and stepped back with a sheepish grin. "I'm a hugger. He might as well get used to it."

Ren frowned. "Commander, the comms system on the bridge has been buzzing nonstop."

Luxuth glanced at me with pursed lips, seeming reluctant to leave.

"Go ahead," I said. "It will give me time to debrief my crew."

He nodded once and swiftly strode away. I sighed, watching his fine ass as it disappeared into the hall.

"What the hell was that?" Ren balled her hands on her hips.

"What?" I shifted. "Just appreciating the view while I have it."

"A damn fine view at that." Zenda fanned her face dramatically. "Spill. What happened between you two down there? If those fuck me eyes he just sent you are any clue, I'm willing to bet it got plenty steamy."

Ren groaned. "Don't we have more important things to discuss?"

"Ren's right. Business first." I sent Zenda a conspiratorial wink. "I'll give you the dirty details after."

"Ooo it got dirty!" She hopped up and down. "I knew it."

Ren rolled her eyes. "I'm almost finished with the repairs over here. A few more hours and everything will be back in working order."

"So soon? That's incredible, Ren. Good work." I cocked a brow. "But tell me this; you were supposed to be fixing the landing gear on the Destiny. What possessed you to take apart the engine and power down the AI while we were stuck on that planet?"

"The landing gear was a simple fix. I had it done within the first hour." Ren cringed and rubbed the back of her neck. "I was only trying to help. How was I supposed to know you would be abducted?"

Ren might put on a tough act, but deep down, she had a giving soul. Her going above and beyond to fix Lux's ship proved it.

I smiled gently. "It's okay. I wasn't trying to reprimand you, just curious. So, once you're finished, the Destiny will be back in working order?"

"Yep. I figured it was the least I could do for the commander after he swooped in to save us from those slavers."

"Great work, Ren. Lux will be happy to hear that." I widened my smile, but my heart clenched. That meant Lux was one step closer to leaving for Earth. I should've been happy for him, but I couldn't stop the sinking sensation from expanding in my gut.

Zenda's gaze darted between both of us. "That it? We good on the business yet? I'm dying over here."

I crossed my arms. "I don't know. Maybe I should have Ren take me through her repairs step by step. Make sure she didn't miss anything."

Zenda gasped. "Don't you dare. You've left me in suspense long enough."

I chuckled. Zenda was too easy to rile. I glanced at Ren. With the way she avoided men like they were radioactive, I didn't want to make her uncomfortable. "You sure you want to stick around for this? I wasn't kidding when I said it got dirty."

Zenda whooped. "Yes, girl!"

I kept my gaze trained on Ren. She toed the floor with her boot before shrugging. "I-I'm a little curious too."

Hm, interesting. I'd always assumed she would be the last woman to look for a partner, but maybe Ren was coming around to the idea.

I started walking toward the hatch to the Verne, waving for them to follow. "C'mon ladies."

"Where are we heading?" Zenda asked.

"Our mess hall. If I'm about to spill the tea, I'm gonna need a mug of the good stuff while I'm at it."

24

Bad News

I slid into my pilot's chair, sighing at the welcoming embrace of a seat made to my exact dimensions. Arda's ship had been surprisingly comfortable on the inside, compared to how much of a junker it appeared from outside, but everything was just a touch too small for someone my size.

I rubbed my hand along the control panel, ignoring the frantically beeping comms. *First things first.* "Destiny. Damage report."

"The ship is performing at 97 percent nominal capacity."

"97 percent," I repeated under my breath. "Not bad."

Arda's crew must have stayed busy while we were trapped on the planet. I'd been expecting to find the landing gear fixed—since Ren had been so confident and appeared capable—but I'd expected to have to complete the repairs to the FTL on my own. From a cursory examination of the maintenance readouts, it looked like Ren had fixed nearly everything.

Instead of bolstering my spirits, the news left me oddly deflated. *Arda—I don't want to part from her.* I shoved the thought aside and activated the comm panel.

I clicked on the oldest message. My sister's panicked voice filled the room. "Lux, why are Garcuk demanding a premium for your safe return? Please tell me this is a joke, and you didn't do something stupid."

I sighed as I shut off the message and scanned the rest—all from Elys. They were probably all a variation of the same thing. Nothing for it but to call her.

I punched in a code and waited. It was early morning back on Pheria, but I might as well leave her a message. It was likely too early for Elys to be up. She was so not a morning—

"Lux? Dral's teeth—where have you been?" Elys answered, her voice groggy.

"Relax. I'm all right. We had a little run in with Saenov but I handled it."

"Saenov. That idiot. He contacted the palace through an intermediary, demanding a hefty ransom. Mother has been absolutely livid."

I cringed. "Well, you can tell her I'm safe. Nothing to worry about."

"I'm pleased to hear it." She blew out a relieved breath. "What happened exactly?"

I spent a few minutes filling her in, leaving out how close Arda and I had become during our captivity. "And then we left him there, tied up and forced to listen to the mating frenzy without being able to take part."

"I have to admit, that's a fitting punishment—without you having to stand trial for murder."

"It was all Arda's idea." I smiled to myself, remembering the cute smirk that painted her full lips as we'd abandoned the squealing alien to his fate.

"Speaking of your stowaway... I have some bad news."

My heart seized. "What bad news?"

"When the Garcuks contacted the palace with their demands, they gave them Arda's name. Her *full name*." She paused, and I sensed the reluctance in her tone. "Has she mentioned anything about her family to you?"

"Yes. She told me about her grandmother's crimes. What of it?"

"Well... someone in the inner circle had loose lips. The media pounced on the story. Particularly that aspect."

"I don't see how that matters. It's ancient history." Even as I spoke, my stomach clenched. The media on Pheria were relentless. A member of the royal family spending time with anyone even slightly scandalous always made a splash. Arda's connection with a mass murderer would have them salivating. They wouldn't let this go easily. But luckily, I was headed to Earth and not back home anytime soon.

"Yeah, I know it shouldn't, but I just thought I'd warn you. Last time we spoke, you seemed a little—infatuated. If you were to take her for your mate and return to Pheria, that little tidbit of information will be a challenge to sweep under the rug."

I rubbed my forehead, considering the problem. It would be ages before I returned to Pheria. Years at the earliest. Surely the media would forget by then... I sucked in a breath as I realized exactly where my mind had gone.

Did I want Arda as my mate?

I pushed the question aside for the moment, ignoring my racing heart. "Thank you for telling me, Elys. I'll think on that carefully."

"I understand. I suppose you need to return to the repairs?"

"Yes. I should." I didn't bother filling her in on all the progress Ren made in my absence. If she dug hard enough into the ship's readouts she had remote access to, she could figure it out on her own. For now, I wasn't ready to hear her urging me to complete my mission to Earth as quickly as possible.

I had much to consider, and I planned to take my time doing it.

Arda

Steam curled above my cup in the mess hall, the delicious aroma of cinnamon chai lighting up my senses. I sighed, lifting the mug to my lips. I'd just finished telling the girls what happened in that Garcuk cabin, leaving out some of the more intimate details—including anything to do with blood. They'd listened without interrupting, but I sensed they wouldn't keep silent for long.

"You lucky bitch," Zenda exclaimed. "Why can't I find a man with that kind of staying power?"

Ren shuddered and tilted her head, eyeing my neck. "I don't understand how you could even be remotely in the mood after he pulled that implant out of you. Sex would've been the last thing on my mind."

I bit my lip. I loved my crew, but how much did I want to tell them? I'd spent so long hiding my past and my strange desires, it was hard to open up to anyone.

I trusted Lux, and look at how amazing that turned out... Maybe I should come clean to my crew, too.

I sucked in a deep breath and looked both of them in the eyes. "Can I tell you guys something personal?"

Ren grinned. "Like *that* wasn't personal already?"

Zenda leaned forward and clasped my hand where it rested on the table. "Of course you can, Arda. You can tell us anything."

The humor drained from Ren's face, and she nodded in confirmation.

"I told you about how Vamphere drink animal blood," I began.

Zenda wrinkled her nose. "Yeah, I remember."

"Well, they don't just drink blood to survive." I slipped my hand out from Zenda's and clutched the warm mug to my chest. "They share blood during sex, too."

Ren gasped, her gaze darting back to my neck. "So he drank your blood while you..."

"While we fucked? Yeah. He did." I watched them both closely, gauging their reactions before I told them the rest. Ren looked slightly horrified, her normally tan face a ghostly white. But Zenda tilted her head and scrunched her brow, her expression mirroring how she always looked when studying an interesting new species.

"Did you like it?" Zenda's voice was heavy with curiosity.

I gulped and nodded. "Yeah, I did. And I tasted his blood too."

Ren's eyes bulged. "Really?"

"Not much. Just a drop. Well, two." I set the mug down. "There's an aphrodisiac in Vamphere blood. Lux gave it to me to distract me from the pain."

"Oh." Ren leaned back in her chair. "Now I get why you were horny."

I grinned. "Extremely." I sighed, recalling the incredible wash of arousal that overcame me. "When the women back home get an inkling of how potent that stuff is, I wouldn't be surprised if they started selling Vamphere blood on the black-market."

"That good, huh?" Zenda chuckled.

"It was incredible," I confirmed. "But that might have a little something to do with me, too." I sucked in a breath, incredibly nervous suddenly. "This is where the personal stuff comes in."

Ren leaned her elbows on the table and met my gaze. "It's okay if you don't want to tell us."

"No." I shook my head. "I'm tired of hiding who I am." I steeled my spine and when I spoke, my voice didn't waver in the slightest. "I've always had this urge to have sex with blood involved. I just assumed it was a weird kink I'd inherited. You see, my grandmother was Cora Jenson."

I stared at Zenda and Ren, certain they would gasp and cover their mouths, recoiling at the news. But instead, they gazed back at me calmly with compassion in their eyes.

"You knew about my grandmother already?" I asked.

They both nodded sheepishly. Zenda cleared her throat. "From the first day we signed on to your crew. Ren looked you up on the web." She shrugged. "We both agreed then that it didn't matter. What your grandmother did shouldn't come back to haunt you."

Tears pooled in my eyes, and I blinked them back.

"I guess we should have said something right away," Ren added. "I didn't realize keeping it a secret was bothering you."

I shook my head. "No. It's all right. I wasn't ready to talk about it then. Not until Lux helped me come to terms with my unique genetics."

Zenda perked up, and I held back a giggle. She always got excited when science was mentioned. "What kind of genetics?"

"Apparently, someone messed with the genetic code of one of my ancestors. They gave her Pherian markers. I'm willing to bet it was my grandmother."

Ren rubbed her forehead. "So, is that why she did what she did?"

I shook my head sadly. "I don't know if we'll ever know for sure, but Lux seems to think so. He said the same thing can happen to Pherians if they deny their desire for blood."

Ren brightened. "I bet that's why you like blood while you're getting freaky. Makes sense."

Zenda's eyes widened, and she tapped her chin. "Fascinating."

Warmth pooled in my belly. Zenda and Ren were taking this so well. *I can't believe I was worried my blood kink would sicken them.*

"So, what now? What are you planning to do about your alien hunk?" Zenda asked.

I lifted the mug and sucked down a delicious gulp of chai. *That was the ultimate question, wasn't it? What was I going to do about Lux?*

"Will you keep seeing Lux now that the ships are fixed?" Ren leaned on her elbow.

I set down my empty mug on the table. "I don't know. Probably not."

"Seriously? Why not?" Zenda quirked a brow. "It sounds like you two have a good thing going."

Ren nodded. "Yeah, sounds like you're pretty compatible to me."

"Can the man fuck like a god? Definitely. But I wouldn't say we're compatible. Not outside of the bedroom, at least."

"Arda, a guy like that doesn't come around often," Zenda said.

"You think I don't know that?" I sighed, wishing Lux was a little less amazing. Then maybe the idea of never seeing him again would sting less. "Luxuth is unlike anyone I've ever met. I wish things were different, but the way things are, it will never work."

"Why not?" Ren asked.

I frowned, tracing a finger idly on the table. "He's looking for a wife, for one. A mate."

Ren shrugged. "It doesn't sound like sleeping with him would be an issue for you."

I rolled my eyes and grinned. "Yeah, all those orgasms would be so annoying."

Zenda adjusted her glasses. "Do you not want kids?"

"No, I do. Just not right now. But I don't think Lux is willing to wait. He wants an heir."

"Oh." Zenda frowned.

"Get this." I leaned back and crossed my arms. "He's planning to knock up an older woman, so he's not stuck with her for long."

"Wow. That's pretty cold." Ren shook her head.

"Did he tell you this before or after you slept together?" Zenda asked.

"Before. Why?"

Zenda rested her chin on one fist. "Hm. Are you sure his plans haven't changed?"

My stomach clenched as what Lux said in the shower flashed through my mind. *"What if I told you I am not so sure about that plan any longer?"*

I shook the memory aside. "Say he's given up on that idea; it still won't work. We're too different."

"Are you, though?" Ren quirked a brow.

How didn't they see it? I held out a hand and started ticking off all the things that meant Lux and I could never be. "Luxuth is moving to Earth and I work in space. He wants a child now, and I don't. I drive him crazy practically every minute of the day. Not to mention, I'm entirely too problematic for him."

"Problematic? What's that supposed to mean?" Zenda asked.

"He's here to open trade negotiations between our species. How will it look when he picks the granddaughter of Cora Jenson for his mate?"

Ren's brow furrowed. "That's—I see what you mean."

"Yep." I picked up my mug and spun it in my hands. "Alien royalty doesn't end up marrying into the family of a mass murderer."

"Wait, Lux is royal?" Zenda's voice squeaked, and she hopped out of her chair. "You didn't tell us that. You bagged an alien prince!"

"Actually, I'm more like a lord than a prince," Lux's deep voice announced from the doorway.

I spun to face him, my face burning. How much of that had he heard? "Lux, hi. Did you get your communications sorted?"

He nodded curtly and opened his mouth, but Zenda jumped in before he could reply.

"A fucking space lord is in our presence." She scrambled in front of him with a huge grin and curtsied so low I'm surprised her knee didn't scrape the floor. Lux just stared at her, a tiny wrinkle on his brow. "My lord," she purred as she rose, sending me a wink.

I scowled at her, my cheeks so hot I could boil my next mug of tea with them. Across the table, Ren snickered, until I shot her a hard glare and she tried to pass it off as a cough.

"Don't you have repairs to finish?" I bit out.

Ren rose from the table, hiding her grin. "Sure. Back to work. Come on, Zen."

"I'll meet you back there," Zenda replied, stubbornly not taking the hint. "So, Luxuth, what are your plans after this? Arda tells us you're going to Earth, but not where."

Ren sent me a sympathetic smile before she disappeared into the hall. I buried a groan. *There's no way I'll escape Zenda's twenty ques-*

tions without her asking him something embarrassing. Or more likely, embarrassing me.

Butterflies swirled in my stomach, but I couldn't think of an excuse to send Zenda packing. All my brainpower was focused on Lux and hearing his answers.

Goddamn it, how much of that conversation had he overheard?

25

Expectations

Lux

I stood in Arda's mess, a dozen thoughts sucking at me with all the ferocity of a black hole.

I'd spent a long while lingering on my bridge, considering Elys' words. I'd finally come to the conclusion that the connection Arda and I had was too good to throw away. Mind made up, I hurried to find her, only to discover her listing off all the reasons we didn't belong together.

Guess she doesn't feel the same...

Dral knows what possessed me to burst into her conversation. I should've just slunk away. Instead, Arda's perplexing medical officer was performing elaborate human greetings and asking me questions.

That's right—she just asked me a question.

I cleared my throat, forcing myself to focus on Zenda. "I've been told Earth's underwater settlements are quite pleasant for my species. I am expected at the largest, Subralia."

Zenda's smile fell. "Subralia," she repeated in a quiet voice.

"Do you know it?" I asked.

Zenda's smile returned, looking a touch too bright. "I do. I lived there once, actually. You'll be perfectly comfortable. One of my best friends still lives there. He's a Vorill. The alien community is well established at Subralia."

"That's great to hear." Arda's voice dripped with false cheer. "Didn't you have—"

"You'd love it there too." Zenda swung her gaze to Arda. "It's a lovely place to visit." Her expression turned wistful. "It's so breathtaking living underneath the sea. The entire city is made of glass everywhere it touches the ocean. You can watch the fish swim whenever you want."

"Perhaps you both can come visit sometime," I offered.

"No." Zenda shook her head vehemently. "I can't. I-It's a long story." She grimaced and edged toward the hatch. "I-I ought to help Ren with those repairs."

Arda rose from her chair as Zenda disappeared into the hall. "I thought she'd never take a hint."

"Are you so eager to have the repairs completed?" I stepped closer—close enough to touch—but I stuffed my hands into my skinsuit pockets.

Arda gulped, gazing up at me with those brilliant blue eyes. "What about you? I'm sure you're late enough as is. You're expected at Subralia, right?"

"I am."

Ask her to come with you.

The request was on the tip of my tongue, but all those excuses of hers bombarded me. Besides, I'd already offered her to visit with Zenda, but she'd left that invitation hanging in the wind.

Arda twisted her hands and stared down at the floor. "Well, I won't keep you."

My heart sank. She truly believed it all. Even after everything we'd shared. Our secrets. Our desires. Our bodies. I forced myself to remain calm while inwardly my mind was screaming.

"And what will you do?" I asked.

She shrugged. "Mine enough jesillium to pay off the Verne. Then, whatever I want. I've always wanted to explore space. I thought it would be fun to start a delivery service between worlds."

I lifted a brow. "Would you believe that's what I've been planning for my retirement?"

"Seriously?" Arda met my eyes, her face fully animated for the first time since I'd wandered into the mess. "We make a pretty good team. Maybe we should join forces?"

I sighed. "I can't. Not now."

Arda frowned. "Your responsibilities. Got it."

My stomach clenched as her hopeful expression faded. "What about Earth? Will you ever return?"

"And face all those people with their judgmental whispers?" She shuddered. "Yeah, I'll pass."

"You'll let the words of strangers keep you from your home?"

Arda crossed her arms and replied with a voice coated in menace. "Who says I even want to go there? I *like* exploring. This is my choice."

Her choice... A choice that kept her far away from me. "Is it really? Or are you just hiding?"

Arda

Hiding? Where did Lux get off accusing *me* of hiding? This, from the same guy who was avoiding love. He was fine marrying any woman who would spread her legs and birth his precious heirs—and, of course, die a few decades later.

God, the man was *cold*. I had to remember that. He didn't want me. Not really. I was just convenient. Right place, right time to screw.

Fuck. I can't believe I asked him to team up. And what did he do? Turned me down flat. My temples throbbed with the beginning of a headache, and I nearly unleashed a tirade on Lux.

No. That was the wrong play. The man might be cold, but he was the best sex of my life. If he was intent on leaving, then I might as well use him just like he'd used me.

I forced the frown etched on my face to smooth into a coy smile. "If this is goodbye, then I don't want to spend it fighting." I closed the distance between us and planted my hands on his hard chest.

"No?" He leaned down, capturing my gaze. "Tell me what you want, Arda."

I slid my hands down, enjoying the way his abs twitched beneath my questing fingers. *Mm, this is much better than arguing.* I unlocked my gaze from his silvery eyes as my fingers closed around the hilt of a knife strapped to Lux's belt. I pulled the dagger free and lifted it between us. "You know what I want."

Lux's eyes glazed over. He grasped the blade, his breathing heavy. I licked my lips, longing for the rich taste of his blood on my tongue.

The blade clattered on the floor. I lifted a brow.

"We can't share our blood again," Lux said, his tone thick with regret.

"What if I ask you extra nicely?" I slid my hands back up Lux's chest, my veins swimming with desperation. Surely, he was just playing hard to get? I glanced down, spotting the obvious bulge tenting his pants. Lux wanted me too. That much was clear.

Lux groaned as I rolled over his nipple and clamped my hands against his chest with his own. "I told you Pherians mate for life, but not why."

I met his eyes and my stomach clenched. There was no hint of playfulness in his expression. I had a sinking suspicion that whatever he was about to tell me, I wouldn't like. "So tell me."

Lux let out a heavy sigh and grabbed my hips, pulling me flush against him. I wrapped my arms around his back, rested my cheek against his cold chest, and waited uneasily. Lux stroked my hair a few times before speaking. "When Pherians share their blood during sex often enough, it causes a blood bond to form."

I backed away, peering up at his face. "A blood bond? What the hell is that?"

Lux didn't let me get far. He held tight to my hands, lightly caressing my knuckles. "Don't worry. We don't have one. Not yet, at least. With most couples, it takes a dozen or so instances for the bond to form."

"Okay... and what is it, exactly?"

"It's like a marriage, but on a physical level. Instead of craving sex with anyone, you crave only your blood bonded mate. No other partner will ever satisfy you. Till death."

"Wow. That's intense."

Lux nodded.

"And you didn't tell me this until now?" I glared at him. "Seems like something we should have discussed before we fucked."

"You were hurting, Arda. I couldn't let you go on like that." He shrugged. "Pherians still share blood with casual bed partners. They just avoid repeat sharing with anyone except for their mate."

"Oh." I tried to pull away further, but Lux's grip on my hands tightened.

His eyes burned into mine, and his voice lowered an octave. "Don't think I don't want to. The taste of you... I've tasted nothing sweeter. I'll be tasting you in my dreams for the rest of my days."

I shivered. "We haven't done it even close to a dozen times. What's one more for the road?"

Lux shook his head. "There have been a few cases where the bond formed earlier. We shouldn't chance it."

"Guess that means fucking is out, too."

Lux winced, his gaze burning a trail to my neck. "If I had that tight cunt of yours wrapped around me again, I wouldn't be able to resist tasting you."

I bit my lip, need pulsing between my legs—a need I ignored. "Well, I guess this really is goodbye then."

I almost begged him to stay. But the memory of his earlier refusal stilled my tongue. I tugged on my hands again. This time, Lux let me go.

"Goodbye, Arda. I hope you find what you're looking for while you're exploring."

I sent him a crooked smile. "You too, Lux. I hope you find what you want on Earth." I sighed and opened the hatch.

Too bad it couldn't be me.

26

Drained

Lux

The comms panel beeped, the incessant noise igniting a spark in my gut. I pounded on the panel. "What?"

"Dral's sake, Lux. You're in a mood lately," Elys replied.

I rubbed my temples. "I'm about to land. Can't the badgering wait?"

"You know as well as I do that a final report is required. I don't know what's gotten into you."

Might have something to do with the maddening blue-eyed beauty I'd left behind...

I shook off the thought with a sigh. "Sorry, Elys. I skipped breakfast, that's all."

"Hm, if you say so." I could sense she wasn't buying my lame excuse, but she was sensible enough to let it slide. "I'm waiting for that report."

I gritted my teeth but didn't waste any time, hurrying through the list of ship's functions and readouts she expected. Once she was satisfied all was well, I sucked in a deep breath and blurted, "What about my med-readouts?"

"Oh, I have them right here. Let me send them through to your dash," she replied cheerily. Much too cheerily for them to be anything other than perfectly normal.

I scanned them, confirming my guess. "Nothing," I muttered.

Elys chuckled. "You sound like you were expecting something to be wrong."

I cleared my throat. "I had an open wound on an alien world. Can't be too careful."

"Funny, it didn't seem like the queries you fed to the med-bot were focused on infection." Elys was silent for a long moment, then she asked, "Were you expecting a blood bond to form between you and some of those microbes?"

No. I needed to make sure this longing for Arda wouldn't be permanent. My stomach clenched. "It doesn't matter. Drop it."

Elys took pity on me for once and changed the subject. "Your approach couldn't have been timed better. You'll be landing on the night side of Earth. Once you've breached the atmosphere, feel free to remove the protective shielding over the viewport to soak in the view."

"Will do." I leaned forward, my hand hovering over the comm panel. "Is that all?"

"Yep. That should do it. Just one more thing."

"What?"

"Make sure you eat before you meet the mayor. We don't want his first impression of us to be while you're grumpy."

I rolled my eyes. "Don't worry. I'll handle it."

"Good luck, brother."

I signed off and collapsed into the pilot's chair, feeling drained. The last few days on my own, in route to Earth, were challenging, to say the least. Until now, the voyage had been peaceful. I had Smudge for companionship, and Elys to chat with if need be. I'd never struggled with my solitude.

Now, I couldn't turn a corner without hearing Arda's sweet laughter echoing in my ears. I couldn't enjoy my breakfast without the memory of her licking her lips returning to plague me. I couldn't even sleep in my bed without her scent invading my dreams.

At least the voyage was almost over. Once I made it to Earth, it would be much easier to shake off the hold my stowaway had on me.

I straightened in the pilot's chair and scanned the nav readouts. Almost... Now. I keyed in the code to pull back the shielding on the viewport, revealing a world lit by a single moon. Dark oceans sparkled, surrounding land covered in millions of dots of light, like so many stars in the night sky.

Smudge hopped in the co-pilot's chair and peered out the viewport with me. "What do you think? Our new home is pretty incredible, isn't it?" I petted her head gently, warmth radiating up my arm.

If only I didn't feel like something was missing.

Within minutes, the Destiny sank through the atmosphere and breached the ocean. Subralia appeared ahead, a sprawling compound perched on the Pacific Ocean's sea bottom. The outer hull was lit with tiny lights, revealing its shape even in the dark water so far below the surface.

Subralia called over docking instructions. Soon Destiny was hunkered inside the seaport, and I made my way to the outer hatch after placing Smudge securely in her carrier. I wasn't expecting much fanfare. With my delays, I'd arrived well after the city went to sleep, but surely there would be someone to show me to my new living quarters.

"Commander Luxuth."

I startled as a huge Vorill barreled toward me as I stepped out of my ship, arms spread wide in welcome. "Hello." I thrust out a hand, but the alien ignored it and pulled me into a hug, wrapping his lanky arms around me and squeezing tightly.

"I'm Mayor Prim. I'm so glad to meet you, my boy."

This is interesting. Elys hadn't told me the mayor was an alien. The Vorill were an aquatic species, with green-hued skin and long lean limbs they kept covered with skinsuits when they weren't swimming.

"It's a pleasure to meet you as well."

The mayor pulled back, scanning me up and down. "You must be exhausted. Come, I'll show you to your new home."

27

The Outer Rim

Arda

"Pleasure doing business with you, too." I hid a smirk behind my hand as I exited the loan office. Pleasure getting the fuckers off my ass for a couple months was more accurate.

We'd made it to the outer rim with the jesillium just in time. Now I could breathe easy—until the next payment was due, at least. I let out a relieved breath, staring up at the dark of space overhead. The asteroid we'd landed on was one of the biggest in the rim. A state-of-the-art see-through environmental dome protected the surface from the cold vacuum of space.

Zenda grabbed my elbow, her eyes wide beneath her cat's eye glasses. "What did he say?"

"We made it. No penalties or extra interest." I grinned. "In fact, that haul was big enough it bought us three months until the next payment is due."

"Really? That's awesome!" Zenda's grin turned mischievous. "Sounds like a celebration's in order. You fancy a trip to the brothels?"

Not so long ago, I couldn't imagine wanting anything more... but after Lux. I shook my head. "I'm gonna pass this time, Zen."

Zenda lifted a brow. "You sure? I bet they've got a Vampherian model stashed away somewhere."

I sighed. "Yeah. I'm sure."

"You all right, Capt?"

I squeezed her arm. "I'll be fine. Don't let me stop you. Go, celebrate."

Zenda shrugged. "Sure. But if you want to talk, you know where to find me."

We split up, Zenda strolling happily toward the brothel, and me back to the ship. I cursed under my breath and nearly spun on my heel and trailed after her. It would be weeks before we visited here again. I really ought to get my jollys off while I could. But I just couldn't muster up the desire to fuck a machine with the memory of Lux fresh in my mind.

It wasn't fair. *Why did I have to fall for a guy who was determined to live in the one place I couldn't stand to be?* I froze as the thought ricocheted through my brain. I hadn't *fallen* for him. Surely not.

I bit my lip and forced my feet to move. My boots clattered across the hard stone asteroid, the ground pounded smooth into a flat walkway between the neatly lined up buildings. I strode past the stone houses and storefronts without really looking at any of them.

No, my mind was too caught up with Lux. It had only been a few days since we'd parted, but I couldn't help but miss him. I missed his silver eyes and his big hands wrapped around me. I missed his dumb attempts at jokes. I even missed his ugly little skinball of a pet.

Most of all, I missed the way he supported me without question. Yeah, he liked to bark orders, but when it really mattered, he had no problem following my lead. I hadn't lied when I'd told him we made a good team. But that was all over now.

I arrived at the airstrip where the Verne was docked. I climbed aboard, so wrapped up in my head that I squeaked when someone grabbed my shoulder.

"Fuck, Ren. You scared me." My speeding heart slowed as I spotted her beside me.

Ren curved a hand through her short blonde curls. "Sorry, Capt. I didn't mean to."

I swept my gaze down Ren's outfit, surprised to find her in a loose pink nightgown rather than the oil-stained skinsuit she always wore. "You look comfortable."

She blushed, her hands tangling in the fabric billowing around her legs. "I-I thought you and Zenda would be out all night."

I sighed, brushing past her and wandering into the mess. "I wasn't in the mood." I stopped in front of the food processor and ordered a cup of hot water.

Ren sank into a chair at the table. "You miss him, don't you?"

"Is it that obvious?" I grabbed my stash of tea bags, selecting a chamomile blend.

"'Fraid so." Ren frowned. "You know how I feel about men. Normally, I'd be the first to say you're better off without him. But Lux seemed different. Hell, he didn't have to come with you to save us. He didn't have to help us track down our stolen jesillium either. He seems like one of the good ones."

"He is," I said quietly, dunking my tea bag into the mug.

"Then why did you let him go?"

"You heard all my reasons."

Ren cocked her head. "Do they really matter all that much in the grand scheme? I mean, I'm no expert, but I thought when you loved someone, you *made* it work."

My stomach roiled, and I plunked down in the chair opposite her. "You make it sound so easy."

Ren snorted. "I never said that. I bet it's the hardest thing in the universe making a relationship work." She leaned forward. "But the best captain I know doesn't shy away from tackling hard challenges." Ren winked and rose from her chair. "I'm off to bed. Talk to you later, Capt."

I sat there sipping my tea and digesting her words. I was happy exploring space. When I pictured my future, the dream of having my ship paid off and the freedom to explore had always sustained me. Now I couldn't shake the suspicion that when I succeeded, there would be something missing.

What was I going to do about it? Lux was already gone, probably wrapped up in some gorgeous older woman by now. My stomach churned. Was he already tasting her, the way he'd tasted me?

I groaned, laying my head in my hands atop the table. I should just drag Zenda out of that brothel and hightail it back to sector G.

Fuck. I sat up, realizing exactly where my thoughts had led me. Lux was right. I *was* running. I could run out into space, like I'd run from the rumors and the ugly whispers my whole life. Or I could stay and tackle the hard challenge.

A smile slowly spread across my face. I knew exactly where to head next.

28

What If

Lux

I paused my morning walk, staring out the window as a large predator swam past. Zenda was certainly right about it being breathtaking. If only I could enjoy it. But in the two weeks I'd been at Subralia, every waking minute that wasn't filled with work had been consumed with thoughts of Arda.

I couldn't stop wondering *what if*. What if I hadn't overheard her list of all the things keeping us apart? What if I asked her to come with me? Would she have turned down a direct request to be with me, instead of the lame offer to visit I'd settled for?

The creature locked eyes with me, and as if it sensed my foul mood, it turned tail and swam away.

"Luxuth. How's it going?" a chipper voice asked behind me.

I spun around, spotting a familiar Vorill approaching down the blue walled corridor. "Nash. Your uncle told me I might run into you here."

Nash's muscles bunched beneath his turquoise skinsuit as he jogged over to greet me. He stopped beside me and grinned, his long tongue snaking out and quickly passing over his face. "Yeah. I like it here. Not quite as comfortable as back on Vorillion but the perks are nice."

I lifted a brow and opened my mouth, curious to learn more about the *perks*, but at that moment, a human female turned the corner ahead. She was an attractive specimen, with curly black hair and lush curves—not so lush as the ones I was desperate to forget. The female locked eyes on Nash and added a slink to her stride and a coy smile to her lips.

"Good morning," she purred. She stopped directly in front of Nash and cocked a hip. "If you're headed to the main mess, you better hurry. They just put out the fresh catch. I know how much you like it."

Nash's eyes lit up. "How thoughtful, Bethany."

"Of course. I'm on my way to my quarters if you want to thank me properly after."

Nash's smile widened. Then he slipped his tongue out again and rubbed it over his face, much slower this time. I didn't miss the way Bethany followed the action with her gaze. By the time Nash retracted his tongue, she was flushed pink. "See ya soon, Bethany." Nash winked, then grabbed my elbow, towing me toward the mess. "C'mon, Lux. Join me for breakfast."

Normally, I would make excuses to leave, but my curiosity got the better of me. "What was that?"

"What? You mean with the tongue? I thought you knew already. We Vorill's have to keep our skin moist—"

"Not the tongue. The girl."

"Oh." Nash leaned in, dropping his voice. "The females here are quite the eager bed partners. I'm surprised you haven't figured that out already, considering what you came here for."

I sighed heavily. "I haven't been in the mood to hunt for a mate yet." It did not surprise me Nash had learned of my mission. His uncle was the mayor of Subralia and my plans weren't exactly a secret.

We arrived at the main mess, a sprawling cafeteria flooded with tables, chairs and the aroma of roasted meat. Humans and at least five different species of aliens crowded the space. They hunched over tables slurping and chomping, and lined up to grab food from the massive spread set up buffet style.

Nash and I each grabbed a tray loaded with roasted fish and a drink. Nash selected an oversized mug of water and I went for a small mug of animal blood. Thankfully there were already a few species here at Subralia who also enjoyed my breakfast of choice, proving mine and Elys' fears unfounded.

We settled down at a table and Nash finally addressed my confession. "Don't suppose you not wanting to hunt for a mate has anything to do with a certain mining vessel's captain, would it?"

What? How did Nash learn about Arda? I hadn't mentioned her to anyone besides Elys. Certainly no one here at Subralia. I racked my brain until the answer hit me.

"Zenda. She said she had a Vorill friend living in Subralia."

Nash leaned back. "Guilty. Just chatted with Zen the other day and she had a lot to say about you."

"She did, did she?" I frowned down at my plate, suddenly not in the mood for a single bite of the delectable dish.

"Yep." He waggled his brows and leaned closer. "Apparently you were the best Arda ever had. Poor Zen sounded a little jealous."

I chuckled. "Don't know if that's saying much when the competition's a machine."

Nash nodded knowingly. "You'd be surprised. I think some of these Terran females prefer the bots to their men." He sipped his water and cocked his head. "Can I ask, if you like Arda, then why not make her your mate?"

"It's not that simple."

"Why not?"

I rubbed my temples. "A half dozen reasons, at least. She doesn't want to live on Earth, for one."

Nash chewed a bite of fish thoughtfully. "Why don't you go with her? Don't I recall you admitting to an itch to explore when we were discussing all those ship's plans a few years back?"

I scoffed. "Sure. I'll just wait a year for another Pherian to come and replace me."

"Don't be so dramatic." Nash set his fork down. "You've set up most of the basics of the Terran/Pherian exchange program already. You'll need to pop in from time to time, but most of the paperwork can be done remotely."

I rubbed my clammy hands against my thighs. If that was true... "Remotely. That is interesting." Still, there was so much between us. So many obstacles. Who's to say Arda would even agree to give me another chance? Why tie herself to a Pherian with a blood bond when she could keep her options open?

"You mind if I give you some friendly advice?" Nash asked.

I wanted to tell Nash to take his advice and shove it, but I knew that was just my foul mood coming into play. I sighed. "Fine."

"If you have feelings for her, any feelings at all, don't let them go unsaid. You'll only regret it. Trust me." Nash looked away, his normal easy smile absent and replaced with such intense longing, it made me wonder if he was speaking from experience. Before I could dig any deeper, he shoved his chair back and stood. "Thanks for the company, Lux. I hope you talk to your captain." He waggled his brows. "I have a thank you to give."

Nash lifted his empty tray and left me sitting there with my swirling thoughts and an ache in my chest.

29

The Detour

Arda

"Hey Capt, why are we headed in the wrong direction?" Zenda asked.

I spared a glance over my shoulder, then bent back to the ship's controls. "I'm making a detour. There's something I need to do."

"You're the boss." Zenda plopped down in the co-pilot's chair and tapped the armrests. "This have anything to do with a sexy space lord?"

"No. Well, not directly." I twisted my lips. "Lux made me realize I need to stop running from my past. I'm sick of being ashamed. It's time I discover what happened to my grandmother to make her commit her crimes."

"How are you planning to do that? She's long dead, isn't she?"

I nodded. "Hung herself while she was awaiting trial."

It had been all over the news when Cora Jenson killed herself. That fact made me even more certain I needed to uncover the truth. I'd always assumed my grandmother had done it to escape justice.

Now, I couldn't help but wonder if she'd been suffering from a guilty conscience for crimes committed while overtaken with bloodlust.

"So, how do you expect to learn anything?" Zenda asked.

"There's one person who might know something. I've looked into it, and whoever was next of kin would receive all my grandmother's medical records and personal belongings upon her death."

"Who was that?"

I gulped, dreading the answer. "It's time I paid a visit to my mother."

Zenda's gaze traced my face. "I'm guessing you're not exactly close."

"You could say that..."

"Don't worry. Ren and I will be here if you need us." She grabbed my hand and gave it a squeeze.

"Thanks. I can handle her on my own, but it's good to know I have you in my corner."

The rest of the trip passed smoothly. All the same, the pit in my stomach grew so large it felt like it had its own gravitational pull.

Did my mother know the truth about my grandmother? It was hard to believe she didn't when she'd been given all her medical files. Maybe even a diary. Why would she keep changes to Cora's genetic code a secret from me when those changes were part of my code as well?

Ren breezed onto the bridge as we touched down. She squinted through the viewport. "Where are we? Mars?"

"Nope." I chuckled dryly, eyeing the rusty sand and rock formations outside. "We're in Australia, Earth. Home sweet home."

Ren whistled. "I've never been in this part of the world. Looks...hot."

"It is. Sorry, but there isn't much out here. The closest town is miles away. Mom's a bit of a hermit these days. If you leave the ship, don't wander far. And take water with you."

Zenda gripped my wrist as I stood. "Do you want us to come with you?"

"No. I got this."

Zenda smiled and dropped my wrist. "Call us if you need anything."

I sent them both a nod and strolled toward the outer hatch. It'd been years since I'd set foot on Earth. Even longer since I'd last spoken to Mom.

She wasn't a terrible mother, just distant. When I was a child, she'd floated from one job to another, and left me to my own devices more often than not. It hadn't given us much time to develop the tight-knit bond some families have.

After I became a ship's captain and began my life in space, we drifted even further apart. I couldn't place all the blame for the distance between us at her feet. Truthfully, it would be nice to see her again, even if it was under such strange circumstances.

I stepped into the sweltering heat of an Australian summer. Mom bought this plot of land dirt cheap. For a long while, certain areas in Australia had been deemed unlivable, due to the extreme heat brought on by climate change. Luckily, the terraforming equipment we'd been gifted by the Vorill after the war fixed that.

The place was deserted. Off in the distance, I spotted a few more houses scattered across the sandy horizon, but no one was out and about. As sweat pooled down my back on the short hike to my mother's small bungalow, I could see why she was one of the few who'd brave this heat.

I cocked a brow, spotting several political signs jammed into the dirt beside the lone road to town. Each one belonged to the newest political party making a splash in planetary news—the Isolationists. They were busy advocating for Earth to push all the aliens out and give up faster than light travel.

Did Mom turn into an extremist while I've been gone?

Guess I wouldn't be telling her about Lux anytime soon. *If she wants all the aliens to leave, what will she say about her daughter banging a Pherian royal?* I snorted and shook my head, then headed for the front door. I lifted my fist and pounded on the wood. Footsteps sounded from within, then the door cracked open enough for a pair of blue eyes to peek out. "Arda?"

"Hi, Mom. I'm home."

The door swung wide open, and she waved me in. "Hurry, you'll let all the cold out." I sighed as the air-conditioning welcomed me into its cool embrace. Mom closed the door firmly behind me. "This is a surprise. I wasn't expecting you."

She tucked a strand of brown hair behind her ear that had escaped from her bun. Mom looked the same as she had when I left for space, no new wrinkles on her face or her crisply pressed black shorts and linen top. "You look good, Mom."

"You do too. I guess space travel is agreeing with you." She smiled benignly and ushered me into the kitchen. She pulled a chair out from the small wooden table and bustled over to the tiny stove. "I'll put the kettle on. Make you a cuppa. Sit."

"Thanks." I settled into the chair, flicking a glance across the room. The neatly stacked dishes on the open-shelved cabinets stared down at me. Everything in its perfect place. "I actually came to talk about Grandmom."

Mom stiffened, and the kettle clattered loudly on the stove. "Why would you want to talk about that wretched woman?" She turned the burner on and whipped around, hands on her hips. "I've heard enough about her to last a dozen lifetimes. Haven't you?"

I frowned. *Why so evasive, Mom?* "I had a medical scan done. They found some interesting markers in my DNA. You wouldn't know anything about that, would you?"

Her eyes darted to the ceiling, and she shook her head. "No. Can't say that I do. What's that have to do with *her*?"

"You have her medical records, don't you? Can I see them?"

Mom's gaze flashed down the hall and landed on the door to her study. The same door she always kept locked. *Bingo.*

"I don't have them. Got rid of all her junk the day they handed it to me."

Sure you did. It wasn't hard to spot the telltale signs of her lying. She fidgeted in place, unable to meet my eye. I didn't call her on it, though. "Darn. That's too bad. Oh well. No biggie." I leaned back in my chair and sent her an easy grin.

"Sorry I couldn't help, dear." Mom visibly calmed, smoothing her twitchy hands across her shorts with a sigh.

Now, I just need to get her out of here so I can search that study...

The answer came to me instantly. We weren't the closest mother-daughter pair in existence, but I knew one thing about my mother. Her love language was baking.

"Hey, Mom. You don't have any apple pie to go with that tea, do you? I sure miss having a slice of your homemade pie now and then. The food processors just can't get it right."

"No. I haven't baked a pie in ages." She pursed her lips. "How long are you staying?"

Too easy. My smile widened. "I could be persuaded to stick around for dinner, if you're thinking what I'm thinking."

She hustled over to the side door, grabbing her pocketbook off a hook on the wall. "I'll run out and grab all the ingredients. Can't let my baby go back to space on an empty stomach."

A twinge of guilt set in as the rumble of her truck started up outside just as the kettle whistled. Yeah, I shouldn't deceive my mother—but she shouldn't lie to me either. I stood and turned off the burner, then crossed the kitchen. My hands closed on the cold metal handle of the study door.

Locked. Even living in a house all alone, she still kept it locked. My heart hammered. My grandmother's files were in there—they had to be.

I tapped on my neck, activating my new implant. "Verne, come in."

"Here Capt," Zenda replied.

"Is Ren there with you?" I asked.

"Ren," Zenda yelled, making me wince. "She'll be here in a sec. How's it going with your mom? Do you need backup after all?"

"Something like that."

"Hey, Capt. I'm here," Ren said.

"Any chance you know how to pick a lock?" I asked with a grin.

30

Change of Plans

Lux

The fluorescent lights in my quarters flickered as I sat down at my call screen. The mayor provided me with one of the largest and most opulently furnished personal quarters in Subralia. Comfortable seating for meetings dominated the space, along with an enormous bed built for my larger than human frame. But even the best rooms below the sea seemed to suffer from the occasional electrical issue.

I forced the frown off my face and punched in the details for my call. My stomach churned as I waited for the line to connect. My dignitary status meant I'd been allotted my own holovidscreen in my room. But even with a dedicated line, a call to a planet halfway across the universe took forever to connect.

Ages later, a slim shape coalesced, hovering in the small space atop the vidscreen; a handsome woman wearing a white dress the same shade as her long, straight hair. "Luxuth. To what do I owe the pleasure?" The dignified voice rang in my ears, and even the lightyears between us couldn't slow the ache that spread through my chest.

"Do I need a reason to call my mother?" I asked.

"No, but it hasn't happened yet, so I imagine something is amiss."

She knew me too well. Though I loved my mother with all my heart, she was a busy woman. As one of the political heads of Pheria, it was hard to lock down a moment of her time. Even this brief call had to be prearranged through her secretary to ensure she could fit me into her hectic schedule. It was much simpler to keep contact with Elys and allow her to fill Mother in. Still, some things were too important to discuss through an intermediary.

"I've decided to make some changes to my plans here on Earth."

"Oh?" Mother crossed her arms, one slim brow lifting. "And what changes should we be expecting?"

My heart skittered. I knew my mother wanted me happy, but when it came to the future of our entire civilization, I couldn't be certain she'd be civil about any changes. I'd just have to prove to her that my reasons are well thought out and sound. *Here goes nothing.*

"I've spoken with Mayor Prim, and with the head of the Pherian/Terran exchange program we've elected. They've both agreed that my contributions to the program are not needed on a day-to-day basis any longer. In light of that, I've decided to maintain an occasional presence here on Earth and to spend most of my time in space."

"In space? Doing what?"

"I've always yearned to travel. To explore. I assumed those dreams would have to wait until my retirement, but now I believe I can fulfill that desire now."

"I see." Mother uncrossed her arms and tapped her chin thoughtfully. "What of your promises to be the first Pherian to mate a Terran? To produce an heir?"

Now for the clincher.

"I still intend to mate. The heir will come, in time."

"Hm. I suppose that is acceptable. After all, we have the reports of Terran and Pherian DNA mixing in a living individual already, thanks to you." Mother's gaze turned shrewd. "And when shall I meet my new daughter?" She peered around him, as if hopeful of finding someone lingering behind me. "It is her, isn't it? Your stowaway captain, Arda Jenson? Elys said you were infatuated."

"She's not here, Mother. But yes, I hope she will be my mate."

Mother frowned. "Where is she?"

I gulped. "She's a captain, remember? And I had to come here."

Mother pursed her lips. "Well, it sounds like I'm not the only one you need to discuss your future with."

"So, you approve of my plans?" I held my breath, waiting for her answer. I'd already decided to see this plan through, no matter what, but I still hoped she would give me her blessing.

"Of course, Lux." She grinned. "Go find your mate. I'll tell my secretary to make room in my schedule for another call when I can meet her."

"Goodbye, Mother."

I ended the call, feeling lighter than air. I was one step closer to living the life I'd always dreamed of, and I had Arda to thank for it. Without her, I would have never arranged this. Now I could travel the stars, here and now, instead of waiting for my retirement.

If only I can find Arda and take her up on her offer to join forces. And if she agrees to be my mate, I'll have everything I want.

Of course, that was easier said than done. It had been weeks since I last saw Arda. She might be anywhere by now, even halfway across the galaxy. Luckily, I knew just the guy who had an in with one of her crew.

Lux

My knuckles rapped against the door, and I shuffled from foot to foot, waiting for an answer. "Come on, open up."

Footsteps sounded a few moments later. The door slipped open. Nash stood in the entryway, eyes widening. "Lux. I wasn't expecting you." He cinched a robe tightly around his waist, hiding his green skin.

"Can I come in? I need a favor."

"Sure. Just give me a sec, okay?" The door slammed closed. I gritted my teeth and leaned against the hall. At least the sea life was there to entertain me while I waited for Nash to get decent—or whatever he was doing inside. I watched a school of fish swim past the glass windows. By the time they'd disappeared out of sight, the door reopened.

Instead of Nash, a slim redhead appeared in the doorway. She pinned me with an evil glare before turning back to Nash as he followed her through the doorway. "I'm going to hold you to that raincheck."

"I'm counting on it, Stasia." Nash winked at her, then turned to me. "Sorry to keep you waiting."

"It's not a problem." I followed him inside, frowning. "You didn't have to get rid of your company on my account."

Nash grinned, closing the door. "Don't worry. Stasia can be a bit clingy. You're doing me a favor." He tugged on the sleeves of his turquoise skinsuit. He'd clearly had time to dress while I'd been alone with the fishes. I wasn't about to complain when I was here to beg for his help.

"What brings you by?" Nash asked. He led me into a modest sitting room with furniture nearly identical to the set I'd been assigned. But while my quarters were still devoid of personal touches, knickknacks and artwork littered the shelves and walls. There were colorful renditions of swamp lands reminiscent of his home world. That and strange sculptures that reminded me of a quirky type of human art called caricatures, where the figures sported a much larger head than body.

Nash chuckled as I tapped one and the head wobbled. "I have a thing for bobble heads," he explained with a shrug. "You'll pick up a few new interests too, if you stick around on Earth long enough."

"That's actually what I wanted to talk about. I took your advice. I've arranged it with your uncle and my family back home so that I can work remotely."

"Ah. I see." Nash plunked down in an oversized chair. "Here to say goodbye before you venture out to explore space on your own?"

"I'm hoping I won't be alone. That's why I need a favor."

Nash sat up straight. "Let me guess. You're hoping I can track down a certain vessel for you?"

I stared at him and nodded. "I am."

Nash popped up and slapped me on the back. "Taking *all* of my advice, I see. I'm happy for you, Lux. I hope Arda gives you another chance."

I tamped down the discomfort that statement raised. *I hope so too.* "Thank you."

Nash strode across the room to a holovidscreen much like the one back in my room. "Zen doesn't have holo-tech on the Verne, but I can send her a voice call."

I hovered behind Nash as he worked the controls. I drew in a deep breath, prepared to wait for a long connection. Surely, wherever they might be in space would—

"Hello? That you, Nash?" Zenda's voice piped in almost immediately.

That means they're close! My heart picked up speed. I might reunite with Arda sooner than I thought.

"Yeah, it's me, Zen. How are you doing?" Nash replied.

"Two calls in less than a week." Zenda tsked. "Are you finally running out of tail to chase in Subralia so you're bugging me?"

Nash chuckled. "Not quite. I have something I want to send you. Can you ping me your location?"

Her voice came back, sounding incredulous. "You want to—" she paused, "Nash, give me a sec. I need to put you on hold."

I frowned, resisting the urge to tear my hair out of my scalp.

Zenda returned a few moments later. "Hey Nash, sorry I have to cut this call short. I just pinged you our location, but if I were you, I'd send that delivery express. I don't think we'll be here long."

"Everything all right?" Nash's casual demeanor slipped away, revealing a face creased with concern.

"Nothing we can't handle. Gotta go. Talk to ya later."

The connection cut off and Nash leaned back in his chair, rubbing his chest. A moment later, the panel chimed.

"Is that their location?" I asked.

"Hm?" Nash frowned, then leaned forward. "Yeah, I've got it. Huh..."

"What is it?"

"No wonder the connection picked up so fast. They're on Earth. Australia. Let me send the details to your ship." Nash tapped away at the console, all the while my heart pounded out of my chest.

Arda was on *Earth*? After she insisted so vehemently that she didn't want to return? What did that mean? Was she lying to me? Or perhaps... Was something wrong?

Whatever the case, I had to find her fast. "Thanks Nash. I owe you one." I stalked toward the door.

"Hold on. You can't go now."

I didn't even deign that statement with a response, just continued marching away.

"Lux." Nash caught me at the door with a hand on my elbow.

"What?" I growled.

"They're in the middle of the Australian outback at noon."

I jerked my arm out of his hold. "So what?"

"The sun, Lux. If you go after her now, you'll die."

31

Surprise Delivery

Arda

"What's taking them so long?" I grumbled to myself as I paced beside the front door.

Knock, knock.

"Finally." I jerked the door open and ushered Zenda and Ren inside. "Took you long enough."

Zenda adjusted her cat's eyeglasses and peered around the dusty entryway. "Sorry, Capt."

"Yeah, sorry," Ren chimed in. She dumped a gigantic box of tools on the floor beside her boots and dug her hands into her lower back. "I had to round up all my tools, and Zen was busy chatting up that boyfriend of hers."

"He's just a friend." Zenda plucked at a speck of dirt on her pink skinsuit.

"Didn't sound like that to me." Ren waggled her brows. "What kind of friend sends out a surprise express delivery?"

I cocked a brow as Zenda's cheeks flushed. It was kind of nice gossiping about someone else's love life for a change.

"I mean it. Surprise or not, we're just friends. I haven't even seen Nash in person since we were teens." She shrugged. "Besides, he's a great friend, but Nash is definitely not boyfriend material. He goes through women like they're toilet paper."

Ren gagged. "Gross. Thanks for putting that image in my mind."

I chuckled. "Come on. I'll show you the door we have to unlock."

Ren hefted her tools in her arms. Then Zenda and Ren trailed me through the house to the study, giggling at the pictures on the wall of me as a goofy child and awkward teen. We halted outside the study, and Ren kneeled down to examine the handle and keypad. "How long do I have?"

"Mom went into town. It's an hour's drive each way and it will take her a little while to shop. Two and a half hours, I'd wager."

Ren grimaced and scratched her short blonde curls. "Hate to break it to ya, but I might not crack this in time."

"Seriously?" Zenda cocked a hip. "What's your mother keeping in there? Family jewels?"

I scoffed. "No. Just my grandmother's medical records—I hope."

"Whatever she's got in there, she doesn't want found. This lock is top of the line." Ren opened her tool box and dug inside. "I'll try my best, but I'm not promising anything."

"Thanks, Ren." I squeezed her shoulder. "You got this."

Zenda leaned back on her heels. "What do you want to do while we wait?"

I shrugged. "You want a tour of the house? There's really not much to—"

Knock, knock, knock.

All three of us startled at the pounding on the front door. "Who could that be?" I asked.

"Bet it's loverboy's delivery." Ren smirked.

"Already?" I bit my lip and walked down the hall.

"That was fast." Zenda grinned and hurried toward the door, quickly outpacing me. She threw the door open and gasped. She backed away, her arms flailing and a shriek spilling out of her lips.

I rushed forward, my heart hammering. *What the fuck's at the door?*

Shoving Zenda behind me, I nearly bit my tongue when I spotted a monstrous creature in the doorway. The hulking beast was covered head to toe in a thick layer of gloopy white ooze. It staggered on two shaky legs, groaning and shuddering.

It took everything in me not to scream when the beast lurched inside. "Arrr," it gurgled, lumbering closer.

Zenda screeched behind me. "Monster!"

I threw up my fists, prepared to battle the intruder with my bare hands.

Ren appeared with a wrench clenched in her fist. "The fuck?"

"Arrrda," the monster roared. Then it collapsed in a heap just inside the entryway.

"Did that thing just say your name?" Zenda shuddered.

I inched closer. "I think it did." I peered at the beast closely. Where it lay on the floor, some of the goo sloughed off, revealing pale skin and golden hair.

Oh no. A sick feeling of recognition struck me.

I slammed the door closed. "Quick, Zen. Draw the curtains. Now! Help me!"

Zenda hurried to help, and soon we cast the entryway into shadow.

"What's going on, Arda?" Ren shook her wrench at the intruder. "Who's the new guy?"

I kneeled beside the unconscious figure on the floor and wiped the thick gloop off his face. "It's not a monster. It's Lux." I slapped Lux's sticky face. "Wake up, big guy."

"What's Lux doing here?" Ren hovered over us, squinting. "And what the hell is all that slime?"

I grimaced, tap, tap, tapping on his cheek. "He said he can't go out in the sun." What was he thinking, looking for me during the day? *If he dies because of me, I'll never forgive myself...*

"I bet that stuff acts as a barrier to protect his skin," Zenda mused.

"I don't think it helped much." My hands shook. The heat sinking into my palms with every slap made my stomach clench. "He's always been so cold. Now he's burning up. What are we going to do?"

Zenda twisted her hands. "I haven't trained in Pherian anatomy. Maybe we should cool him down?"

"I don't think the slapping is helping," Ren said gently.

I grabbed Lux's shoulders and shook. "Wake up! I don't know how to help you."

Nothing. He just lay there, passed out and overheated. My crew was right. *Time to try something else.*

I gripped the colossal idiot's shoulders, hefting his head off the floor. "Come on, guys. Help me move him."

"Where are we taking him?" Zenda lifted his leg.

Ren set down her wrench and grabbed the other leg. "Damn, he's slippery."

Together, we started dragging him down the hall. The ooze made our grips precarious, and his huge body was a struggle to lift. But at least the goo helped slide him across the hardwood floors a little easier.

"Fuck, he's heavy too," Ren grumbled.

"We don't have to go far," I insisted. "Let's get him in the tub. Cool him down."

"Smart plan," Zenda said. "You think it will work?"

"No idea, but it's worth a shot." I paused long enough to throw open the bathroom door. The small space wasn't built with the intention of holding four people at once, much less one of them a giant alien. Somehow, we piled inside and lifted Lux enough to roll him into the tub. He landed on his side, with his big booted feet sticking out, but at least he was in.

Zenda tugged at one of his boots, but I reached straight for the faucet.

"Shouldn't we undress him first?" Ren asked.

"No time." I spun the knob for the cold water. An icy rush of liquid chugged out of the spout. I flicked on the showerhead. As the cold droplets rained down, Lux jolted awake.

"Thank fuck!" I clutched my chest. "Jesus, you scared me half to death, you big oaf!"

"Arda? What happened?" Lux sputtered, while struggling to sit up and wiping water out of his face.

Zenda clapped me on the back. "I think we'll leave you to it."

Ren chuckled. "Yeah, I have a lock to pick."

As they left, closing the door, my speeding heart finally slowed. I settled on the floor beside the tub. "Take it easy." I gripped the neck of Lux's sopping wet skinsuit and pushed him back. "You need to cool down." I rested the back of my hand against his forehead and sighed. He still wasn't as cold as the water trickling out of the shower, but he was cooling quickly.

Lux blinked and scanned his soaked body. The ooze trickled off wherever the water hit him, revealing a black skinsuit molded to his muscles.

God, he looked so good, all wet and sexy. A bolt of desire shot straight to my core, but I forced myself to ignore it.

Not now, Arda. The guy almost died.

Lux squinted at my mom's tiny bathroom. At the flower shower curtain and dated pink tile walls. "Where am I?"

"My mom's bathroom. What are you doing here, Lux?"

32

Perfect

Lux

"Arda." I stared into the most beautiful blue eyes. I was slightly woozy from the effects of Earth's sun, but thanks to my lovely stowaway's quick thinking, I was still in one piece. "I had to find you."

"Seriously?" She crossed her arms. "And that couldn't wait until, I don't know, you weren't in danger of dying?" She frowned and her brows dipped, clearly angry enough to spit. "You got so mad about me staying safe. Well, you need to stay safe too, you idiot."

If she's already angry... I grabbed her wrist and jerked her into the tub on top of my lap.

"Cold!" she shrieked. "Fuck, that's too cold." Arda twisted around and adjusted the knobs. As soon as the water shifted from icy to lukewarm, I pulled her back against my chest.

"I missed you. Did you miss me?" I found the zipper on her skinsuit and eased it down her neck.

"Are you for real right now?" she squeaked. "Aren't we going to talk about what the hell you're doing here in my mother's bathtub?"

I flicked her wet hair out of my way and licked her neck, making her shiver. "We'll talk later." I reached her ear and tugged the lobe gently between my teeth.

"Lux," she said, her voice husky.

"Shh." I worked the zipper down to her belly button and slipped my hand inside, curving around her breast. Arda arched into my touch and turned her head, gifting me her sweet lips. I dove for them, kissing her with all the pent-up passion from our long weeks apart.

Arda met me with just as much fervor. Our tongues dueled, lips nipping. I plumped her sweet flesh, loving the way she shuddered. It wasn't long before I needed more. But I couldn't get her naked from this position.

I surrendered her lips and pulled my hand out of her skinsuit. My cock twitched when she mewled in protest. I pushed her gently forward. "Stand up."

Arda hopped up and turned to watch me. I kicked off my lone boot—no idea what happened to the other one—and struggled to stand on the slippery tub bottom.

Arda bit her lip and reached down to aid me. "Maybe we should wait. You almost died."

I shook my head. "It's just slippery with that barrier ointment trapped beneath me. I am fine." I clambered to my feet and tugged her into my arms. "Better than fine, now."

I silenced the questions in her gaze with another lingering kiss. Then I stripped her slowly, leaving a trail of kisses on every exposed inch. By the time I plopped her wet skinsuit on the tile floor, she was quivering and gasping.

She captured my hands when I reached for her bra. "Your turn." She jerked on my zipper, and I didn't have the heart to argue. Arda treated me to the same slow exploration. Everywhere her questing fingers and mouth lingered felt like it had been kissed by flames.

She dropped to her knees and wrapped her hand around my length. "Dral's teeth," I cursed under my breath. Arda peeked up at me with a smirk on her wicked mouth. Then she bent forward and sucked me in. I groaned and slammed my fists against the wall for balance.

Her hot mouth wrapped around me, those bright blue eyes swimming with desire, was more than I could stand. "I need you now." I tugged her to her feet and tore off the rest of her clothes. My fingers slid between her thighs. She moaned, soaking my fingers with her heat.

Perfect. I grabbed her luscious thighs and lifted her, pressing her back against the cool tiles. She wrapped her legs around me just as I thrust inside.

"Fuck, Lux. Fuck me," she moaned.

I swiveled my hips, hitching her higher on the wall. She bounced on my cock, her head lolling back, eyes half-lidded. She felt so perfect wrapped around me. Only one thing could make it better. My gaze locked on her neck and my mouth watered. I shook my head and focused on her gorgeous face.

I wanted to taste her more than anything, but not until I knew I could keep her forever. The next time Arda's blood was on my tongue, she would be my mate.

Arda slid her hand from around my neck and cradled my cheek, her blue eyes locking on mine as I pounded into her. "Lux," she moaned in a throaty purr.

There was no doubt in my mind. Arda was the one for me. She could throw up all the excuses she wanted until the end of time, and

I would knock them all down. I'd chase her across the galaxy. Hell, I'd brave the blistering sun a thousand times—for her.

"You're mine," I told her, my voice more growl than words.

Arda screamed as she came, legs shaking and her core clenching me like a vise. I followed her seconds later. My release slammed into me like a meteor crash, raining pleasure through every cell of my body.

"Fuck, that was," Arda gulped, "incredible."

I kept her pinned to the wall, not wanting to break our connection. Her cunt clenched around me with the remnants of her orgasm. I groaned and leaned my forehead against hers. "Mm, I'm just getting started."

Arda shoved at my chest. "Let me down."

I thrust my hips, hoping to distract her.

Arda moaned, but she shook her head and pushed harder. "I'm serious. We can't just fuck all day, Lux. I need to talk to you."

I dropped her reluctantly. She shut off the water and climbed out of the shower.

I followed her and grabbed the towel she thrust into my arms. I quickly rubbed the moisture off my skin and patted down my hair. Arda eyed me warily as she dried her perfect curves.

"What shall we talk about?" *How about you admit that you're crazy about me, for starters?* I stalked closer, letting the towel fall at my side.

Arda's gaze darted across my chest, then lower. She frowned. "Hold on. I can't concentrate with you all," she waved her hand toward me, "naked and sexy."

I smirked as she toed the sodden pile of skinsuits. Sighing, she wrapped her towel around her waist, cracked open the door, and stuck her head out. "Zenda, you out there?"

Footsteps clattered down the hall. "What's up, Capt?"

"Would you mind running over to the Verne to grab a fresh skinsuit out of my closet?"

Zenda's laughter echoed beyond the doorway. "Sure. I think I can handle that."

Arda turned to me, her cheeks flushed a pretty pink. "Do you have a change of clothes with you?"

I nodded and rattled off the code that unlocked Destiny's outer hatch.

"Did you catch that, Zen?" Arda asked.

"Yep. Be back soon."

Arda eased the door closed as Zenda's footsteps trailed down the hall. I tied my towel around my waist, hoping that would be enough to appease Arda. *I don't know how she expects me to sit here without touching her.* My fingers tingled, desperate to slide over her smooth skin.

Arda glared at me and groaned. "Here." She dug in the linen closet and thrust a fluffy pink bundle in my arms. "Put this on."

I shook out the fabric, my brows raising as I examined the oversized robe. Well—it was oversized for a human. I tugged it on my arms, finding it a snug fit. "Happy?" I cinched the waist and spun around with a cocky grin.

She giggled. "Yep. That's just ridiculous enough to stave off my hormones."

"So, let's talk."

Arda sighed. "Not in here. Come on." She led me out of the bathroom and through the house. I spotted Ren crouched in front of a door, hard at work digging into the locking mechanism beside it. She was so engrossed with the task that we were practically atop her before she glanced up.

She snickered loudly, her gaze zeroing in on my pink robe. "Looking good, Commander."

"Do you like it?" I deadpanned, fluffing the collar. "I wasn't sure it worked with my coloring, but Arda insisted." I leaned closer and stage whispered, "She can get a bit bossy."

Arda yanked my elbow. "Follow me, your lordship."

"See what I mean?" I said.

Ren ignored me and shared a crooked smile with Arda. "With that getup, he looks more like a lady." Ren cracked up at her own joke.

Arda shoved open a door at the end of the hall. I cringed as bright sunlight spilled out, blinding me and making my skin crawl. "One second." Arda disappeared inside, slamming the door closed behind her. Rustling sounded on the opposite side of the door, then she said, "All right. You can come in."

Much better. I entered to find the curtains closed and the room dimly lit from the residual light leaking through the fabric. Posters and memorabilia decorated the walls. A narrow bed sat in the center, flanked by a pair of matching wooden dressers on either side. It was a cozy space, made all the more intimate when I realized where I must be.

"Is this your bedroom, Arda?"

33

Speed of Light

Arda

I tugged my towel firmly as I sat down, then patted the spot on the bed beside me. "Yeah. This was my room, a long time ago."

I sighed, taking in the posters of exotic Earth landscapes and even more exotic alien worlds tacked to the wooden walls. Mom hadn't changed a thing. It was like she was just waiting for me to fail at being a space captain, hoping I would return to reclaim it.

Lux gave the room a curious appraisal before sinking down next to me. Mom's fluffy robe gaped open at the bottom, showcasing his muscular legs. I tore my eyes up, determined to have a serious conversation despite his near nakedness.

"What are you doing here, Lux? You never answered me."

He claimed my hand and looked me dead in the eyes. "I came for you."

"Ok..." I bit back the giddy smile that fought to surface. "But why? I hope you weren't risking your life just for a quickie."

Lux rubbed my knuckles, sending sparks racing up my arms. "I haven't stopped thinking about you, Arda. I begged Zenda's friend Nash to hunt down the Verne for me. When he told me you were on Earth, I assumed something must be wrong."

And he came racing to help me... My heart squeezed, welling with warmth for the big oaf gazing at me so protectively.

"I took your advice." I squeezed his hand. "You were right. I have been running from my past. I'm here to figure out what really happened to my grandmother. I know I can't change what happened, but maybe if I learn the full story, I can come to terms with why she committed such horrible crimes."

"So that's why Ren is breaking into a room down the hall?" Lux asked.

I nodded. "My mother has Cora's medical records. I'm hoping they'll hold the answers. Or at the least, a clue where to look next."

Knock, knock.

"Come in," I said.

Ren peeked inside, a wide smile on her face. "It's open."

"Great work! I knew you could crack it." I hopped up to my feet, ready to search immediately, but Lux held tight to my hand. I scanned his face and turned to Ren. "I'll be there in a minute."

"Sure. I'm gonna clean up and bring my tools back to the Verne."

"Thanks, Ren."

Ren shut the door, and I sank back beside Lux on the bed. I could sense he was still itching to say something. "What is it?"

"I took your advice too."

My brow furrowed. "You did?"

"Yes. It didn't take me long to realize my original plan was hopelessly flawed. I haven't sought any older women to be my mate."

After what we just did in the bathroom, I would certainly hope not. "Oh. Well, that's a relief."

Lux chuckled. "I've given my future a lot of thought these weeks we've spent apart. Still, I have responsibilities to my people. The Pherians are counting on me."

I swallowed thickly, gazing down at the floor. "I understand that."

"I don't think you do." Lux tipped up my chin. "I can't live without you, Arda. These weeks we spent apart, a day didn't go by where I wished I'd said the hell with my plans and took you up on your offer to explore space together."

"But you didn't." *Why tell me this when he still has all those responsibilities to fulfill?* I bit my lip, staring into his eyes. "Sounds like you still can't."

"Actually, I can." He smiled. The sight of his lips curling up with pleasure on his normally stoic face nearly did me in. "Does the offer still stand, Arda? Would you like to team up?"

My heart hammered as I stared into Lux's eyes. "You want to team up? But what about your responsibilities?" I frowned. "I still don't want to live on Earth."

"I'm not asking you to." He traced an icy finger gently across my cheek. "I want to come with you."

"You do?"

I can't believe it! He can't mean that, can he? My thoughts swirled about me at the speed of light. What about his people and their exchange program? What about his desperate need for an heir?

"Most of what I needed to do to set up the program, I finished quickly. I've arranged it so that I can continue my work remotely. I'll still need to return to Earth occasionally, but I don't have to put off my dream of exploring until retirement any longer."

"Really, Lux?" It all sounded too good to be true. "That's amazing."

"There is still one promise I must keep."

Of course, there was a catch. "What promise?"

"Now that I can explore space freely, there's no rush for an heir, but I must find a human to be my mate." My pulse sped up as he met my gaze. "Be my mate, Arda."

I stared into his eyes, and my heart overflowed with glee. At the same time, my stomach twinged with disbelief. This protective, gorgeous, alien lord really wanted me? Was he for real?

I smoothed the bedspread nervously. "You could have anyone you wanted. Certainly, someone without such a notorious past."

Lux grabbed my hands. "I don't care about any of that. If anyone ever tries to use your grandmother's crimes to push us apart, I'll set them straight. You don't deserve to be punished for a past you had no part of. You're not a criminal." The corners of his lips inched up. "I might have mistaken you for a thief when we first met, but now I've seen what a kind, hard-working, beautiful woman you are. You've brought laughter and passion into my life. I can't imagine anyone better as my mate."

Hell, when the guy lays it out like that, how can I say no?

"Yes, Lux. I'll be your mate." I leaped on his lap and drowned him in kisses, my heart erupting with bliss. Lux wrapped me in his arms and I sighed into his mouth. *Nothing could possibly be better than this.*

Then he flipped me on my back atop the bed and rocked his length against my towel covered core. *I take that back. This is better. Much better.*

My towel landed on the floor and Lux's hands were everywhere. He followed his cool touch with his hot mouth, driving me wild. I moaned, clutching at him desperately.

The door slammed open. "Arda, the study's been broken into. Are you all—" My mother stood wide-eyed in the doorway; a shotgun clutched in her hands. "Take your grimy alien paws off my daughter!" she demanded.

"Holy shit! Mom! Get out." I shoved at Lux, trying to reach for my towel. My cheeks burned. *This is just perfect. She's not supposed to be back yet!*

"Get over here, baby. I won't let that fiend violate you."

My gaze darted between her and Lux. I remembered those signs on the lawn—all the anti-alien slogans. *Now she finds Lux groping me with her house broken into. She's gotta be pissed.*

Lux growled deep in his throat, shoving me behind him and away from the rifle.

"Leave her alone," Mom yelled, waving the shotgun menacingly.

"Mom, stop." I darted from behind Lux, whipping my towel up and covering myself. "He's not attacking me. I love him."

I stilled as the words rushed out unbidden. I hadn't meant to say it. Clearly, it was much too soon. But I couldn't deny the rightness that rang through me as soon as the truth was out.

"What?" My mother's brows drew down, at the same time she tucked the shotgun under her arm. "You love him?"

I turned to Lux. "I do." I smiled gently, then turned back to my mother. "Meet my mate, Mom. Commander Luxuth of the planet Pheria."

Lux tugged that ridiculous pink robe closed and stood, his hand lifted for a shake. "Pleasure to meet you, Mother."

Lux

I stood with my hand outstretched, awaiting Arda's mother's response. I aimed a soft smile at her as she stared me down. I bit my tongue, deciding to keep silent rather than beg her forgiveness for the scene she'd walked in on. Truth of the matter was, I couldn't find it in myself to be sorry about it. But this *was* the mother of my mate. I wanted her to like me.

They look so much alike. Arda and her mother shared the same brown curls and blue eyes. To an impartial observer, they might have passed for sisters. And clearly, I didn't need to wonder any longer where Arda inherited her fierce temperament.

The tiny woman pursed her lips and eyed my hand long enough for sweat to break out across my chest beneath the puny robe.

Go on, shake it. I held my breath, praying she wasn't planning to shoot me instead.

Finally, she hitched the weapon more firmly under her arm and reached out. She shivered before clasping my hand with her small fingers in a grip far more crushing than I would have expected of a woman her size. "Commander Luxuth. Call me Lexie."

I bit back a smirk. *Guess she's not ready to be called Mother yet.*

Lexie released me from her death grip and whipped around as a doorway slammed. The familiar chatter of Arda's crew spilled into the house before cutting off abruptly.

Zenda hovered in the doorway a moment later, two folded bundles of cloth in her arms. Ren shifted on her feet behind her. Zenda's gaze shot between all of us, before narrowing in on the weapon. "Capt? Everything all right?"

"It is now." Arda rushed forward and plucked the skinsuits out of Zenda's arms. She turned to her mother with a wobbly smile. "Mom, this is Zenda and Ren, my crew." They all muttered tense pleasantries, then Arda said, "Can you give us a minute to dress?"

Lexie backed up warily with a nod. "*Just* a minute. You have a lot of explaining to do, young lady." She tugged the door closed, leaving Arda and I alone once more.

Arda's shoulders slumped. She held out my black skinsuit. "Here, we better—"

I didn't let her finish. I claimed her mouth, quenching the burning desire that had consumed me since those three little words left my mate's lips. My fears that Arda wouldn't return my feelings had evaporated with her hasty confession, replaced with an all-consuming need—for her.

My mate loves me.

Hearing that, then her introducing me as her mate to her mother lit a fire in my loins. I yearned to claim Arda completely. To taste her sweet blood and her even sweeter cunt. It took every ounce of self-control I could muster to stop the kiss before it went too far.

Arda's eyes were cloudy with desire when I pulled away. I tucked an errant curl behind her ear. "Did you mean what you said, my mate?"

Arda's gaze locked onto mine. She flushed and set her hands on her hips. "I know it's too soon. But it's out there now, and I won't take it back."

I chuckled. My fiery mate. Even while confirming her feelings, she was ready to bicker. "Why would I want you to take it back?"

She shoved my skinsuit at my chest, turning away with a huff.

I tugged her into my arms. "I love you too, Arda."

Her face lit up with a jaw dropping grin. "You do?"

"Yes." I eased her gently away, patting her plump behind. "Now get dressed before I prove to you how much I crave you. I doubt your mother would appreciate waiting."

Arda hurried across the room with a squeak. I averted my eyes as her towel hit the floor.

No way I can see her naked right now without throwing her on that bed.

I made quick work of shucking off the silly robe and slipping into my skinsuit.

"Are you ready for the grand inquisition?" Arda tugged her zipper up her chest.

Lexie was certainly fearsome with that antique weapon aimed at me, but now that we'd been introduced, how bad could she be? I tugged open the door. "Lead the way, my mate."

34

Signs

Arda

Lux strode into the hall, seemingly unbothered by the prospect of facing my mother. That and he was apparently now obsessed with calling me "my mate."

A goofy grin split my face before the pit in my stomach chased it away. It was hard to stay excited about my upcoming nuptials when I was about to face a one-woman firing squad.

Hell, I almost pissed myself when she burst in on us. And now she was bound to have a million questions. Questions she might not like the answers to.

Put on your big girl panties and get it over with.

With that goal planted in my mind, I trailed Lux down the hall. A sudden thought made me hurry in front of him.

"Wait." I grabbed his elbow, halting him before he reached the kitchen. "Let me go first. There's a lot of windows."

Lux nodded and stood waiting. I sucked in a deep breath and rounded the corner.

Well, that's interesting.

The curtains were already closed, washing the room in shadow. Mom hovered above the counter; a bag of Granny Smiths perched beside her elbow. She'd lost the shotgun, only to replace it with a gleaming blade. It flashed in the dim room while she chopped an apple into even slices.

"Come in. Both of you. Your crew told me about the sunlight." Mom raised her voice. "It's safe in here for you, Commander."

I gulped as she waved the knife while speaking. *Safe* felt a little premature when Mom was still armed.

Lux appeared beside me. "No need to stand on formalities with family. You can call me Lux."

"Lux," Mom repeated. She frowned at me. "About that. When were you planning to tell me about your *mate*?" She spit out the last word like it pained her. "Did you get married without inviting me?"

"No," I hurried to explain. "We're not married, yet. We haven't even set a date."

"Oh." Mom smiled. "Good. I want to be there when you do."

My jaw dropped. "You do?" Mom and I weren't exactly close. And then there were those anti-alien signs on her front lawn...

But from the affronted glare she speared me with, clearly, I was mistaken. "Of course I do." Mom set down the knife and crossed her arms. "What kind of awful mother wouldn't want to watch her only daughter tie the knot with the man she loves?"

Tears pricked at the corners of my eyes.

Lux grabbed my hand and spoke smoothly. "We would love to have you there, wouldn't we, my mate?"

I nodded, my cheeks splitting with a wide smile. But I had to know... "What about the signs? Are you *really* happy I'm marrying an alien?"

Mom's brows scrunched. "What signs?"

"The ones on your lawn. They're full of Isolationists' slogans."

Lux stiffened beside me. *Guess he didn't spot them while the sun was roasting him.*

"Oh, those." Mom chuckled and waved a hand. "I just put them up for Ruth."

"Who?" I asked.

Mom lifted the knife and went back to chopping. "One of my new neighbors. Biggest loudmouth busybody I've ever met. Can't stand the woman."

I pursed my lips. "I don't get it..."

"Her grandson is running for office," she leaned forward and waggled her brows, "for the other side. I couldn't care less about politics. I just wanted that old witch to leave me alone."

I burst out laughing. "Mom, that's devious."

Lux chuckled, too. "I bet it worked."

Mom winked. "Like a charm." She set down the knife again and walked over to us. "Don't worry, love. I'm thrilled for you. The way you two look at each other, it's obvious you're made for each other—different species or not. And nothing in the universe could stop me from being there to watch my baby girl get married."

I grabbed Mom and pulled her in for a hug. With her arms wrapped around me, and Lux there at my side, contentment washed over me. I'd been prepared to argue about Lux being a suitable match for me. Having Mom's acceptance just handed to me without question was a gift I'd not been expecting.

"Thanks Mom."

"You're welcome, baby." Mom pulled away and met my eyes. "Now that we have that settled, do you mind telling me why you broke into my study?"

I pulled away from my mother's arms, but I refused to show any guilt over my actions. "It's about grandmother. I *need* to know what happened to her."

Mom's gaze shot to the floor. She shook her head. "I told you. I don't—"

"And I don't believe you." I flung my arm out, aiming a finger at the study. With the lock torn apart, it wouldn't latch. The door hung open and light spilled into the hallway like a beacon, leading me to the answers I *knew* it held. "Why else would you keep that room locked up like Fort Knox?"

"And why can't you just let it go? Nothing good will come out of learning more. Nothing at all."

"That's not true. I'm tired of being kept in the dark. You never told me what they did to her. If you had, then maybe I wouldn't have spent most of my life feeling like a freak."

Mom backed away like I'd slapped her. "What they did..." She gulped. "What do you know? And what do you mean, you felt like a freak?" Her lower lip quivered and for a second I was sure she was about to cry before she steeled her spine and barked, "Tell me, Arda."

Lux grabbed my hand and squeezed. I took comfort in his presence. With him beside me, I finally had the strength to speak my truth.

Time to stop hiding.

My hands grew clammy and my heart pounded. I choked out, "When I was a teenager, I started having unusual cravings."

Mom blanched. "Cravings for what?"

Lux squeezed my fingers tighter. I sucked in a breath and blurted, "Sex and blood."

"Oh, Arda. I—"

"Let me finish." I held up a hand and Mom nodded. "I never told you back then because I was ashamed. I was afraid I would turn out just like her. It wasn't until I met Lux, and the med-bot on his ship fixed me I learned the truth. Someone tweaked Cora's genetic code, didn't they?"

Mom hung her head. "Yes."

"Why didn't you tell me?" My voice cracked. Lux tugged me into his side and stroked my shoulders.

"I didn't find out until after she died." Mom retreated to the counter and picked up the knife. Her hands shook, but as soon as she started chopping apples again, the shaking leveled off and her voice steadied. "When I was given all of Cora's medical records and personal effects, you were just a baby. I didn't know what to do. I tracked down the prison doctor who signed all her records. We had a long talk, and I took his advice."

"What did he say?" Lux asked.

Mom sighed. "You must understand, I've never felt what you and Cora felt. I don't know how or why, but the cravings you have—I don't have them."

"How is that possible?" I scrunched my nose.

"What they did to Cora was unregulated genetic testing." Lux scratched his chin. "Sounds like the effects skipped a generation. It's not uncommon with genetic mutations."

Mom frowned. "That makes sense." She turned to me, her gaze soft and pleading. "But you have to believe me, love. I thought those cravings would only be a problem for Cora. The doctor told me that by adding more human fathers into the mix, the genetic abnormalities were being diluted. He said they wouldn't cause us any problems."

"So since your dad and my dad were human, that was supposed to overpower the Vampherian DNA?"

"Yes. But if I had any idea you were feeling those things..." Mom cringed. "I guess it was stupid to assume you'd talk to your mother about your sex life when you were a teenager."

I bit back a laugh. *Yeah, I can't imagine many teens spill all the dirty details of their sexual fantasies to their parents.*

"Do you still have her files?" I asked.

Mom dropped the knife and wiped her hands on a dishcloth. "I do. You were right. They're in the study. I don't know what exactly you're looking for by reading them, but you're welcome to take them."

"Thanks Mom." I turned to leave the kitchen.

"Arda?" Mom's voice stopped me in my tracks. I spun around slowly. Tears pooled in her eyes as she rounded the counter and shuffled closer. "I'm sorry for keeping the truth from you, baby. I was only trying to protect you. I—"

My voice hitched as I flung myself into her arms. "It's okay. I'm sorry, too. I wish I'd trusted you with my secret back then. Things would have been different if I had."

I held my mother while she silently cried. Despite her tears, warmth rushed through me. This whole crazy experience had brought me closer to Mom than ever before. Now that all our secrets were out in the open, maybe we could have the close relationship I'd always secretly wished for.

Movement behind her caught my eye. I smiled at Lux as he leaned against the kitchen wall, watching us embrace.

It was baffling to think all this change started from one little mistake. If I hadn't crashed into his ship, setting off the chain of events that led me here, then I might have gone my entire life without rebuilding trust with my mother.

And I had my sexy space lord to thank for it.

35

Heads or Tails

Lux

Arda called her crew with her personal communicator and asked them to come back into the house. Night was beginning to fall outside, but she still insisted on entering the study first to pull the heavy drapes closed tightly. "Come in."

It warmed my heart to see her so eager to protect me. *My mate.*

I strode in as she tugged the chain on a desk lamp, illuminating the homely space. Bookshelves lined the walls, and the dusty scent of old paper tickled my nose. An oversized desk stood in the center of the room and a ratty old loveseat sat in the corner beside the window.

Lexie walked inside and exhaled. She wrung her hands, gazing at Arda. "Baby, are you sure you want to see this? It's not pretty."

My brave mate stood firm and nodded. "I do. I need to know what happened back then. Who did this to her? Why all the secrecy and lies?" Arda turned to me. "Lux helped me get a handle on my bloodlust so I never have to worry about acting out violently like grandmother, but what if there are others? There could be more people out there struggling with bloodlust like I was. What if something in that file can help me find them?"

It did not surprise me Arda wanted to find others. To help them. She was a strong woman with a caring heart, and I couldn't be prouder to call her mine.

Lexie's gaze softened. "I never even considered…" She spun around and moved to the bookshelf behind the desk. She kneeled down and trailed her hands along the third row from the bottom.

Zenda and Ren returned, their excited chatter preceding them into the room. "What's going on?" Ren asked.

"Mom agreed to give me Cora's files." Arda leaned her head sideways, studying Lexie as her lips moved, counting silently while her fingers trailed across the dusty tomes.

"Here's one." Lexie plucked a book off the shelf triumphantly. She set it on her desk, then moved to another shelf across the room. She started the process again, on a high row this time. A second book landed atop the first and Lexie moved on to a third shelf.

Zenda's eyes widened, and she nudged Arda with her elbow. "No way we would have found everything in time, even if your mother was gone for the rest of the night."

It's good they made up—for more reasons than one.

"I've been meaning to ask you, Mom. How did you get home so quickly? I thought you'd be gone for a couple of hours." Arda strode to the desk, picking up the first book to examine it closer. I walked beside her just as she opened it, revealing a hollow compartment cut into the pages of the thick hardback. Folded paper was stacked inside. Arda shuffled through the top few sheets and I spotted neat, even handwriting covering the yellowed pages.

"There's a new general store, half the distance from where we shopped before you left for space." Lexie cocked a brow at Arda and adopted a teasing tone. "Maybe if you came to visit once in a while, you'd have known about it."

"I promise I won't wait so long next time." Arda rubbed the back of her neck, her cheeks pinking adorably. It was clear my mate had a strained relationship with her mother, but the love they felt for each other shone through the awkwardness.

"Good." Lexie set a third book on the desk. "This is everything."

"Thanks, Mom."

"You're welcome. I hope you find what you're looking for, although I don't know if anything in there will help you find any others." Her face lit up, and she flashed me a crooked grin. "Unless..." Lexie tugged the first book out of Arda's hands. "There was one paper hidden within all the rest. I could never make heads or tails of it, but I wonder if you could, Lux."

Lexie dug through the book and all of us leaned forward, eager for a glimpse at the mystery paper. After what felt like ages, but was likely only a few seconds, her nimble fingers caught on a crumpled sheet.

The paper crinkled in my hands as I spread it on the desk. "Hm, let me see." I smoothed it out and squinted at the tiny letters on the page. They weren't in galactic standard, that was for sure. But despite that, it was a language I recognized. "I know why you can't understand this."

"You do?" Lexie leaned over the table, scrutinizing the lettering with pursed lips. "I knew it was alien!"

Arda tugged on my elbow. "Can you read it?"

"No. But I've seen it before. This is the native language of the Vorill."

"That's Nash's species," Zenda chimed in. "Why would your grandmother have something in her file written in Vorillian?"

"I don't know," I replied. "But it will be simple enough to have this translated. Destiny can have it readable within the hour."

"Destiny?" Lexie asked.

"His ship," Arda explained.

Lexie shook her head and smiled at me. "All these years, I've wondered what that paper said. You've been here for less than a day and the mystery is solved."

"Happy to help." I smirked. *Let's try this again...* "Mom."

Lexie eyed me sideways, but her smile widened. She nodded at the paper. "What are you waiting for?" She winked. "Son."

Arda

Lux beamed at Mom. Tingles spread through my chest. All she had to do to get my stoic mate to smile was call him son. *And here I was worried about having to call him daddy...maybe he'd like it.*

I chuckled under my breath. Lux arched a brow as he spun to the door. "Would you care to join me on Destiny?"

"Baby, could you hang back for a sec?" Mom asked before I could reply. "I have one more thing I need to tell you." Mom toed at the floor, her gaze downcast.

My stomach churned at her odd behavior. *Maybe a little privacy is in order for this chat.*

"Okay." I nodded to my crew. "You guys want to keep Lux company?"

Ren hopped up from the dusty old loveseat and brushed her hands down her oil-stained skinsuit. "Sure, I'm game."

Zenda clapped her hands together. "Did you bring Smudge with you?" she asked Lux.

"I did."

"Ooo, then count me in."

The three of them trailed down the hall. Mom waited for the front door to bang closed before she raised her gaze from the floor and cleared her throat. "There's something I've been meaning to tell you for a while now, love. It seemed like the kind of thing I needed to say face to face."

My skin prickled at the seriousness in her voice. "Fuck, Mom, you're scaring me."

She crossed her arms. "Arda. Language."

"Sorry," I replied sheepishly.

Mom shook her head. Then she sucked in a big breath. "You don't need to be scared. It might take some *adjusting,* though."

The suspense was killing me. I pursed my lips and waved a hand. *Get on with it, Mom.*

"Your grandmother's notoriety isn't the only reason we moved around so much when you were growing up."

My brow furrowed. "Huh?"

Mom grabbed my hands gently. "How old do you think I am?"

Chills spread down my spine. *She'd said she had me when she was eighteen, and I'm twenty-four.* I did the math quickly. "Forty-two."

She met my eyes. "How old do I *look*?"

I took a second to scrutinize her closely. Mom had always looked more youthful than other women her age. Even now, her skin was wrinkle-free and her hair was fully brown without a single gray strand. As soon as I grew as tall as her, the comments about us being sisters started. My stomach clenched. Even as I aged, those comments had never stopped.

Mom looked as young today as she had when I was a child. How had I never noticed before now?

"I wasn't eighteen when I had you," Mom whispered.

"What?" My jaw dropped. "How old were you?"

"Forty-seven."

"Forty-seven? That would make you…" I paused. *God damn math!*

"I'm seventy-one."

"Jesus, Mom. Are you serious?" How was that possible? A light-bulb lit up in my head. "The Vampherian DNA."

Mom nodded. "Yes, baby. When I got Cora's medical records, the doctor told me her real age. She was in her nineties when she passed. They found out when they performed her autopsy."

I gasped. I'd seen all the pictures and holovids from when she'd been captured. "But she looked so young…"

"I know. There's no way to know what age she would have lived to if she hadn't taken her own life." Mom squeezed my hands. "But you need to be prepared for the same thing to happen to you. When the time comes, I can introduce you to my contact. We'll have fake papers drawn up so you can fudge your age. If you move around enough, people won't notice."

I drew back, frowning. "That's what you did? Every time we moved—from city to city, planet to planet. You were hiding who you really are."

"Yes, baby. I didn't want to tell you until I had to. You deserved a normal life. Well, as normal as I could make it with Cora as your grandmother."

My stomach clenched. How lonely it must have been. Having to uproot her life every few years. Never making friends that last. Could it be that the lack of closeness I always sensed sprang from this? No wonder Mom was distant when she was forced to keep so many secrets. All to make sure I had a normal childhood.

Mom sighed. "It's about time for me to move again. Maybe I can find a home on an alien planet for a while. You'll come visit me, won't you?"

"No," I said sharply.

"Oh." Mom's lip quivered.

I clutched her hands. "Wait. That's not what I meant. You're not moving again. Not unless you really want to."

"Arda—"

"No, Mom. Listen. You deserve a life where you can put down roots. Make friends. Not have to constantly hide who you are." I sent her a wobbly smile, fighting to keep the emotion out of my voice. "Now that we know who the Vampherians are—hell, now that Lux and I are together—the truth needs to come out. We'll face it—together."

Tears pooled in her eyes. "Are you sure that's what you want, baby?"

I didn't even need to think about it for a second. "Yes. I spent so long hiding. I didn't have to hide my age, like you, but I hid my cravings. Lux helped me see I don't need to keep my truth hidden any longer. We'll uncover what happened to Cora. We'll let the whole universe know her crimes were not so black and white. And that what they did, made us who we are—long lifespans and all. We don't have to be ashamed anymore."

Mom nodded, tears spilling down her cheeks. "My baby. You are so strong. I'm amazed by you."

"You're not the only one," Lux said from the doorway.

"Hey." I twisted around and sent Lux a watery smile. "How much of that did you hear?"

"Enough." Lux crossed the room and clutched me and Mom in his massive arms. Mom laughed, wiping tears off her cheeks. Lux bent his head, staring into my eyes. "My mate, I will help you solve Cora's mystery every step of the way."

Mom pushed her way out of Lux's arms, sniffing dramatically. "I better check on that pie in the oven." She hurried out of the study, leaving us alone.

"Do you really mean that?" I asked. "You're not disappointed we won't be exploring space together, like we planned?"

Lux snagged my hand and led me to the loveseat. He sat down and tugged me into his lap. "I don't see why we can't do both." He trailed his thumb across my cheek. "Have you ever been to Vorillion?"

I frowned at the change of subject. "No."

"The paper in Cora's file, Destiny didn't take long to translate it."

My heart raced. "What does it say?"

Lux settled me more firmly across his lap. "Not much we can use, unfortunately. But it belongs to a medical research facility in a tiny town on their home world. Perhaps a trip there is in order?"

"Hm. Good idea." I beamed at him, my fingers stroking his muscular chest. *God, he's so sexy. And he's all mine.* But there was one more thing we had to discuss before I let my hands head south like they were itching to.

"My mom told me she's been hiding her real age." I leaned back, biting my lip. "Sounds like I might stick around for a lot longer than expected. I know you were looking forward to spending your retirement single—"

Lux gripped the back of my head and tilted my face up to his. He hovered there, his mouth closing the space between us until his breath whispered across my lips. "I couldn't ask for a better gift than a full lifetime with the woman I love."

Our mouths collided, and I melted against Lux's chest. I could spend forever there, wrapped up in the strong shelter of my alien lord's arms. *Nothing in the universe will ever feel as perfect as I do right now.*

A throat cleared loudly, breaking us apart. "Pie's ready." Mom peeked inside the doorway, then walked away, her voice trailing behind her. "Get it while it's hot."

I smiled at Lux. "Are you hungry? Mom's apple pie is to die for."

Lux trailed a finger over my neck, staring at me with enough hunger to make me shiver. "I can wait." He set me on my feet and swatted my behind playfully. "Eat up, my mate. You'll need your strength for what I'm planning to do to you later."

I giggled and strode away, adding an extra swing to my hips. The heavenly scent of apples and cinnamon perfumed the air. We found Ren and Zenda seated at the kitchen table, their mouths full of pie.

"Hey, Capt." Zenda slid a chair out with the toe of her boot. "Saved ya a slice."

Mom settled a hot cup of tea in front of me as I sat. "Here you go, baby."

"Thanks." I sighed, my gaze trailing around the faces of my family and friends. I might have a mystery to solve, and a ship to pay off, but I pushed those worries to the back of my mind. I took a sip of my favorite chai and smiled. Who would have guessed it would take crashing into an alien ship to find the love of my life? Definitely not me.

But you won't catch me complaining. Not a chance in hell.

36

Last Chance

I stretched my sore muscles, body aching from a long day of hard work. It had taken us weeks to finish remodeling the Verne, but now it was finally close to completion.

The decision to sell Destiny to provide the funds for all the repairs had been easy. Verne might look like a hunk of junk from the outside, but with its larger size, it was far more suited for a future ferrying passengers through space. And I had to admit, with most of the bulky mining attachments removed, the ship looked a little—

Oh, who am I kidding? The Verne would never be fit to grace the cover of an engineering manual. But being here with my mate made her happy.

The day I sold Destiny and paid off Arda's debt flashed in my mind, and my dick twitched in my skinsuit. She'd been plenty happy then, and not at all shy about showing it—in bed, and the ionic shower. Even on the table in the mess.

I traced my fingers across the smooth leather of the new, much larger, pilot and co-pilot chairs I just finished installing.

Perhaps we should add to our list...

Before I could turn to find my mate, the comms panel lit up, blinking incessantly. I sighed and dropped into the pilot's chair before flicking the speakers on.

"Elys, for Lux. Is he available?"

"It's me." I grinned, in a far better mood for my sister's needling today than usual. Of course, she caught on immediately.

"Don't you sound chipper? I guess mated life is agreeing with you?"

"You could say that. Being with Arda, preparing to explore space—it's more than I've ever dreamed."

"I'm happy for you, big brother." Elys cleared her throat and her tone shifted, taking on a note of caution. "I wanted to update you on how the Pherian media is handling your upcoming nuptials."

I frowned. "That bad, huh?" I'd known they'd latch onto Arda's grandmother's story like a vorhound on carrion.

"It's not good. But mother wanted me to tell you she's handling it and not to worry."

My heart squeezed. Even before meeting her, my family was banding around Arda. It nearly brought a tear to my eye. "That's right. I still owe her an introduction call."

"I'll make sure she schedules you in." Elys' voice grew excited. "Mother's dying to meet Arda. Even more now, since I started chatting with Arda and told Mother what a character your mate is." Elys giggled, likely remembering some joke Arda had fed her. Most of them were about me—the little minx.

I rolled my eyes and was a second away from making my excuses and ending the call when another thought popped into my mind. "I almost forgot. Did you get our most recent med-scans back?"

"Hold on, let me check." Elys went silent for a long moment that seemed to stretch forever. "Here they are."

"Well? What do they say?" My heart pounded, and I tapped my fingers on the armrest.

"It's not active yet, but it's close. Once more, twice maybe, ought to clinch it."

I blew out a shaky breath. "Thanks, Elys. I-I need to go."

"Talk to you soon, Lux."

I killed the comms and stalked out of the bridge, searching for my mate. Chances were, she'd be happy to hear the news. All the same, a trickle of fear wormed its way into my gut.

If Arda wasn't ready... Dral help me. If she'd changed her mind, I don't think I could bear it.

I found my mate in the mess hall, sipping from a steaming mug. She glanced up from scrolling through her tablet and graced me with a carefree smile. "Hey. You're not gonna believe—" Her words cut off and her smile morphed into a frown. "What's wrong?"

I joined her at the table, plunking into the seat across from her. "We need to talk."

She set the tablet aside and grabbed my hands. "What is it?"

With her tiny, warm hands wrapped around me, I found the strength to tell her. "I just spoke with Elys. Our latest med-scans have come back."

Her perfect lips pursed and her brows dipped. "Is everything okay?"

"Yes. Nothing to worry about. It's just... our blood bond is nearly complete."

"Really?" Arda lit up. "That's good news, isn't it?"

"I think so. Only, it's customary on Pheria for mating pairs to renew their vows before the bond becomes permanent. To give each other a last chance to back out."

Arda scoffed. "And what? You want out?"

I squeezed her hands. "No. Of course not."

Arda's expression softened. "Don't tell me you were worried I'd jump ship?"

My racing pulse began to slow. I met her beautiful blue eyes and sent her a crooked smile. "Maybe a little."

Arda let go of my hands and stood. She rounded the table and straddled my lap, wrapping her arms around me. "You're not getting rid of me now, big guy. I'm keeping you." She licked her lips. "How about we make it official?"

How can I say no to that? My beautiful mate. I couldn't be more thankful that a faulty radio beacon sent her crashing into my life.

I lifted her without warning, making her squeal. With her sweet curves cradled against my chest, I fled the mess, heading toward the bridge.

"Where are you going?" Arda giggled.

"I want to show you the new chairs I installed. They could use some *testing*." I waggled my brows.

Arda shifted in my arms. "Wait, I have a better idea."

Arda

I clutched Lux's neck as he strode down the hall to my—scratch that—*our* quarters. He slammed the hatch controls with his elbow and carried me over the threshold.

His brow arched. Surprise was evident on his chiseled face as he stared at the massive bed sitting in the space my tiny bunk used to occupy. "I thought the delivery company couldn't fit us in until tomorrow?"

I shrugged, hopping down from his arms. "They had an opening. What do you think?"

We'd knocked down a wall to enlarge my quarters. No way a Pherian-sized bed would fit inside otherwise. But I wasn't mad about it. Especially since the money Lux got selling Destiny was enough to add a new addition to the Verne.

The extra module would be perfect for hauling passengers. The furniture we'd purchased for the new rooms could even be stowed. We could easily make extra space for cargo, should we run out of traveling explorers and dignitaries to ferry from system to system.

Everything was shaping up just like I'd always imagined—only better. With my mate by my side, I would never need to worry about my unusual cravings ruining my life. I'd always have someone in my corner, a true partner in life. Lux still drove me crazy sometimes, but he always had my back. That was priceless.

Lux scratched his chin, surveying the bed. "Hm. It's missing something."

I stacked my hands on my hips. "It's perfect and you know—" My words cut off with a squeal when Lux tossed me on the bed.

"Now it's perfect." He smirked, his big mitts already working the zipper of his skinsuit.

"Verne," I called.

The comm box on the wall lit up and the computer's voice chimed in, "Captain Arda. How can I help you?"

"Set a 'do not disturb' on my quarters." I swallowed thickly as Lux peeled the black fabric from his upper body, revealing all those delicious muscles I was dying to lick. "Emergencies only." Zenda and Ren were down on the planet buying supplies, but I didn't want any calls interrupting us.

"Of course, Captain."

I tore my zipper down to my navel, but my hands stilled when Lux jerked the rest of his clothes off. A weird sense of déjà vu washed over me as he stared at me, naked and hungry.

My mouth quirked up as I remembered the silly VR program I used to rely on to get my rocks off. Lux stood in the same position as that nameless hunk in the simulation. It was my secret fantasy, come to life. Only this time, it wasn't some random man with soulless eyes.

I shivered, meeting Lux's silver gaze. His eyes burned with heat. That and something so much more.

"I love you, my mate," he said, confirming the depth of emotion I sensed in his gaze.

"And I love you, Lux." I stretched out my arms. "Make me yours. Forever."

Lux kneeled down and plucked a knife from his discarded clothes. He stalked closer, the silver blade glinting in the fluorescent cabin light. The bed sank as he joined me.

"Are you sure you're ready?" Lux's throat worked as he gulped. "If you need to wait, I'll understand."

I tugged the knife gently out of his fingers and turned his hand over. The sharp point of the blade dented the pad of his thumb. I met his eyes before pressing hard enough to draw blood.

Lux shivered. He nodded. His breath leaked out in a hiss as a drop of burgundy liquid pooled on the digit. I lifted it to my lips. "You're mine," I told him before flicking my tongue out to taste him. His unique flavor exploded on my tongue and made my pussy throb.

Lust burned in Lux's gaze. I pointed the blade at my chest and nicked my collarbone. He fell on me, ravenous. "Mine," he growled into my chest, his hot mouth licking and suckling my skin like he'd never get enough.

I tore at my skinsuit, desperate to press my overheated flesh against his cool skin. Lux helped me peel off my clothes. His hand slid between my thighs before the last layer hit the ground.

He groaned, finding me drenched. "I need you, mate."

"Yes." I moaned at the delicious shock of his icy fingers stroking me where I burned for him. But I needed more. "Take me. Now."

Lux tugged me beneath him and lined his cock up to my entrance. Then, with his eyes locked onto mine, he sank into me on a long, slow thrust. At that moment, something in my soul burst. A supernova screamed through my veins and exploded, erupting in my heart and reforming it anew—with Lux twined inside.

I watched the play of emotion on Lux's face and knew he felt it, too.

"Is that the bond?" I asked, voice thick with wonder.

"I think so." Lux grinned down at me. Then he pulsed his hips and pleasure took over. Mind-blowing, toe-curling pleasure raced through me, setting off the orgasm to end all orgasms. I screamed so loud it's a miracle everyone on Earth couldn't hear it—even though we were in orbit. Lux grunted and his hot seed shot inside me, making me warm all over.

As we lay there in each other's arms, catching our breath, I turned to him and smiled. "Guess you're stuck with me now, big guy."

Lux rolled me atop him and brushed my curls off my face. "Mm. The last time I was stuck with you, it turned out all right."

"Damn right it did." I sealed my words with a blistering kiss. *It sure was an incredible ride.* I pulled my lips away a fraction. "Ready for what comes next?"

Lux gripped my hips. "What's that?"

I pushed off his chest and hopped out of bed. "I hear there are some new chairs that need *testing*." I crooked my finger and raced for the door. "Come and get me, mate."

About the Author

Leda Palmer loves dreaming about alien worlds and star-crossed lovers finding each other. When she's not writing, you'll find her with her nose in a book or her eyes on the stars. The Cosmic Lovers series is her debut series.

Find out more about her future projects on her Facebook page Leda Palmer – Author. Or on follow her on Instagram at ledapalmer-author.

Also By

Upcoming novels in the Cosmic Lovers Series:

Betrothal Voyage — 2024

For early access to Betrothal Voyage, and all Leda's work, look for her stories on Kindle Vella.

www.ingramcontent.com/pod-product-compliance
Lightning Source LLC
Chambersburg PA
CBHW021307190726
48288CB00003B/729